I0575351

John S. C. Abbott

History of Joseph Bonaparte

King of Naples and of Italy

John S. C. Abbott

History of Joseph Bonaparte
King of Naples and of Italy

ISBN/EAN: 9783337239190

Printed in Europe, USA, Canada, Australia, Japan

Cover: Foto ©Andreas Hilbeck / pixelio.de

More available books at **www.hansebooks.com**

HISTORY

OF

JOSEPH BONAPARTE,

KING OF NAPLES AND OF ITALY.

By JOHN S. C. ABBOTT,

AUTHOR OF

"THE HISTORY OF NAPOLEON BONAPARTE," "THE
FRENCH REVOLUTION," &o.

NEW YORK:

HARPER & BROTHERS, PUBLISHERS,

FRANKLIN SQUARE.

Entered, according to Act of Congress, in the year 1869, by

HARPER & BROTHERS,

In the Clerk's Office of the District Court of the United States for
the Southern District of New York.

———

Copyright, 1897, by SUSAN ABBOTT MEAD.

PREFACE.

THE writer trusts that he may be pardoned for relating the following characteristic anecdote of President Lincoln, as it so fully illustrates the object in view in writing these histories. In a conversation which the writer had with the President just before his death, Mr. Lincoln said:

"I want to thank you and your brother for Abbotts' series of Histories. I have not education enough to appreciate the profound works of voluminous historians, and if I had, I have no time to read them. But your series of Histories gives me, in brief compass, just that knowledge of past men and events which I need. I have read them with the greatest interest. To them I am indebted for about all the historical knowledge I have."

It is for just this purpose that these Histories are written. Busy men, in this busy life, have now no time to wade through ponderous folios. And yet every one wishes to know the general character and achievements of the illustrious personages of past ages.

A few years ago there was published in Paris a life of King Joseph, in ten royal octavo volumes of nearly five hundred pages each. It was entitled "*Mémoires et Correspondance, Politique et Militaire, du Roi Joseph, Publiés, Annotés et Mis en Ordre par A. du Casse, Aide-de-camp de S. A. I. Le Prince Jerome Napoleon.*" These volumes contained nearly all the correspondence which passed between Joseph and his brother Napoleon from their childhood until after the battle of Waterloo. Every historical statement is substantiated by unequivocal documentary evidence.

From this voluminous work, aided by other historical accounts of particular events, the author of this sketch has gathered all that would be of particular interest to the general reader at the present time. As all the facts contained in this narrative are substantiated by ample documentary proof, the writer can not doubt that this volume presents an accurate account of the momentous scenes which it describes, and that it gives the reader a correct idea of the social and political relations existing between those extraordinary men, Joseph and Napoleon Bonaparte. It is not necessary that the historian should pronounce judgment upon every transaction. But he is bound to state every event exactly as it occurred.

No one can read this account of the struggle in Europe *in favor of popular rights* against the old dynasties of *feudal oppression*, without more highly appreciating the admirable institutions of our own glorious Republic. Neither can any intelligent and candid man carefully peruse this narrative, and not admit that Joseph Bonaparte was earnestly seeking the welfare of the *people;* that, surrounded by dynasties strong in standing armies, in pride of nobility, and which were venerable through a life of centuries, he was endeavoring to promote, under monarchical forms, which the posture of affairs seemed to render necessary, the abolition of *aristocratic usurpation*, and the establishment of *equal rights for all men.* Believing this, the writer sympathizes with him in all his struggles, and reveres his memory. The universal brotherhood of man, the fundamental principles of Christianity, should also be the fundamental principles in the State. Having spared no pains to be accurate, the writer will be grateful to any critic who will point out any incorrectness of statement or false coloring of facts, that he may make the correction in subsequent editions.

This volume will soon be followed by another, " The History of Queen Hortense," the daughter of Josephine, the wife of King Louis, the mother of Napoleon III.

JOHN S. C. ABBOTT.

FAIR HAVEN, CONN., }
    May, 1869.

CONTENTS.

ENGRAVINGS.

JOSEPH BONAPARTE.

CHAPTER I.

SCENES IN EARLY LIFE.

THE island of Corsica, in the Mediterranean Sea, sixty miles from the coast of Tuscany, is about half as large as the State of Massachusetts. In the year 1767 this island was one of the provinces of Italy. There was then residing, in the small town of Corté, in Corsica, a young lawyer nineteen years of age. He was the descendant of an illustrious race, which could be traced back, through a succession of distinguished men, far into the dark ages. Charles Bonaparte, the young man of whom we speak, was tall, handsome, and possessed strong native powers of mind, which he had highly cultivated. In the same place there was a young lady, Letitia Raniolini, remarkable for her beauty and her accomplishments. She also was of an ancient family. When but sixteen years of age

Letitia was married to Charles Bonaparte, then but nineteen years old.

About a year after their marriage, on the 7th of January, 1768, they welcomed their first-born child, Joseph Napoleon Bonaparte. In nineteen months after the birth of Joseph, his world-renowned brother Napoleon was born. But in the mean time the island had been transferred to France. Thus while Joseph was by birth an Italian, his brother Napoleon was a Frenchman.

Charles Bonaparte occupied high positions of trust and honor in the government of Corsica, and his family took rank with the most distinguished families in Italy and in France. Joseph passed the first twelve years of his life upon his native island. He was ever a boy of studious habits, and of singular amiability of character. When he was twelve years of age his father took him, with Napoleon and their elder sister Eliza, to France for their education. Leopold, the grand duke of Tuscany, gave Charles Bonaparte letters of introduction to Maria Antoinette, his sister, who was then the beautiful and admired Queen of France.

Leaving Joseph at the college of Autun, in Burgundy, the father continued his journey to

Paris, with Napoleon and Eliza. Eliza was placed in the celebrated boarding-school of St. Cyr, in the metropolis, and Napoleon was taken to the military school at Brienne, a few miles out from the city. The father was received as a guest in the gorgeous palace of Versailles. Joseph and Napoleon were very strongly attached to each other, and this attachment continued unabated through life. When the two lads parted at Autun both were much affected. Joseph, subsequently speaking of it, says:

"I shall never forget the moment of our separation. My eyes were flooded with tears. Napoleon shed but one tear, which he in vain endeavored to conceal. The abbé Simon, who witnessed our adieus, said to me, after Napoleon's departure, 'He shed only one tear; but that one testified to as deep grief in parting from you as all of yours.'"

The two brothers kept up a very constant correspondence, informing each other minutely of their studies, and of the books in which they were interested. Joseph became one of the most distinguished scholars in the college of Autun, excelling in all the branches of polite literature. He was a very handsome young man, of polished manners, and of unblemished purity of life. His natural kindness of heart, combined with these attractions, rendered him a universal favorite.

Autun was in the province of Burgundy, of which the Prince of Condé, grandfather of the celebrated Duke d'Enghien, was governor. The prince attended an exhibition at the college, to assist in the distribution of the prizes. Joseph acquitted himself with so much honor as to attract the attention of the prince, and he inquired of him what profession he intended to pursue.

Joseph, in the following words, describes this eventful incident:

"The solemn day arrived. I performed my part to admiration, and when we afterward went to receive the crown, which the prince himself placed on our heads, I was the one whom. he seemed most to have noticed. The Bishop of Autun's friendship for our family, and no doubt also the curiosity which a little barbarian, recently introduced into the centre of civilization inspired, contributed to attract the prince's attention. He caressed me, complimented me on my progress, and made particular inquiries as to the intentions of my family with respect to me. The Bishop of Autun said that I was destined for the Church, and that he had a living in reserve, which he would bestow upon me as soon as the time came.

" 'And you, my lad,' said the prince, ' have you your own projects, and have you made up your mind as to what you wish ?'

" ' I wish,' said I, ' to serve the king.' Then seeing him disposed to listen favorably to me, I took courage to tell him that it was not at all my wish, though it was that of my family, that I should enter the Church, but that my dearest wish was to enter the army.

" The Bishop of Autun would have objected to my project, but the prince, who was colonel-general of the French infantry, saw with pleasure these warlike dispositions on my part, and encouraged me to ask for what I wanted. I then declared my desire to enter the artillery, and it was determined that I should. Imagine my joy. I was proud of the prince's caresses, and rejoiced more in his encouragement than I have since in the two crowns which I have worn.

" I immediately wrote a long letter to my brother Napoleon, imparting my happiness to him, and relating in detail all that had passed; concluding by begging him, out of friendship for me, to give up the navy and devote himself

2

to the artillery, that we might be in the same regiment, and pursue our career side by side. Napoleon immediately acceded to my proposal, abandoned from that moment all his naval projects, and replied that his mind was made up to dedicate himself, with me, to the artillery— with what success the world has since learned. Thus it was to this visit of the Prince of Condé that Napoleon owed his resolution of entering on a career which paved the way to all his honors."

In 1784, Joseph, then sixteen years of age, returned to Corsica. During his absence he had entirely forgotten the Italian, his native language, and could neither speak it nor understand it. After a few months at home, during which time he very diligently prosecuted his studies, his father, whose health was declining, found it necessary to visit Paris to seek medical advice. He took his son Joseph with him. Arriving at Montpellier, after a tempestuous voyage, he became so ill as to be unable to proceed any farther. After a painful sickness of three months, he died of a cancer in the stomach, on the 24th of February, 1785. The dying father, who had perceived indications of the exalted powers and the lofty character of his son

Napoleon, in the delirium of his last hours repeatedly cried out,

"Napoleon! Napoleon! come and rescue me from this dragon of death by whom I am devoured."

Upon his dying bed the father felt great solicitude for his wife, who was to be left, at the early age of thirty-five, a widow with eight children, six of whom were under thirteen years of age. Joseph willingly yielded to his father's earnest entreaties to relinquish the profession of arms and return to Corsica, that he might solace his bereaved mother and aid her in her arduous cares. Napoleon says of this noble mother.

"She had the head of a man on the shoulders of a woman. Left without a guide or protector, she was obliged to assume the management of affairs, but the burden did not overcome her. She administered every thing with a degree of sagacity not to be expected from her age or sex. Her tenderness was joined with severity. She punished, rewarded all alike. The good, the bad, nothing escaped her. Ah, what a woman! where shall we look for her equal? She watched over us with a solicitude unexampled. Every low sentiment, every ungenerous affection was discouraged and discarded. She suffered nothing but that which was grand and elevated to take root in our youthful understandings. She abhorred falsehood, and would not tolerate the slightest act of disobedience. None of our faults were overlooked. Losses, privations, fatigue had no effect upon her. She endured all, braved all. She had the energy of a man combined with the gentleness and delicacy of a woman."

Madame Permon, mother of the Duchess of Abrantes, a Corsican lady of fortune who resided at Montpellier, immediately after the death of Charles Bonaparte, took Joseph, the orphan boy, into her house. Madame Permon and Letitia Raniolini had been companions and intimate friends in their youthful days. "She was to me," says Joseph, "an angel of consolation ; and she lavished upon me all the attentions I could have received from the most tender and affectionate of mothers."

Joseph soon returned to Corsica. Napoleon had just before been promoted to the military school in Paris, in which city Eliza still continued at school. Lucien, the next younger brother, had also now been taken to the Continent, where he was pursuing his education. The four remaining children were very young.

"My mother," says Joseph, "moderated the expression of her grief that she might not excite mine. Heroic and admirable woman! the model of mothers; how much thy children are indebted to thee for the example which thou hast given them!"

Joseph remained at home about a year, devoting himself to the care of the family, when Napoleon obtained leave of absence, and, to the great joy of his mother, returned to Corsica. He brought with him two trunks, a small one containing his clothing, and a large one filled with his books. Seven years had now passed since the two affectionate brothers had met. Napoleon had entirely forgotten the Italian language; but, much chagrined by the loss, he immediately devoted himself with great energy to its recovery. "His habits," says Joseph, "were those of a young man retiring and studious." For nearly a year the two brothers prosecuted their studies vigorously together, while consoling, with their filial love, their revered mother. After some months Napoleon left home again, to rejoin his regiment at Valence. During this brief residence on his na-

tive island, with his accustomed habits of industry, he employed the hours of vacation in
writing a history of the revolutions in Corsica.
At Marseilles he showed the manuscript to the
abbé Raynal. The abbé was so much pleased
with it that he sent it to Mirabeau. This distinguished man remarked that the essay indi-
cated a genius of the first order.

Joseph decided, being the eldest brother, to
remain at home with his mother, to study law,
and commence its practice in Ajaccio, where
his mother then resided. He accordingly went
to Pisa to attend lectures in the law school
connected with the celebrated university in
that place. His rank and character secured
for him a distinguished reception, and he was
presented by the French minister to the grand
duke. Here Joseph became deeply interested
in the lectures of Lampredi, who boldly advoca-
ted the doctrine, then rarely heard in Europe,
of the *sovereignty of the people*. There were
many illustrious patriots at Pisa, and many
ardent young men, whose minds were imbued
with new ideas of political liberty. Freely and
earnestly they discussed the themes of aristocratic usurpation, and of the equal rights of all
men. Joseph, with enthusiasm, embraced the

cause of popular freedom, and became the unrelenting foe of that feudal despotism which
then domineered over all Europe. His associates were the most illustrious and cultivated
men of the liberal party. At that early period
Joseph published a pamphlet advocating the
rights of the people.

Having finished his studies and taken his
degree, Joseph returned to Corsica. He was
admitted to the bar in 1788, being then twenty
years of age, and commenced the practice of
law in Ajaccio. Upon this his return to Corsica he met his brother Napoleon again, who,
a few days before, had landed upon the island.
Napoleon was then intensely occupied in writing a treatise upon the question, "What are
the opinions and the feelings with which it is
necessary to inspire men for the promotion. of
their happiness?"

"This was the subject of our conversations,"
says Joseph, "in our daily walks, which were
prolonged upon the banks of the sea; in saun-
tering along the shores of a gulf which was as
beautiful as that of Naples, in a country fra-
grant with the exhalations of myrtles and or-
anges. We sometimes did not return home
until night had closed over us. There will be

found, in what remains of this essay, the opinions and the characteristic traits of Napoleon,
who united in his character qualities which
seemed to be contradictory—the calm of reason, illumined with the flashes of an Oriental
imagination; kindliness of soul, exquisite sensi-
bility; precious qualities which he subsequently deemed it his duty to conceal, under an ar-
tificial character which he studied to assume
when he attained power, saying that men must
be governed by one who is fair and just as
law, and not by a prince whose amiability might
be regarded as weakness, when that amiability is not controlled by the most inflexible justice.

"He had continually in view," continues
Joseph, "the judgment of posterity. His heart
throbbed at the idea of a grand and noble action which posterity could appreciate.

"'I would wish to be myself my posterity,'
he said to me one day, 'that I may myself
enjoy the sentiments which a great poet, like
Corneille, would represent me as feeling and
uttering. The sentiment of duty, the esteem
of a small number of friends, who know us as
we know ourselves, are not sufficient to inspire noble and conscientious actions. With

such motives one can make sages, but not heroes. If the movement now commenced continue in France, she will draw upon herself
the entire of Europe. She can only be defended by men passionate for glory, who will
be willing to die to-day, that they may live
eternally. It is for an end remote, indetermi-
nate, of which no definite account is taken, that
the inspired minority triumphs over the inert
masses. Those are the motives which have
guided the legislators, who have influenced the
destinies of the world.'"

It is remarkable that at so early a period
Napoleon so clearly foresaw that the opinions
of political equality, then struggling for existence in Paris, and of which he subsequently
became so illustrious an advocate, would, if
successful, combine all the despots of Europe
in a warfare against regenerated France. Joseph and Napoleon both warmly espoused the
cause of popular liberty, which was even then
upheaving the throne of the Bourbons.

At this time, June, 1789, the Constituent
Assembly commenced its world-renowned session in Paris. As soon as the liberal constitution, which it adopted, was issued, Joseph, who
was then president of the district in Ajaccio,

published an elementary treatise upon the constitution both in French and Italian, for the
benefit of the inhabitants of his native island.
This work conferred upon him much honor,
and greatly increased his influence.

The mayor of the city, Jean Jérôme Levie,
was a very noble man, and a particular friend
of the Bonapartes. Very liberally he contributed of his large fortune to aid the poor. "Napoleon," says Joseph, "honored him at Saint
Helena in his last hour, and left him a hundred
thousand francs. This proves the truth of
what I have often said of the kindness and
tenderness of Napoleon's heart. It was this
which led him in his last moments to remember the abbé Recco, Professor of the Royal College of Ajaccio, who in our early childhood,
before our departure for the Continent, kindly
admitted us to his class, and devoted to us his
attention. I recall the incident when the pupils
were arranged facing each other upon the opposite sides of the hall under an immense banner, one portion of which represented the flag
of Rome, and the other that of Carthage. As
the elder of the two children, the professor
placed me by his side under the Roman flag.

"Napoleon, annoyed at finding himself be-

JOSEPH AND NAPOLEON—TOUR IN CORSICA.

neath the flag of Carthage, which was not the
conquering banner, could have no rest until he
obtained a change of place with me, which I
readily granted, and for which he was very
grateful. And still, in his triumph, he was
disquieted with the idea of having been unjust
to his brother, and it required all the authority
of our mother to tranquilize him. This abbé
Recco was also remembered in his will."

On one occasion Napoleon accompanied Joseph on horseback to a remote part of the isl-
and, to attend a Convention, where Joseph was
to address the assembly.

" Napoleon was continually occupied," says
Joseph, " in collecting heroic incidents of the
ancient warriors of the country. I read to him
my speech, to which he added several names
of the ancient patriots. During the journey,
which we made quite slowly, without a change
of horses, his mind was incessantly employed
in studying the positions which the troops of
different nations had occupied, during the many
years in which they had combatted against the
inhabitants of the island. My thoughts ran in
another direction. The singular beauty of the
scenery interested me much more."

Louis Napoleon, in an article which he wrote

while a prisoner at Ham, upon his uncle, King Joseph, just after his death, says:

"Joseph was born to embellish the arts of peace, while the spirit of his brother found itself at ease only amid events which war introduces. From their earliest years this difference of capacity and of inclination was clearly manifested. Associated in the college at Autun with his brother, Joseph aided Napoleon in his Latin and Greek compositions, while Napoleon aided Joseph in all the problems of physics and mathematics. The one made verses, while the other studied Alexander and Cæsar."[1]

During the meeting of the Convention at Bastia, above alluded to, the tidings came of the death of Mirabeau. By the request of the President, Joseph Bonaparte announced the event to the Convention in an appropriate eulogy. The two brothers had but just returned to Ajaccio when the grand-uncle of the Bonaparte children died. He had been a firm friend of the family, and was greatly revered by them all. A few moments before his death he assembled them around his dying bed, and took an affectionate leave of each one. Joseph was

[1] Quelques Mot sur Joseph Napoleon Bonaparte; Oeuvres de Napoleon III., tome ii. p. 452.

now a member of the Directory of the depart-
ment. We have the testimony of Joseph that
the dying uncle said to his sobbing niece,

"Letitia, do not weep. I am willing to die
since I see you surrounded by your children.
My life is no longer necessary to protect the
family of Charles. Joseph is at the head of
the administration of the country; he can
therefore take care of the interests of the family. You, Napoleon, you will be a great man."

The French Revolution was now in full career. Napoleon returned to Paris, and witnessed the awful scenes of the 10th of August,
1792, when the palace of the Tuileries was
stormed, the royal family outraged, and the
guard massacred. He wrote to Joseph,

"If the king had shown himself on horseback at the head of his troops, he would have
gained the victory; at least so it appeared to
me, from the spirit which that morning seemed
to animate the groups of the people.

"After the victory of the Marseillaise, I saw
one of them upon the point of killing one of
the body-guard; 'Man of the South,' said I,
'let us save the poor fellow.' 'Are you from
the South?' said he. 'Yes,' I replied. 'Very
well,' he rejoined, 'let him be saved then.'"

The French monarchy was destroyed. France, delivered from the despotism of kings, was surrendered to the still greater despotism of irreligion and ignorance. Faction succeeded faction in ephemeral governments, and anarchy and terror rioted throughout the kingdom. Thousands of the nobles fled from France and joined the armies of the surrounding monarchies, which were on the march to replace the Bourbons on the throne. The true patriots of the nation, anxious for the overthrow of the intolerable despotism under which France had so long groaned, were struggling against the coalition of despots from abroad, while at the same time they were perilling their lives in the endeavor to resist the blind madness of the mob at home. With these two foes, equally formidable, pressing them from opposite quarters, they were making gigantic endeavors to establish republican institutions upon the basis of those then in successful operation in the United States. Joseph and his brother Napoleon with all zeal joined the Republican party. They were irreconcilably hostile to despotism on the one hand, and to Jacobinical anarchy upon the other. In devotion to the principles of republican liberty, they sacrificed their fortunes, and

placed their lives in imminent jeopardy. Anx·
ious as they both were to see the bulwarks of
the old feudal aristocracy battered down, they
were still more hostile to the domination of the
mob.

"1 frankly declare," said Napoleon, "that if
I were compelled to choose between the old
monarchy and Jacobin misrule, I should infi-
nitely prefer the former."

General Paoli had been appoined by Louis
XVI. lieutenant-general of Corsica. This il·
lustrious man, disgusted with the lawless vio-
olence which was now dominant in Paris, and
despairing of any salutary reform from the
revolutionary influences which were running
riot, through an error in judgment, which he
afterward bitterly deplored, joined the coalition
of foreign powers who, with fleets and armies,
were approaching France to replace, by the
bayonet, the rejected Bourbons upon the throne.
Both Joseph and Napoleon were exceedingly
attached to General Paoli. He was a family
friend, and his lofty character had won their rev·
erence. Paoli discerned the dawning greatness
of Napoleon even in these early years, and on
one occasion said to him,

"O Napoleon! you do not at all resemble

3

the moderns. You belong only to the heroes
of Plutarch."

Paoli made every effort to induce the young
Bonapartes to join his standard; but they, be·
lieving that popular rights would yet come out
triumphant, resolutely refused. The peasantry
of Corsica, unenlightened, and confiding in General Paoli, to whom they were enthusiastically
attached, eagerly rallied around his banner.
England was the soul of the coalition now formed against popular rights in France. Paoli, in
loyalty to the Bourbons, and in treason to the
French people, surrendered the island of Corsica to the British fleet.

The Bonaparte family, in wealth, rank, and
influence, was one of the most prominent upon
the island. An exasperated mob surrounded
their dwelling, and the family narrowly escaped
with their lives. The house and furniture were
almost entirely destroyed. At midnight Madame Bonaparte, with Joseph, Napoleon, and all
the other children who were then upon the isl-
and, secretly entered a boat in a retired cove,
and were rowed out to a small vessel which was
anchored at a short distance from the shore.
The sails were spread, and the exiled family,
in friendlessness, poverty, and dejection, were

Their Arrival in France.

landed upon the shores of France. Little did
they then dream that their renown was soon to
fill the world ; and that each one of those children was to rise to grandeur, and experience reverses which will never cease to excite the sympathies of mankind.

CHAPTER II.

DIPLOMATIC LABORS.

IT was the year 1793. On the 21st of January the unfortunate and guilty Louis XVI. had been led to the guillotine. The Royalists had surrendered Toulon to the British fleet. A Republican army was sent to regain the important port. Joseph Bonaparte was commissioned on the staff of the major-general in command, and was slightly wounded in the attack upon Cape Brun. All France was in a state of terrible excitement. Allied Europe was on the march to crush the revolution. The armies of Austria, gathered in Italy, were threatening to cross the Alps. The nobles in France, and all who were in favor of aristocratic domination, were watching for an opportunity to join the Allies, overwhelm the revolutionists, and replace the Bourbon family on the throne.

The National Assembly, which had assumed the supreme command upon the dethronement of the king, was now giving place to another assembly gathered in Paris, called the National

Convention. Napoleon was commissioned to obtain artillery and supplies for the troops composing the Army of Italy, who, few in numbers, quite undisciplined and feeble in the materials of war, were guarding the defiles of the Alps, to protect France from the threatened Austrian invasion in that quarter. He was soon after named general of brigade in the artillery, and was sent to aid the besieging army at Toulon. Madame Bonaparte and the younger children were at Marseilles, where Joseph and Napoleon, the natural guardians of the family, could more frequently visit them. On the last day of November of this year the British fleet was driven from the harbor of Toulon, and the city recaptured, as was universally admitted, by the genius of Napoleon.

In the year 1794 Joseph married Julie Clary, daughter of one of the wealthiest capitalists of Marseilles. Her sister Eugenie, to whom Napoleon was at that time much attached, afterward married Bernadotte, subsequently King of Sweden. Of Julie Clary the Duchess of Abrantes says:

" Madame Joseph Bonaparte is an angel of goodness. Pronounce her name, and all the indigent, all the unfortunate in Paris, Naples, and

Madrid, will repeat it with blessings. Never did she hesitate a moment to set about what she conceived to be her duty. Accordingly she is adored by all about her, and especially by her own household. Her unalterable kindness, her active charity, gain her the love of every body."

The brothers kept up a very constant correspondence. These letters have been published unaltered. They attest the exalted and affectionate character of both the young men. Napoleon writes to Joseph on the 25th of June, 1795:

"In whatever circumstances fortune may place you, you well know, my dear friend, that you can never have a better friend, one to whom you will be more dear, and who desires more sincerely your happiness. Life is but a transient dream, which is soon dissipated. If you go away, to be absent any length of time, send me your portrait. We have lived so much together, so closely united, that our hearts are blended. I feel, in tracing these lines, emotions which I have seldom experienced; I feel that it will be a long time before we shall meet again, and I can not continue my letter."

Again Napoleon writes on the 12th of August: " As for me, but little attached to life, I contemplate it without much anxiety, finding myself constantly in the mood of mind in which one finds himself on the eve of battle, convinced that when death comes in the midst, to terminate all things, it is folly to indulge in solicitude."

In these letters we see gradually developed the supremacy of the mind of Napoleon, and that soon, almost instinctively, he is recognized as the head of the family. On the 6th of September he writes from Paris:

"I am very well pleased with Louis.' He responds to my hopes, and to the expectations which I had formed for him. He is a fine fellow; ardor, vivacity, health, talent, exactness in business, kindness, he unites every thing. You know, my friend, that I live for the benefits which I can confer upon my family. If my hopes are favored by that good-fortune which has never abandoned my enterprises, I shall be able to render you happy, and to fulfill your desires. I feel keenly the absence of Louis. He was of great service to me. Never was a man more active, more skillful, more

' Napoleon's younger brother, father of Napoleon III.

winning. He could do at Paris whatever he wished."

None of the members of the Bonaparte family were ever ashamed to remind themselves of the days of their comparative poverty and obscurity. "One day," writes Louis Napoleon, now Napoleon III., "Joseph related that his brother Louis, for whom he had felt, from his infancy, all the cares and tenderness of a father, was about to leave Marseilles to go to school in Paris. Joseph accompanied him to the diligence. Just before the diligence started he perceived that it was quite cold, and that Louis had no overcoat. Not having then the means to purchase him one, and not wishing to expose his brother to the severity of the weather, he took off his own cloak and wrapped it around Louis. This action, which they mutually recalled when they were kings, had always remained engraved in the hearts of them both, as a tender souvenir of their constant intimacy."[1]

On the 6th of March, 1796, Napoleon was married to Josephine Beauharnais. "Thus vanished," writes Joseph Bonaparte, "the hope which my wife and I had cherished, for sev-

[1] Œuvres de Napoleon III., tome deuxième, p. 451.

JOSEPH GIVING HIS CLOAK TO HIS BROTHER LOUIS.

eral years, of seeing her younger sister Eugenie
united in marriage with my brother Napoleon.
Time and separation disposed of the event otherwise."

A few days after Napoleon's marriage he
took command of the Army of Italy, and hastened across the Alps to the scene of conflict.
After the victory of Mondovi, Napoleon, cher-
ishing the hope of detaching the Italians from
the Austrians, sent Joseph to Paris to urge
upon the Directory the importance of making
peace with the Court of Turin.   General Junot
accompanied Joseph, to present to the Directory the flags captured from the enemy.   The astonishing victories which Napoleon had gained
excited boundless enthusiasm in Paris.   Carnot, one of the Directors, gave a brilliant entertainment in honor of the two ambassadors,
Joseph and Junot.   During the dinner he
opened his waistcoat and showed the portrait
of Napoleon, which was suspended near his
heart.   Turning to Joseph, he said,.

"Say to your brother that I wear his minia-
ture there, because I foresee that he will be the
saviour of France.   To accomplish this, it is
necessary that he should know that there is no
one in the Directory who is not his admirer
and his friend."

The measures which Napoleon had suggested were most cordially approved by all the members of the Government. One of the most important members of the Cabinet proposed that Joseph Bonaparte should immediately, upon the ratification of peace, be appointed ambassador of the French Republic to the Court of Turin. Joseph, with characteristic modesty, replied, that though he was desirous of entering upon a diplomatic career, he did not feel qualified to assume at once so important a post. He was however prevailed upon to enter upon the office.

From this mission, so successfully accomplished, Joseph returned to his brother, and joined him at his head-quarters in Milan. Napoleon pressed forward in his triumphant career, drove the Austrians out of Italy, and soon effected peace with Naples and with Rome.

Having accomplished these results, Napoleon immediately fitted out an expedition for the reconquest of Corsica, his native island, which the British fleet still held. The expedition was placed under the command of General Gentili. The troops sailed from Leghorn, and disembarked at Bastia. Joseph accompanied

them. Immediately upon landing, the Corsi-
cans generally rose and joined their deliverers,
and the English retired in haste from the isl-
and. Joseph gives the following account of
his return to his parental home :

"I was received by the great majority of
the population at the distance of a league from
Ajaccio. I took up my residence in the mansion of Ornano, where I resided for several
weeks, until our parental homestead, which
had been devastated, was sufficiently repaired
to be occupied. I could not detect the slightest trace of any unfriendly feelings toward our
family. All the inhabitants, without any exception, hastened to greet me. In my turn, I
reorganized the government without consulting any other voice than the public good. A
commissioner from the Directory soon arrived,
and he sanctioned, without any exception, all
the measures which I had adopted.

"Having thus fulfilled, according to my
best judgment, the mission which fraternal
kindness had intrusted to me, and leaving our
native island tranquil and happy in finding itself again restored to the laws of France, I prepared to return to the Continent, having made
a sojourn in Corsica of three months."

On the 27th of March, 1797, Joseph was appointed ambassador to the Court of Parma. He presented to the duke credentials from the Directory of the French Republic, containing the following sentiments:

"The desire which we have to maintain and to cherish the friendship and the kind relations happily established between the French Republic and the Duchy of Parma, has induced us to appoint Citizen Bonaparte to reside at the Court of your Royal Highness in quality of ambassador. The knowledge which we have of his principles and his sentiments is to us a sure guarantee that the choice which we have made of his person to fulfill that honorable mission will be agreeable to you, and we are well persuaded that he will do every thing in his power to justify the confidence we have placed in him. It is in that persuasion that we pray your Royal Highness to repose entire faith in every thing which he may say in our behalf, and particularly whenever he may renew the assurance of the friendship with which we cherish your Royal Highness."

The Duke of Parma had married an Austrian duchess, sister of Maria Antoinette. She was an energetic woman, and in conjunction with the ecclesiastics, who crowded the palace, had great control over her husband. But the spirit of the French Revolution already pervaded many minds in Parma. Not a few were restive under the old feudal domination of the duke and the arrogance of the Church. One day Joseph was walking through the gardens of the ducal palace with several of the dignitaries of the Court. He spoke with admiration of the architectural grandeur and symmetry of the regal mansion.

"That is true," one replied, "but turn your eyes to the neighboring convent; how far does it surpass in magnificence the palace of the sovereign! Unhappy is that country where things are so."

After the peace of Leoben Napoleon returned to Milan and established himself, for several months, at the chateau of Montebello. Joseph soon joined his brother there. In the mean time their eldest sister, Eliza, had been married to M. Bacciochi, a young officer of great distinction. He was afterward created a prince by Napoleon. He was a man of elegant manners, and had attained no little distinction in literary and artistic accomplishments.

"We have often been amused," say the au-

thors of the " Napoleon Dynasty," " to see British writers, some of whom doubtless never
passed beyond the Channel, speak deprecia-
tingly of the manners and refinement of these
new-made princes and nobles of Napoleon's
Empire. Those who are familiar with the elegant manners of the refined Italians read such
slurs with a smile. Whatever may be the
crimes of the Italians, they have never been
accused, by those who know them, of coarse-
ness of manner, or lack of refinement of mind
and taste. Eliza is said to have possessed
more of her brother's genius than any other
one of the sisters. Chateaubriand, La Harpe,
Fontanes, and many other of the most illustrious men of France sought her society, and have
expressed their admiration of her talents."

At Montebello the second sister, Pauline,
was married to General Leclerc. Pauline was
pronounced by Canova to be the most peerless
model of grace and beauty in all Europe. The
same envenomed pen of slander which has
dared to calumniate even the immaculate Josephine has also been busy in traducing the
character of Pauline. We here again quote
from the " Napoleon Dynasty," by the Berke-
ley men :

" No satisfactory evidence has ever been adduced, in any quarter, that Pauline was not a virtuous woman. Those who were mainly instrumental in originating and circulating these slanders at the time about her, were the very persons who had endeavored to load the name of Josephine with obloquy. Those who saw her could not withhold their admiration. But the blood of Madame Mère was in her veins, and the Bonapartes, especially the women of the family, have always been too proud and haughty to degrade themselves. Even had they lacked what is technically called moral character, their virtue has been intrench-ed behind their ancestry, and the achievements of their own family; nor was there at any time an instant when any one of the Bonapartes could have overstepped, by a hair's breadth, the bounds of decency without being exposed. None of them pursued the noiseless tenor of their way along the vale of obscurity. They were walking in the clear sunshine, on the topmost summits of the earth, and millions of enemies were watching every step they took.

" The highest genius of historians, the bitter-est satire of dramatists, the meanest and most malignant pens of the journalists have assailed them for more than half a century. We have written these words because a Republican is the only one likely to speak well even of the good things of the Bonaparte family. It was, and is, and will be, the dynasty of the people standing there from 1804 a fearful antagonism against the feudal age, and its souvenirs of oppression and crime."

On the 7th of May, 1797, Joseph was promoted to the post of minister from the French Republic to the Court at Rome. He received instructions from his Government to make every effort to maintain friendly relations with that spiritual power, which exerted so vast an influence over the masses of Europe. Pope Pius VI. gave him a very cordial reception, and seemed well disposed to employ all his means of persuasion and authority to induce the Vendeans in France to accept the French Republic. The Vendeans, enthusiastic Catholics, and devoted to the Bourbons, were still, with amazing energy, perpetuating civil war in France. The Allies, ready to make use of any instrumentality whatever to crush republicanism, were doing every thing in their power to encourage the Vendeans in their rebellion. The Austrian ambassador at the Papal Court was unwearied in his endeavors to circumvent the peaceful mission of Joseph.

Though the Pope himself and his Secretary of State were inclined to amicable relations with the French Government, his Cabinet, the Sacred College, composed exclusively of ecclesiastics, was intent upon the restoration of the Bourbons, by which restoration alone the Catholic religion could be reinstated with exclusive power in France.

By the intrigues of Austria, General Provera, an *Austrian officer*, was placed in command of all the Papal forces. Joseph immediately communicated this fact to the Directory in Paris, and also to his brother. This Austrian officer had been fighting against the French in Italy, and had three times been taken prisoner by the French troops.

Napoleon, who had lost all confidence in the French Directory, and who, by virtue of his victories, had assumed the control of Italian diplomacy, immediately wrote as follows to Joseph :

"Milan, Dec. 14, 1797.

" I shared your indignation, citizen ambassador, when you informed me of the arrival of General Provera. You may declare positively

to the Court of Rome that if it receive into
its service any officer known to have been in
the service of the Emperor of Austria, all good
understanding between France and Rome will
cease from that hour, and war will be already
declared.

" You will let it be known, by a special note
to the Pope, which you will address to him in
person, that although peace may be made with
his majesty the Emperor, the French Republic
will not consent that the Pope should accept
among his troops any officer or agent belonging to the Emperor of any denomination, except the usual diplomatic agents. You will require the departure of M. Provera from the
Roman territory within twenty-four hours, in
default whereof you will declare that you quit
Rome."

The spirit of the French Revolution at this
time pervaded to a greater or less degree all
the kingdoms of Europe. In Rome there was
a very active party of Republicans anxious for
a change of government. Napoleon did not
wish to encourage this party in an insurrection.
By so doing, he would exasperate still more
the monarchs of Europe, who were already

combined in deadly hostility against republic
an France; neither did he think the Repub.
lican party in Rome sufficiently strong to maintain their cause, or the people sufficiently enlightened for self-government.   Thus he was
not at all disposed to favor any insurrectionary
movements in Rome; neither was he disposed
to render any aid whatever to the Papal Government in opposing those who were struggling
for greater political liberty.   He only demanded that France should be left by the other governments in Europe in entire liberty to choose
her own institutions.   And he did not wish
that France should interfere, in any way whatever, with the internal affairs of other nations.

While Joseph was officiating as ambassador
at Rome, endeavoring to promote friendly relations between the Papal See and the new
French Republic, he was much embarrassed by
the operations of two opposite and hostile parties of intriguants at that court.   The Austrians, and all the other European' cabinets,
were endeavoring to influence the Pope to give
his powerful moral support against the French
Revolution.   On the other hand there was a
party of active revolutionists, both native and
foreign, in Rome, struggling to rouse the popu-

lace to an insurrection against the Government, to overthrow the' Papal power entirely, as France had overthrown the Bourbon power, and to establish a republic. These men hoped for the countenance and support of France. But Joseph Bonaparte could lend them no countenance. He was received as a friendly ambassador at that court, and could not without ignominy take part with conspirators to overthrow the Government. He was also bound to watch with the utmost care, and thwart, if possible, the efforts of the Austrians, and other advocates of the old régime.

On the 27th of December three members of the revolutionary party called upon Joseph and informed him that during the night a revolution was to break out, and they wished to communicate the fact to him, that he might not be taken by surprise. Joseph reproved them, stating that he did not think it right for him, an ambassador at the Court of Rome, to listen to such a communication; and moreover he assured them that the movement was ill-timed, and that it could not prove successful.

They replied that they came to him for advice, for they hoped that republican France would protect them in their revolution as soon as it was accomplished. Joseph informed them that, as an impartial spectator, he should give an account to his Government of whatever scenes might occur, but that he could give them no encouragement whatever; that France was anxious to promote a general peace on the Continent, and would look with regret upon any occurrences which might retard that peace. He also repeated his assurance that the revolutionary party in Rome had by no means sufficient strength to attain their end, and he entreated them to desist from their purpose.

The committee were evidently impressed by his representations. They departed declaring that every thing should remain quiet for the present, and the night passed away in tranquillity. On the evening of the next day one of the Government party called, and confidentially informed Joseph that the *blunderheads* were ridiculously contemplating a movement which would only involve them in ruin. The Papal Government, by means of spies, was not only informed of all the movements contemplated, but through these spies, as pretended revolutionists, the Government was actually aiding in getting up the insurrection, which it would promptly crush with a bloody hand.

At 4 o'clock the next morning Joseph was
aroused from sleep by a messenger who informed him that about a hundred of the revolutionists had assembled at the villa Medici,
where they were surrounded by the troops of
the Pope.   Joseph, who had given the revolutionists good advice in vain, turned upon his
pillow and fell asleep again.   In the morning
he learned that there had been a slight conflict, that two of the Pope's dragoons had been
killed, and that the insurgents had been put to
flight; several of them having been arrested.
These insurgents had assumed the French national cockade, implying that they were acting,
in some degree of co-operation, with revolutionary France.

Joseph immediately called upon the Secretary of State, and informed him that far from
complaining of the arrest of persons who had
assumed the French cockade, he came to make
the definite request that he would arrest all
such persons who were not in the service of
the French legation.   He also informed the
secretary that six individuals had taken refuge
within his jurisdiction.   At Rome the residen-
ces of the foreign ambassadors enjoyed the
privilege of sanctuary in common with most

Duphot's contemplated Marriage.

of the churches. Joseph informed the secretary, that if those who had taken refuge in his palace were of the insurgents, they should be given up. As he returned to his residence he found General Duphot, a very distinguished French officer, who the next day was to be married to Joseph's wife's sister, and several other French gentlemen, eagerly conversing upon the folly of the past night. Just as they were sitting down to dinner, the porter informed him that some twenty persons were endeavoring to enter the palace, and that they were distributing French cockades to the passers-by, and were shouting " Live the Republic." One of these revolutionists, a French artist, burst like a maniac into the presence of the ambassador, exclaiming " We are free, and have come to demand the support of France."

Joseph sternly reproved him for his senseless conduct, and ordered him to retire immediately from the protection of the Embassy, and to take his comrades with him, or severe measures would be resorted to. One of the officers said to the artist scornfully, " Where would your pretended liberty be, should the governor of the city open fire upon you?"

The artist retired in confusion. But the tu-

mult around the palace increased. Joseph's
friends saw, in the midst of the mob, well-known
spies of the Government urging them on, shouting *Vive la Republique*, and scattering money with
a liberal hand. The insurgents were availing
themselves of the palace of the French ambassador as their place of rendezvous, and where, if
need be, they hoped to find a sanctuary. Joseph
took the insignia of his office, and calling upon
the officers of his household to follow him, descended into the court, intending to address the
mob, as he spoke their language. In leaving
the cabinet, they heard a prolonged discharge
of fire-arms. It was from the troops of the Government; a picket of cavalry, in violation of the
established usages of national courtesy, had invaded the jurisdiction of the French ambassador,
which, protected by his flag, was regarded as the
soil of France, and, without consulting the ambassador, were discharging volleys of musket-
ry through the three vast arches of the palace.
Many dropped dead; others fell wounded and
bleeding. The terrified crowd precipitated itself into the courts and on the stairs, pursued
by the avenging bullets of the Government.
Joseph and his friends, as they boldly forced
their way through the flying multitude, en-

countered the dying and the dead, and not a
few Government spies, who they knew were
paid to excite the insurrection and then to de-
nounce the movement to the authorities.

Just as they were stepping out of the vesti-
bule they met a company of fusileers who had
followed the cavalry. At the sight of the
French ambassador they stopped. Joseph demanded the commander. He, conscious of the
lawlessness of his proceedings, had concealed
himself in the ranks, and could not be distinguished. He then demanded of the troops by
whose order they entered upon the jurisdiction
of France, and commanded them to retire. A
scene of confusion ensued, some advancing, others retiring. Joseph then facing them, said, in
a very decisive tone, " that the first one who
should attempt to pass the middle of the court
would encounter trouble."

He drew his sword, and Generals Duphot and
Sherlock and two other officers of his escort,
armed with swords or pistols and poniards,
ranged themselves at his side to resist their advance. The musketeers retired just beyond
pistol-shot, and then deliberately fired a general
discharge in the direction of Joseph and his
friends. None of the party immediately sur-

rounding the ambassador were struck, but several were killed in their rear.

Joseph, with General Duphot, boldly advanced as the soldiers were reloading their
muskets, and ordered them to retire from the
jurisdiction of France, saying that the ambassador would charge himself with the punishment of the insurgents, and that he would immediately send one of his own officers to the
Vatican or to the Governor of Rome, and that
the affair would thus be settled. The soldiers
seemed to pay no regard to this, and continued
loading their muskets. General Duphot, one of
the most brave and impetuous of men, leaped
forward into the midst of the bayonets of the
soldiers, prevented one from loading and struck
up the gun of another, who was just upon the
point of firing. Joseph and General Sherlock,
as by instinct, followed him.

Some of the soldiers seized General Duphot,
dragged him rudely beyond the sacred pre-
cincts of the ambassador's palace and the flag of
France, and then a soldier discharged a musket
into his bosom. The heroic general fell, and
immediately painfully rose, leaning upon his
sabre. Joseph, who witnessed it all, in the
midst of this scene of indescribable confusion

called out to his friend, who the next day was
to be his brother-in-law, to return. General
Duphot attempted it, when a second shot pros-
trated him upon the pavement. More than
fifty shots were then discharged into his lifeless
body.

The soldiers now directed their fire upon
Joseph and General Sherlock. Fortunately
there was a door through which they escaped
into the garden of the palace, where they were
for a moment sheltered from the bullets of the
assassins. Another company of Government
troops had now arrived, and was firing from
the other side of the street. Two French officers, from whom Joseph had been separated,
now joined him and General Sherlock in the
garden. There was nothing to prevent the soldiers from entering the palace, where Joseph's
wife and her sister, who the next day was to
have become the wife of General Duphot, were
trembling in terror. Joseph and his friends re-
gained the palace by the side of the garden.
The court was now filled with the soldiers,
and with the insurgents who had so foolishly
and ignominiously caused this horrible scene.
Twenty of the insurgents lay dead upon the
pavement.

"I entered the palace," Joseph writes in
his dispatch to Talleyrand; "the walks were
covered with blood, with the dying, dragging
themselves along, and with the wounded, loudly
groaning. We closed the three gates fronting
upon the street. The lamentations of the be-
trothed of Duphot, that young hero who, constantly in the advance-guard of the armies of
the Pyrenees and of Italy, had always been victorious, butchered by cowardly brigands; the
absence of her mother and of her brother,
whom curiosity had drawn from the palace to
see the monuments of Rome; the fusillade which
continued in the streets, and against the gates
of the palace; the outer apartments of the vast
palace of Corsini, which I inhabited, thronged
with people of whose intentions we were ignorant: these circumstances and many others rendered the scene inconceivably cruel."

Joseph immediately summoned the servants
of the household around him. Three had been
wounded. The French officers, impelled by
an instinct of national pride, heroically emerged
from the palace, with the aid of these domestics,
to rescue the body of their unfortunate general.
Taking a circuitous route, notwithstanding the
fusillade which was still continued, they suc-

ceeded in reaching the spot of his cowardly assassination. There they found the remains of
this truly noble young man, despoiled, pierced
with bullets, clotted with blood, and covered
with stones which had been thrown upon him.

It was six o'clock in the evening. Two
hours had elapsed since the assassination of
Duphot; and yet not a member of the Roman
Government had appeared at the palace to
bring protection or to restore order. Joseph
was, properly, very indignant, and resolved at
once to call for his passports and leave the city.
He wrote a brief note to the Secretary of State,
and sent it by a faithful domestic, who succeeded in the darkness in passing through the crowd
of soldiers. As the firing was still continued,
Joseph and his friends anxiously watched the
messenger from the attic windows of the palace
till he was lost from sight.

An hour passed, and some one was heard
knocking at the gate with repeated blows.
They supposed that it was certainly the governor or some Roman officer of commanding
authority. It proved to be Chevalier Angio-
lini, minister from Tuscany, the envoy of a
prince who was in friendly alliance with the
French Republic. As he passed through the

soldiery they stopped his carriage, and sarcas-
tically asked him "if he were in search of
dangers and bullet-wounds." He courageous-
ly and reproachfully replied, "There can be
no such dangers in Rome within the jurisdiction of the ambassador of France." This was
a severe reproach against the officers of a nation who were indebted to the moderation of
the French Republic for their continued political existence. The minister of Spain soon also
presented himself, braving all the dangers of
the street, which were truly very great. They
were both astonished that no public officer
had arrived, and expressed much indignation
in view of the violation of the rights of the
Embassy.

Ten o'clock arrived, and still no public officer had made his appearance. Joseph wrote
a second letter to the cardinal. An answer
now came, which was soon followed by an officer and about forty men, who said that they
had been sent to protect the ambassador's communications with the Secretary of State. But
they had no authority or power to rescue the
palace from the insurgents, who were crowded into one part of it, and from the Government troops, who occupied another part. No

attention had been paid to Joseph's reiterated demands for the liberation of the palace from the dominion of the insurgents and the troops.

Joseph then wrote to the secretary, demanding immediately his passport. It was sent to him two hours after midnight. At six o'clock in the morning, fourteen hours after the assassination of General Duphot, the investment of the palace by the troops and the massacre of the people who had crowded into it, not a single Roman officer had made his appearance charged by the Government to investigate the state of affairs.

Joseph, after having secured the safety of the few French remaining at Rome, left for Tuscany, and in a dispatch to the French Government minutely detailed the events which had occurred. In the conclusion of his dispatch he wrote:

"This Government is not inconsistent with itself. Crafty and rash in perpetrating crime, cowardly and fawning when it has been committed, it is to-day upon its knees before the minister Azara, that he may go to Florence and induce me to return to Rome. So writes to me that generous friend of France, worthy of dwelling in a land where his virtues and his noble loyalty may be better appreciated."

In reply to this dispatch the French minister, Talleyrand, wrote to Joseph, "I have received, citizen, the heart-rending letter which you have written me upon the frightful events which transpired at Rome on the 28th of December. Notwithstanding the care which you have taken to conceal every thing personal to yourself during that horrible day, you have not been able to conceal from me that you have manifested, in the highest degree, courage, coolness, and that intelligence which nothing can escape ; and that you have sustained with magnanimity the honor of the French name. The Directory charges me to express to you, in the strongest and most impressive terms, its extreme satisfaction with your whole conduct. You will readily believe, I trust, that I am happy to be the organ of these sentiments."

CHAPTER III.

JOSEPH THE PEACE-MAKER.

JOSEPH, after a short tarry at Florence, returned to Paris, where he again met his brother. Napoleon was much disappointed with the result of the embassy to Rome, for he had ardently hoped to cultivate the most friendly relations with that power. Joseph was favored with a long interview with the Directory, by whom he was received with great cordiality. In testimony of their satisfaction, they offered him the embassy to Berlin. He, however, declined the appointment, as he preferred to enter the Council of Five Hundred, to which office he had been nominated by the Electoral College of one of the departments. The Government of France then consisted of an Executive of five Directors, a Senate, called the Council of Ancients, and a House of Representatives, called the Council of Five Hundred.

Preparations were now making for the ex-

pedition to Egypt.   The command was offered
to Napoleon.   For some time he hesitated before accepting it.   One day he said to his
brother Joseph,

"The Directory see me here with uneasiness, notwithstanding all my efforts to throw
myself into the shade.   Neither the Directory
nor I can do any thing to oppose that tendency to a more centralized government, which is
so manifestly inevitable.   Our dreams of a republic were the illusions of youth.   Since the
ninth Thermidor,[1] the Republican instinct has
grown weaker every day.   The efforts of the
Bourbons, of foreigners, sustained by the re-
membrance of the year 1793, had reunited
against the Republican system an imposing
majority.   But for the thirteenth Vendemiaire[2]
and the eighteenth Fructidor,[3] this majority

[1] 9th Thermidor, 28th of July, 1794.   This was the date
of the overthrow of Robespierre, and of the termination of
the Reign of Terror.   The enormous atrocities perpetrated
under the name of the Republic had excited general distrust
of republican institutions.

[2] 13th Vendemiaire, 5th of October, 1795, when Napoleon
quelled the insurgent sections.

[3] 18th Fructidor, 4th of September, 1797.   On this day the
majority of the French Directory overthrew the minority,
who were in favor of monarchical institutions.   Sixty-three
Deputies were banished for conspiring to introduce monarchy.
Both councils renewed their oath of hatred against royalty.

would have triumphed a long time ago. The feebleness, the dissensions of the Directory, have done the rest. It is upon me that all eyes are fixed to-day. To-morrow they will be fixed upon some one else. While waiting for that other one to appear, if he is to appear, my interest tells me that no violence should be done to fortune. We must leave to fortune an open field.

" Many persons hope still in the Republic Perhaps they have reason. I leave for the East, with all means for success. If my country has need of me—if the number of those who think with Talleyrand, Siéyes, and Roederer should increase, should war be resumed, and prove unfriendly to the arms of France, I shall return more sure of the opinion of the nation. If, on the contrary, the war should be favorable to the Republic, if a military statesman like myself should rise and gather around him the wishes of the people, very well, I shall render, perhaps, still greater services to the world in the East than he can do. I shall probably overthrow English domination, and shall arrive more surely at a maritime peace, than by the demonstrations which the Directory makes upon the shores of the Channel.

" The system of France must become that
of Europe in order to be durable. We see
thus very evidently what is required. I wish
what the nation wishes. Truly I do not know
what it wishes to-day, but we shall know better hereafter. Till then let us study its wishes
and its necessities. I do not wish to usurp any
thing. I shall, at all events, find renown in the
East; and if that renown can be made servicea-
able to my country, I will return with it. I will
then endeavor to secure the stability of the happiness of France in securing, if it is possible, the
prosperity of Europe, and extending our free
principles into neighboring states, who may be
made friends if they can profit from our misfortunes."

"Such," says Joseph, " were the habitual
thoughts of General Bonaparte. His happiness was not to depend merely upon the possession of power. He wished to merit the
gratitude of his country and of posterity by his
deeds, and to conform his life to duty, sure that
it was by such renown alone that his name
could pass down to future ages."

Joseph was now a member of the Council
of Five Hundred. His brother Lucien, though
he was still very young, had also been elected

a member of the same body. The brilliant
achievements of the young conqueror in the
East roused the enthusiasm of France. The
conquest of Malta, the landing at Alexandria,
the battle of the Pyramids, and the entrance into
Cairo, had been reported through France, rousing in every hill and valley shouts of exultation. Napoleon was rapidly gaining that renown which would enable him to control and
to guide his countrymen.

The Directory still nominally governed
France, though the affairs of the nation, under
their inefficiency and misrule, were passing rapidly to ruin. The Directors contemplated with
alarm the rising celebrity which Napoleon was
acquiring in the East. They made a formidable attack upon him, through a committee, in
the Council of Five Hundred. Joseph defended his absent brother with so much eloquence
and power, as to confound his accusers, and he
obtained a unanimous verdict in his favor.

The state of things in France was now
very deplorable. The Allies with vigor had
renewed the war. The Austrian armies had
again overrun Italy, and were threatening to
scale the Alps, and to rush down upon the
plains of France. The British fleet, the most

powerful military arm the world has ever
known, had swept the commerce of France
from all seas, had captured many of her colo-
nies, and was bombarding, with shot and shell,
every city of the Republic within reach of its
broadsides.   The five Directors were quarrelling among themselves, some favoring monarchy, others republicanism.   The two councils,
that of the Ancients and that of the Five Hundred, were at antagonism.   Many formidable
conspiracies were formed, some for the support
of the Allies and the restoration of the Bourbons, others for the re-introduction of the Jacobinical Reign of Terror.

France was in a state of general anarchy.
There was no man of sufficient celebrity to gain
the confidence of the people, so that he could
assume the office of leader, and bring order out
of chaos.   The once mighty monarchy of France
was in the condition of a mob, without a head,
careering this way and that way, in tumultuous
and inextricable confusion.   Joseph sent a special messenger, a Greek by the name of Bour-
baki, to Jean d'Acre, to communicate to Napoleon the state of affairs.

Informed of these facts, at this momentous
crisis Napoleon, having attained renown which

caused every eye in France to be fixed upon
him, landed at Frejus, and was borne along,
with the acclamations of the multitude, to Paris.
Immediately upon the young general's arrival,
General Moreau hastened to his humble residence in the Rue de la Victoire, and earnestly
said to him,

"Disgusted with the government of the law-
yers, who have ruined the Republic, I come to
offer you my aid to save the country."

A number of the most distinguished men
of France crowded the small parlors of General Bonaparte. As he was speaking, with that
genius which ever commanded attention and
assent, of the political condition and wants of
France, Moreau interrupted him, saying,

"I only desire to unite my efforts with
yours to save France. I am convinced that you
only have the power. The generals and the
officers who have served under me are now in
Paris, and are ready to co-operate with you."
The little saloon was crowded. General Mac-
donald was present. Generals Jourdan and
Augereau had conversed with Salcetti, and reported that Bernadotte and a majority of the
Council of Five Hundred were in favor of the
movement.

Joseph co-operated diligently with Napoleon in the measures now set on foot to rescue France from destruction. Joseph dined with Siéyes. At the table Siéyes said to his guests,

"I wish to unite with General Bonaparte, for of all the military men he is the most of a statesman."

On the 18th Brumaire[1] the Directory was overthrown, and, without one drop of blood being shed, a new government was organized, and Napoleon was made consul. The world is divided, and perhaps may forever remain divided, in its judgment of this event. Some call Napoleon a usurper. France then called him, and still calls him, the saviour of his country.

In the midst of these tumultuary scenes, when it was uncertain whether Napoleon would gain his ends or fall upon the scaffold, General Augereau came, in great alarm, to St. Cloud, and informed Napoleon that his enemies in the two councils were proposing to vote him an outlaw.

"Very well," said Napoleon calmly, "you and I, General Augereau, have long been acquainted with each other. Say to your friends

---

[1] *18th Brumaire*, Nov. 9th, 1799.

the cork is drawn, we must now drink the wine."

Joseph Bonaparte, who a little before these events had withdrawn from the Council of Five Hundred, was with his brother constantly through these momentous scenes. Immediately after the establishment of the new government he was appointed a member of the legislative body, and soon after of the Council of State. Joseph had become a very wealthy man, having acquired a large fortune by his marriage. He owned a very beautiful estate at Mortfontaine, but a few leagues from Paris. Both Joseph and his wife were extremely fond of the quiet, domestic pleasures of rural life. Neither of them had any taste for the excitement and the splendors of state. But France, in her condition of peril, assailed by the allied despotism of Europe without, and agitated by conspiracies within, demanded the energies of every patriotic arm. Joseph was thus constrained to sacrifice his inclinations to his sense of duty. He rendered his brother invaluable assistance by the energy and the conciliatory manners with which he endeavored to carry out the plans of the First Consul. Lucien Bonaparte, eight years younger than

Joseph, accepted the post of Minister of the Interior.

Before the overthrow of the Directory mob law had reigned triumphant in Paris. Napoleon, as first consul, immediately took up his residence in the palace of the Tuileries. It was proposed to him that he should close the gates of the garden of the Tuileries, that it might no longer be a place of public resort. Joseph strenuously opposed the measure, and it was renounced. The great object Napoleon aimed at was to ascertain the wishes of the people, that he might be the executor of their will. His only power consisted in having cordially with him the masses of the population. He was untiring in his endeavors to ascertain public sentiment, and endeavored to adopt those measures which should, from their manifest wisdom and justice, secure public approbation. In this service Joseph was invaluable to his brother. He gave brilliant entertainments at his chateau at Mortfontaine; and being a man of remarkably amiable spirit and polished manners, he secured the confidence of all parties, and exerted a very powerful influence in healing the wounds of past strife. At these entertainments Joseph made it his constant object to study the wishes and the opinions of the different classes of society.

The Directory had involved the public in serious difficulties with the United States. Napoleon immediately appointed Joseph, with two associates, to adjust all the differences between the two countries. As both parties were disposed to friendly relations, all difficulties were speedily terminated, and a treaty was signed on the 30th of September, 1800, at Joseph's mansion at Mortfontaine.

England and Austria, with great vigor, still pressed the war upon France, notwithstanding the earnest appeals of Napoleon to the King of England and the Emperor of Austria in behalf of peace. This refusal to sheathe the sword rendered the campaign of Marengo a necessity. Napoleon crossed the Alps, and upon the plains of Marengo almost demolished the armies of Austria. The haughty Emperor was compelled to sue for that peace which he had so scornfully rejected. The commissioners of the two powers met at Luneville. Napoleon, highly gratified at the skill which Joseph had displayed in adjusting the difficulties in the United States, appointed him as the ambassador from France to secure a treaty with Austria. The two brothers were in daily, and sometimes in hourly conference in reference to the questions of vast national importance which this treaty involved. But Joseph was again entirely successful. On the 9th of February, 1801, the peace of Luneville was concluded, to the great satisfaction of the Emperor, and to the great gratification of France. Napoleon says, in the conclusion of a letter which he wrote to Joseph upon this subject, "The nation is satisfied with the treaty, and I am exceedingly pleased with it."

France was now at peace with all the Continent. England alone implacably continued the war. But England was inaccessible to any blows which France could strike without making efforts more gigantic than nation ever attempted before. Napoleon resolved to make these efforts to attain peace. He prepared almost to bridge the Channel with his fleet and gun-boats, that he might pour an army of invasion upon the shores of the belligerent isle, and thus compel the British to sheathe the sword. While these immense preparations were going on, the First Consul devoted his energies to the reconstruction of society in France.

Revolutionary fury had swept all the institutions of the past into chaotic ruin. The good and the bad had been alike demolished. Christianity had been entirely overthrown, her churches destroyed, and her priesthood either slaughtered upon the guillotine, or driven from the realm. France presented the revolting aspect of a mighty nation without morality, without religion, and without a God. The masses of the people, particularly in the rural districts of France, had become disgusted with the reign of vice and misery. They longed to enjoy again the quietude of the Sabbath morning, the tones of the Sabbath bell, the gathering of the congregations in the churches, and all those ministrations of religion which cheer the joyous hours of the bridal, and which convey solace to the chamber of death. The overwhelming majority of the people of France were Roman Catholics. Among the millions who peopled the extensive realm there were but a few thousands who were Protestants. Napoleon had not the power, even had he wished it, of establishing Protestantism as the national religion.

He therefore, in accordance with his policy of adopting those measures which were in ac-

cordance with the wishes of the people, resolved
to recognize the Catholic religion as the religion of France, while at the same time he en-
forced perfect liberty of conscience for all other
religious sects. He also determined that all
the high dignitaries of the Church should be
appointed by the French Government, and not
by the Pope. He deemed it not befitting the
dignity of France, or in accordance with her
interests, that a foreign potentate, by having
the appointment of all the places of ecclesiastical power, should wield so immense an influence over the French people.

But to re-establish the Catholic religion, and
to invest it with the supremacy which it had
gained over the imaginations of men, it was
necessary to bring the system under the paternal jurisdiction of the Pope, who throughout
all Europe was the recognized father and head
of the Church.

But the Pope was jealous of his power. He
would be slow to consent that any officers of
the Church should be appointed by any voice
which did not emanate from the Vatican. It
was also an established decree of the Church
that heresy was a crime, meriting the severest
punishment, both civil and ecclesiastical. The

Pope, therefore, could not consent that any·
where within his spiritual domain freedom of
conscience should be tolerated. Under these
circumstances, nothing could be more difficult
than the accomplishment of the plan which
Napoleon had proposed for the promotion of
the peace and prosperity of France.

The eyes of the First Consul were imme·
diately turned to his brother Joseph, as the most
fitting man in France to conduct negotiations
of so much delicacy and importance. He con·
sequently was appointed, in conjunction with
M. Cretet, Minister of the Interior, and the
abbé Bernier, subsequently Bishop of Orleans,
as commissioner on the part of France to a
conference with the Holy See. The Pope sent,
as his representatives, the cardinals Consalvi
and Spina, and the father Caselli. Here again
Joseph was entirely successful, and accomplished his mission by securing all those results
which theFirst Consul so earnestly had desired.

The celebrated Concordat[1] was signed July

[1] "I hold it for certain that in 1802 the Concordat was, on
the part of Napoleon, an act of superior intelligence, much
more than of a despotic spirit, and for the Christian religion
in France an event as salutary as it was necessary. After
the anarchy and the revolutionary orgies, the solemn recog-

15th, 1801, at the residence of Joseph in Paris, in the Rue Faubourg St. Honoré. It was two o'clock in the morning when the signatures of the several commissioners were affixed to this important document.

"At the same hour," writes Joseph, "I became the father of a third infant, whose birth was saluted by the congratulations of the plenipotentiaries of the two great powers, and whose prosperity was augured by the envoys of the vicar of Christ. Their prayers have not been granted. A widow at thirty years of age, separated from her father, proscribed, as has been all the rest of her family, there only remains to her the consolation of reflecting that she has not merited her misfortunes."[1]

Thus did Napoleon re-establish the Christian religion throughout the whole territory of France. In this measure he was strenuously opposed by many of his leading officers, and by

nition of Christianity by the State could alone give satisfaction to public sentiment, and assure to the Christian influence the dignity and the stability which it was needful that it should recover."—Meditations sur l'état Actuel de la Religion Chrétienne, par M. Guizot, p. 5.

[1] This daughter subsequently married her cousin, the brother of the Emperor Napoleon III., the second son of Louis Bonaparte. He died at an early age, in a campaign for the liberation of Italy.

The Re-establishment of Christianity.

the corrupt revolutionary circles of France, yet throughout all the rural districts the restoration of religion was received with boundless enthusiasm.

"The sound of the village bells," writes Alison, "again calling the faithful to the house of God, was hailed by millions as the dove with the olive-branch, which first pronounced peace to the green, undeluged earth. The thoughtful and religious everywhere justly considered the voluntary return of a great nation to the creed of its fathers, from the experienced impossibility of living without its precepts, as the most signal triumph which has occurred since it ascended the imperial throne under the banners of Constantine."

Nearly all the powers upon the Continent of Europe were now at peace with France. England alone still refused to sheathe the sword. But the *people* of England began to remonstrate so determinedly against this endless war, which was openly waged to force upon France a detested dynasty, that the English Government was compelled, though with much reluctance, to listen to proposals for peace.

The latter part of the year 1801, the pleni-

potentiaries of France and England met at
Amiens, an intermediate point between London and Paris. England appointed, as her ambassador, Lord Cornwallis, a nobleman of ex-
alted character, and whose lofty spirit of honor
was superior to every temptation. "The First
Consul," writes Thiers, "on this occasion made
choice of his brother Joseph, for whom he had
a very particular affection, and who, by the
amenity of his manners, and mildness of his
character, was singularly well adapted for a
peace-maker, an office which had been constantly reserved for him."

Napoleon, who had nothing to gain by war,
was exceedingly anxious for peace with all the
world, that he might reconstruct French society from the chaos into which revolutionary
anarchy had plunged it, and that he might
develop the boundless resources of France.
Lord Cornwallis was received in Paris, with
the utmost cordiality by Napoleon. Joseph
Bonaparte gave, in his honor, a magnificent
entertainment, to which all the distinguished
Englishmen in France were invited, and also
such Frenchmen of note as he supposed Lord
Cornwallis would be glad to meet.

La Fayette was not invited. Cornwallis had

commanded an army in America, where he had met La Fayette on fields of blood, and where he subsequently, with his whole army, had been taken prisoner. Joseph thought that painful associations might be excited in the bosom of his English guest by meeting his successful antagonist. He therefore, from a sense of delicacy, avoided bringing them together. But Cornwallis was a man of generous nature. As he looked around upon the numerous guests assembled at the table, he said to Joseph,

"I know that the Marquis de la Fayette is one of your friends. It would have given me much pleasure to have met him here. I do not, however, complain of your diplomatic caution. I suppose that you did not wish to introduce to me at your table the general of Georgetown. I thank you for your kind intention, which I fully appreciate. But I hope that when we know each other better, we shall banish all reserve, and not act as diplomatists, but as men who sincerely desire to fulfill the wishes of their governments, and to arrive promptly at a solid peace. Moreover, the Marquis de la Fayette is one of those men whom we can not help loving. During his captivity I presented myself before the Em-

peror (of Germany) to implore his liberation,
which I did not have the happiness of obtaining."

Cornwallis left Paris for Amiens. Joseph
immediately after proceeded to the same place.
As he alighted from his carriage in the court-
yard of the hotel which had been prepared for
him, one of the first persons whom he met was
Lord Cornwallis. The English lord, disregard-
ing the formalities of etiquette, advanced, and
presenting his hand to Joseph, said,

" I hope that it is thus that you will deal
with me, and that all our etiquette will not retard for a single hour the conclusion of peace.
Such forms are not necessary where frankness
and honest intentions rule. My Government
would not have chosen me as an ambassador,
if it had not been intended to restore peace to
the world. The First Consul, in choosing his
brother, has also proved his good intentions.
The rest remains for us."

Louis Napoleon gives the following rather
amusing account of this incident. " When
Joseph, plenipotentiary of the French Republic, journeyed with his colleagues toward Amiens, to conclude peace with England, in 1802,
they were much occupied, he said, during the

CORNWALLIS AND JOSEPH.

route, as to the ceremonial which should be
observed with the English diplomatists. In
the interests of their mission they desired not
to fail in any proprieties. Still, being representatives of a republican state, they did not
wish to show too much attention, *prévenance*,
to the grand English lords with whom they
were to treat.

"The French ambassadors were therefore
much embarrassed in deciding to whom it belonged to make the first visit. Quite inexperienced, they were not aware that foreign diplomatists always conceal the inflexibility of their
policy under the suppleness of forms. Thus
they were promptly extricated from their embarrassment; for, to their great astonishment,
they found, upon their arrival at Amiens, Lord
Cornwallis waiting for them at the door of his
hotel, and who, without any ceremony, himself opened for them the door of their carriage,
giving them a cordial grasp of the hand."[1]

Lord Cornwallis, however, found himself incessantly embarrassed by instructions he was
receiving from the ministry at London. They
were very reluctantly consenting to peace, being forced to it by the pressure of public opin-

[1] Œuvres de Napoleon III. tome ii. p. 456.

ion. They were, therefore, hoping that obstacles would arise which would enable them, with some plausibility, to renew the war. Napoleon continually wrote to his brother urging him to do every thing in his power to secure the signing of the treaty. In a letter on the 10th of March, he writes,

"The differences at Amiens are not worth making such a noise about. A letter from Amiens caused the alarm in London by asserting that I did not wish for peace. Under these circumstances delay will do real mischief, and may be of great consequence to our squadrons and our expeditions. Have the kindness, therefore, to send special couriers to inform me of what you are doing, and of what you hear; for it is clear to me that, if the terms of peace are not already signed, there is a change of plans in London."

The treaty was signed on the 25th of March, 1802. Joseph immediately prepared to return to Paris. Lord Cornwallis, in taking leave of Joseph, said,

"I must go as soon as possible to London, in order to allay the storm which will there be gathering against me."

"When I arrived in Paris," writes Joseph,

Bernardin de St. Pierre.

"the First Consul was at the opera; he caused me to enter into his box, and presented me to the public in announcing the conclusion of the peace. One can easily imagine the emotions which agitated me, and also him, for he was as tender a friend, and as kind a brother, as he was prodigious as a man and great as a sovereign."

Bernardin de St. Pierre, in his preface to "Paul and Virginia," renders the following homage to the character of Joseph at this time:

"About a year and a half ago I was invited by one of the subscribers to the fine edition of Paul and Virginia to come and see him at his country-house. He was a young father of a family, whose physiognomy announced the qualities of his mind. He united in himself every thing which distinguishes as a son, a brother, a husband, a father, and a friend to humanity. He took me in private, and said, 'My fortune, which I owe to the nation, affords me the means of being useful: Add to my happiness by giving me an opportunity of contributing to your own.' This philosopher, so worthy of a throne, if any throne were worthy of him, was Prince Joseph Napoleon Bonaparte."

While the treaty of Amiens was under discussion, Talleyrand wrote to Joseph: "Your lot will indeed be a happy one if you are able to secure for your brother that peace which alone his enemies fear. I embrace you, and I love you. I think that this affair will kill me unless it is closed as we desire."

At the conclusion of the treaty, Talleyrand again wrote: "MY DEAR JOSEPH, — Citizen Dupuis has just arrived. He has been received by the First Consul as the bearer of such good, grand, glorious news as you have just sent by him should be received. Your brother is perfectly satisfied (*parfaitement content*").

Madame de Staël wrote to Joseph: "Peace with England is the joy of the world. It adds to my joy that it is you who have promoted it, and that every year you have some new occasion to make the whole nation love and applaud you. You have terminated the most important negotiation in the history of France. That glory will be without any alloy."

CHAPTER IV.

JOSEPH KING OF NAPLES.

THE peace of Amiens was of short duration. In May, 1803—but fourteen months after the signing of the treaty—England again renewed hostilities without even a declaration of war. This was the signal for new scenes of blood and woe. Napoleon now resolved to assail his implacable foe by carrying his armies into the heart of England. Enormous preparations were made upon the French coast to transport a resistless force across the Channel. Joseph Bonaparte was placed in command of a regiment of the line, which had recently returned, with great renown, from the fields of Italy.

In the midst of these preparations, which excited fearful apprehensions in England, the British Government succeeded in organizing another coalition with Austria and Russia, to fall upon France in the rear. The armies of these gigantic Northern powers commenced their march toward the Rhine. Napoleon broke up the camp of Boulogne and advanced to meet them. The immortal campaigns of Ulm and Austerlitz were the result. Incredible as it may seem, England represented this as an unprovoked invasion of Germany by Napoleon. This incessant assault of the Allies upon France was a great grief to the Emperor. In the midst of all the distractions which preceded this triumphant march, he wrote to his Minister of Finance:

"I am distressed beyond measure at the necessities of my situation, which, by compelling me to live in camps, and engage in distant expeditions, withdraw my attention from what would otherwise be the chief object of my anxiety, and the first wish of my heart — a good and solid organization of all which concerns the interests of banks, manufactures, and commerce."

While Napoleon was absent upon this campaign, Joseph was left in Paris, to attend to the administration of home affairs. This he did, much to the satisfaction of Napoleon, and with great honor to himself. Napoleon was now

Emperor of France, and the Senate and the people had declared Joseph and his children heirs of the throne, on failure of Napoleon's issue.

A gigantic conspiracy was formed in England by Count d'Artois, subsequently Charles X., and other French emigrants, for the assassination of Napoleon. The plan was for a hundred resolute men, led by the desperate George Cadoudal, to waylay Napoleon when passing, as was his wont, with merely a small guard of ten outriders, from the Tuileries to Malmaison. The conspirators flattered themselves that this would be considered war, not assassination. The Bourbons were then to raise their banner in France, and the emigrants, lingering upon the frontiers, were to rush into the empire with the Allied armies, and re-establish the throne of the old régime. The Princes of Condé grandfather, son, and grandson, were then in the service and pay of Great Britain, fighting against their native land, and, by the laws of France traitors, exposed to the penalty of death. The grandson, the Duke d'Enghien, was on the French frontier, in the duchy of Baden, waiting for the signal to enter France arms in hand.

It was supposed that he was actively en-gaged in the conspiracy for the assassination, as he was known frequently to enter France by night and in disguise. But it afterward ap-peared that these journeys were to visit a young lady to whom the duke was much at-tached.

Napoleon, supposing that the duke was in-volved in the conspiracy, and indignant in view of these repeated plots, in which the Bourbons seemed to regard him but as a wild beast whom they could shoot down at their pleasure, resolved to teach them that he was not thus to be assailed with impunity. A de-tachment of soldiers was sent across the border, who arrested the duke in his bed, brought him to Vincennes, where he was tried by court-martial, condemned as a traitor waging war against his native country, and, by a series of accidents, was shot before Napoleon had time to extend that pardon which he intended to grant. The friends of Napoleon do not se-verely censure him for this deed. His enemies call it wanton murder. Joseph thus speaks of this event:

" The catastrophe of the Duke d'Enghien requires of me some details too honorable to

JOSEPH AT MALMAISON.

the memory of Napoleon for me to pass them by in silence. Upon the arrival of the duke at Vincennes, I was in my home at Mortfontaine. I was sent for to Malmaison. Scarcely had I arrived at the gate when Josephine came to meet me, very much agitated, to announce the event of the day. Napoleon had consulted Cambaceres and Berthier, who were in favor of the prisoner; but she greatly feared the influence of Talleyrand, who had already made the tour of the park with Napoleon.

"'Your brother,' said she, 'has called for you several times. Hasten to interrupt this long interview; that lame man makes me tremble.'

"When I arrived at the door of the saloon, the First Consul took leave of M. de Talleyrand, and called me. He expressed his astonishment at the great diversity of opinion of the two last persons whom he had consulted, and demanded mine. I recalled to him his political principles, which were to govern all the factions by taking part with none. I recalled to him the circumstance of his entry into the artillery in consequence of the encouragement which the Prince of Condé had given me to commence a military career. I still remembered the quatrain of the verses composed by the abbé Simon:

> " 'Condé! quel nom, l'univers le vénère;
> A ce pays il est cher à jamais;
> Mars l'honore pendant la guerre,
> Et Minerve pendant la paix."[1]

"Little did we then think that we should ever be deliberating upon the fate of his grandson. Tears moistened the eyes of Napoleon. With a nervous gesture, which always with him accompanied a generous thought, he said, 'His pardon is in my heart, since it is in my power to pardon him. But that is not enough for me. I wish that the grandson of Conde should serve in our armies. I feel myself sufficiently strong for that.'

"With these impressions I returned to Mortfontaine. The family were at the dinner-table. I took a seat by the side of Madame de Staël, who had at her left M. Mathieu de Montmorency. Madame de Staël, with the assurance which I gave her of the intention of the First Consul to pardon a descendant of the great Condé, exclaimed in characteristic language,

[1]   "Condé! what a name! the universe reveres it;
To this country it is ever dear;
Mars honors it during war,
And Minerva during peace."

" ' Ah! that is right; if it were not so, we should not see here M. Mathieu de Montmorency.'

" But another nobleman present, who had not emigrated, said to me, on the contrary: 'Will it then be permitted to the Bourbons to conspire with impunity? The First Consul is deceived if he think that the nobles who have not emigrated, and particularly the historic nobility, take any deep interest in the Bourbons.' Several others present expressed the same views.

" The next day, upon my return to Malmaison, I found Napoleon very indignant against Count Real; whose motives he accused, reproaching him with having employed in his government certain men too much compromised in the great excesses of the Revolution. *The Duke d'Enghien had been condemned and executed even before the announcement of his trial had been communicated to Napoleon.*

" Subsequently he was convinced of the innocence of Real, and of the strange fatality which had caused him for a moment to appear culpable in his eyes. In the mean time, resuming self-control, he said to me, ' Another opportunity has been lost. It would have been admirable to have had, as aid-de-camp, the grandson of the great Condé. But of that there can be no more question. The blow is irremediable. Yes; I was sufficiently strong to allow a descendant of the great Condé to serve in our armies. But we must seek consolation. Undoubtedly, if I had been assassinated by the agents of the family, he would have been the first to have shown himself in France, arms in his hands. I must take the responsibility of the deed. To cast it upon others, even with truth, would have too much the appearance of cowardice, for me to be willing to do it.'

"Napoleon," continues Joseph, "has never appeared with greater éclat than under these sad and calamitous circumstances. I only learned, several years afterward, in the United States, from Count Real himself, the details of that which passed at the time of the death of the Duke d'Enghien. It was at New York, in the year 1825, at Washington Hall, where we met, by an arrangement with M. Le Ray de Chaumont, the proprietor of some lands, a portion of which he had sold to me and to M. Real, that he informed me how a simple emotion of impatience on his part had very involuntarily the effect of preventing the kindly feeling which the First Consul cherished in favor of the Duke d'Enghien.

"M. Real, one of the four counsellors of state charged with the police of France, had charge of the arrondissement of Paris and of Vincennes. A dispatch was sent to him in the night, informing him of the condemnation of the prince. The police clerk, attending in the chamber which opened into his apartment, had already awoke him twice for reasons of but little importance, which had quite annoyed M. Real. The third dispatch was therefore placed upon his chimney, and did not meet his eye until a late hour in the morning.

"Opening it, he hastened to Malmaison, where he was preceded by an officer of the gendarmerie, who brought information of the condemnation and execution of the prince. The commission had judged, from the silence of the Government, that he was not to be pardoned. I need not dwell upon the regret, the impatience, the indignation of Napoleon."

The crown of Lombardy was, about this time, offered to Joseph, which he declined, as he did not wish to separate himself from France. The kingdom of Naples was now influenced by England to make an attack upon

Napoleon. The King of Naples supposed that France could be easily vanquished, with England, Russia, Austria, and Naples making a simultaneous attack upon her. But the great victory of Austerlitz, which compelled Austria and Russia to withdraw from the coalition, struck the perfidious King of Naples with dismay. France had done him no wrong, and the only apology the Neapolitan Court had for commencing hostilities was, that if the French were permitted to dethrone the Bourbons and to choose their own rulers, the Neapolitan might claim the same privilege.

A few days after the battle of Austerlitz Joseph received orders from his brother to hasten to the Italian Peninsula, and take command of the Army of Italy, and march upon Naples. The King of Naples had, in addition to his own troops, fourteen thousand Russians and several thousand English auxiliaries. Joseph placed himself at the head of forty thousand French troops, and in February, 1806, entered the kingdom of Naples. The Neapolitans could make no effectual resistance. Joseph soon arrived before Capua, a fortified town about fifteen miles north of the metropolis of the kingdom. Eight thousand of the

Neapolitan troops took refuge in the citadel, and made some show of resistance. They soon, however, were compelled to surrender.

The Neapolitan Court was in a state of consternation. The English precipitately embarked in their ships and fled to Sicily. The Russians escaped to Corfu. The Court, having emptied the public coffers, and even the vaults of the bank, took refuge in Palermo, on the island of Sicily. The prince royal, with a few troops of the Neapolitan army, who adhered to the old monarchy, retreated two or three hundred miles south, to the mountains of Calabria. On the 15th of February, Joseph, at the head of his troops, marched triumphantly into Naples. He not only encountered no resistance, but the population, regarding him as a liberator, received him with acclamations of joy.

On the 30th of March, 1806, Napoleon issued a decree, declaring Joseph king of Naples. The *decret* was as follows:

"Napoleon, by the grace of God and the constitutions, Emperor of the French and King of Italy, to all those to whom these presents come, salutation.

"The interests of our people, the honor of

our crown, and the tranquillity of the Continent of Europe requiring that we should assure, in a stable and definite manner, the lot of the people of Naples and of Sicily, who have fallen into our power by the right of conquest, and who constitute a part of the grand empire, we declare that we recognize, as King of Naples and of Sicily, our well-beloved brother, Joseph Napoleon, Grand Elector of France. This crown will be hereditary, by order of primogeniture, in his descendants masculine, legitimate, and natural," etc.

The former Government of Naples was detested by the whole people. The warmest advocates of the Allies have never yet ventured to utter a word in its defense. Even the grandees of the realm were heartily glad to be rid of their dissolute, contemptible, and tyrannical queen, who regarded the inhabitants of the kingdom but as her slaves, and the wealth of the kingdom but as her personal dowry, to be squandered for the gratification of herself and her favorites. With great energy Joseph immediately commenced a reform in all the administrative departments. He carefully sought out Neapolitan citizens of integrity, intelligence, and influence, to occupy the important public stations. Accompanied by a guard of chosen men, he made a tour of the country; thus informing himself, by personal observation, of the character of the inhabitants, and of the wants and capabilities of the kingdom. It was indeed a gloomy prospect of indolence and poverty which presented itself to his eye, though the climate was enchanting, with its genial temperature, its brilliant skies, and its fertile soil. The landscape combined all the elements of sublimity and of beauty, with towering mountains and lovely meadows, streams and lakes watering the interior, and harbors inviting the commerce of the world. But the condition of the populace was wretched in the extreme. The Government, despotic and corrupt, seized all the earnings of the people, and consigned nearly the whole population to penury and rags. King Ferdinand and his dissolute queen, Louisa, made an effort to rouse the people to resist the French. Their efforts were, however, entirely in vain. Joseph issued the following proclamation to the Neapolitans, which they read with great satisfaction:

"People of the kingdom of Naples; the Emperor of the French, King of Italy, wishing

to save you from the calamities of war, had
signed, with your Court, a treaty of neutrality.
He believed that in that way he could secure
your tranquillity, in the midst of the vast conflagration with which the third coalition has
menaced Europe.   But the Court of Naples
has zealously allied itself with our enemies,
and has opened its states to the Russians and
to the English.

"The Emperor of the French, whose justice
equals his power, wishes to give a signal example, commanded by the honor of his crown,
by the interests of his people, and by the necessity of re-establishing in Europe the respect
which is due to public faith.

"The army which I command is on the
march to punish this perfidy.   But you, the
people, have nothing to fear.   It is not against
you that our arms are directed.   The altars,
the ministers of your religion, your laws, your
property, will be respected.   The French soldiers will be your brothers.   If, contrary to
the benevolent intentions of his majesty, the
Court which excites you will sacrifice you, the
French army is so powerful that all the forces
promised to your princes, even if they were
on your territory, could not defend it.   Peo-

ple! have no solicitude. This war will be for you the epoch of a solid peace, and of durable prosperity."

Ferdinand, upon retiring to the island of Sicily, had swept the continental coast of every vessel and even boat. Joseph thus found it quite impossible to transport his troops across the strait of Messina to pursue the fugitive king. He, however, made a very thorough survey of the continental kingdom, and having planned many measures of internal improvement of vast magnitude, which were subsequently executed, he returned to Naples. He was here received with congratulations by all classes of his subjects.

The clergy, led by Cardinal Ruffo, and even the nobility, vied with each other in their expressions of satisfaction in a change of dynasty. The great majority of the most intelligent people in the kingdom were weary of the corrupt Court which, swaying the sceptre of feudal despotism, had consigned Naples to indolence, dilapidation, and penury. Joseph immediately selected the most distinguished Neapolitans as members of his council. He made every effort to introduce into his kingdom all the benefits which the French Revolution had

Philanthropic Labors.

brought to France, while he carefully sought to avoid the evils which accompanied that great popular movement.

Though Joseph soon found himself firmly seated on the throne, war still lingered along the coasts, and in the more remote parts of his kingdom. The fortress of Gaëta, almost impregnable, was still held by a garrison of Ferdinand's troops. Marauding bands of Neapolitans, lured by love of plunder, infested and pillaged the unprotected districts. The English fleet was hovering along the coast, watching for opportunities of assault. It landed an army at the Gulf of St. Euphemia, and discomfited a small division of Joseph's troops. Thus the kingdom was in a general state of disorder wherever the influence of Joseph was not sensibly felt.

But the wise and energetic measures he adopted removed one after another of these evils. He found but little difficulty in persuading all those who co-operated with him in the government, both French and Neapolitans, that the interests of each individual class in the community were dependent upon the elevation and improvement of the whole country; and it is a remarkable fact that the principal noblemen in Naples were among the first to appreciate and adopt the great ideas of reform which Joseph introduced. Influenced by his arguments, they, of their own accord, relinquished their feudal privileges, and adopted those principles of equal rights upon which the empire of Napoleon was founded, and which gave it its almost omnipotent hold upon popular affections. Even the ecclesiastics, men of commanding character and intelligence, who had been introduced into the Council of State, voted for the suppression of monastic orders, and for the use of their funds to place the credit of the kingdom upon a solid basis.

Reform was thus extended, wisely and efficiently, through all the departments of Government. And though the masses of the people, being illiterate peasants, incapable of any intelligent administration of public affairs, had but little voice in the Government, every thing was done for their welfare that enlightened patriotism could suggest. All writers, friends and foes, agree alike in their testimony to the wise measures adopted by Joseph. He founded colleges for the instruction of young men, and many other institutions of a high character for male and female education. Splendid

roads were constructed from one extremity of
the kingdom to the other; manufactories of
various kinds were established and encouraged; the arts were rewarded; agriculture received a new impulse; the army was efficiently organized and brought under salutary discipline; a topographical bureau was created,
the whole kingdom carefully surveyed, and a
fine map constructed. The mouldering ram-
parts of the city were rebuilt, and new fort-
resses reared.

Naples had for ages been filled with a miserable idle population, called lazzaroni. They
infested the streets and the squares, and were
devoured by vermin, and half-covered with
rags. With no incitement to industry, indeed
with hardly the possibility of obtaining any
work, they had fallen into the most abject state
of vice and despair. These men, in large numbers, were collected, comfortably clothed, well
fed, well paid, and were employed in constructing a new and splendid avenue to the metropolis. Made happy by industry, and inspired by
its sure reward, they became contented and useful subjects.

The Ministry of the Interior was confided
to Count Miot. It was his duty to devote all

his energies to promote the interests of agriculture, commerce, manufactures, the arts, the sciences, public instruction, and all liberal institutions. The country had been filled with brigands, rioting in violence, robbery, and murder. To repress their excesses, Joseph established a military commission with each army corps, whose duty it was to judge and execute, without appeal, the brigands taken with arms in their hands.

The English fleet commanded the Mediterranean. The Neapolitan troops, under the command of Ferdinand, had fled to Calabria, and, under the protection of the English fleet, had crossed the straits of Messina to the island of Sicily. The British squadron then swept the coasts of Calabria, applying the torch to all the public property which could not be carried away. While these scenes were transpiring, Napoleon wrote to Joseph almost daily, giving him very minute directions. He wrote to him on the 12th of January, 1806: "Speak seriously to M—— and to L——, and say that you will have no robberies. M—— robbed much in the Venetian country. I have recalled S—— to Paris for that reason. He is a bad man. Maintain severe discipline."

Again he wrote on the 19th : " It is my intention that the Bourbons should cease to reign
at Naples.   I wish to place upon that throne a
prince of my family; you first, if that is agreeable to you ; another, if that is not agreeable
to you.   The country ought to furnish food,
clothing, horses, and every thing that is necessary for your army ; so that it shall cost me
nothing."

Again, on the 27th, Napoleon wrote from
Paris : " I have only to congratulate myself
with all that you did while you remained in
Paris.   Receive my thanks, and, as a testimony
of my satisfaction, my portrait upon a snuff-
box, which I will forward by the first officer
I send to you.   Tolerate no robbers.   I have
just received a letter from the Queen of Naples.
I shall not reply.   After the violation of the
treaty, I can no longer trust her promises."

Again, on the 3d of February, 1806, he
writes : " Believe in my friendship.   Do not
listen to those who wish to keep you out of fire,
loin du feu.   It is necessary that you should
establish your reputation, if there should be
opportunity.   Place yourself conspicuously
As to real danger, it is everywhere in war."

The Prince-royal of Naples wrote a letter to

Joseph, with the hope of regaining his crown. He stated that the King and Queen had abdicated in favor of their son. Joseph replied that he could not listen to the appeal; that he could only execute the orders which he received, and that the application was too late.

The city of Gaëta was one of the strongest positions in Europe. The troops of Ferdinand maintained a siege there for many months. They were very efficiently aided by the British fleet, which brought them continual re-enforcements and supplies. Its capture was considered one of the most brilliant achievements in modern warfare. There was now not a spot upon the Continent of Europe where a flag floated in avowed hostility to France. Ferdinand of Naples, with a small army, had fled to the island of Sicily, where, for a short time, he was protected by the British fleet.

In the mean time King Joseph was devoting himself untiringly and with great wisdom to the development of the new institutions of reform, and of equal rights for all, which everywhere accompanied the French banners. Marshal Massena was sent to the provinces of Calabria to put a stop to brigandage. The brigands were merciless. Severe reprisals became necessary. The British fleet, under Sir Sidney Smith, hovered along the shores of the gulfs of Salerno and of Naples, striving to rouse and encourage resistance to the new Government.

There was a renowned bandit, named Michael Pozza, who, from his energy and atrocities, had acquired the sobriquet of *Fra Diavolo*, or brother of the devil. His bands, widely scattered, were at times concentrated, and waged fierce battle. Gradually French discipline gained upon them. Large numbers of the Neapolitans, hating the old régime, and glad to be rid of it, enlisted in defense of the new institutions. The robbers were at length cut to pieces. Fra Diavolo escaped to the mountains, where he was taken and shot. In this warfare with the brigands, the Neapolitan troops, emboldened by the presence and protection of the French army, displayed very commendable courage.

While engaged in these warlike operations, through his able generals, Joseph was much occupied with the employment, more congenial to him, of conducting the interior administration. It was his first endeavor to eradicate every vestige of the old despotism of feudalism —a system perhaps necessary in its day, but which time had outgrown. The whole political edifice was laid upon the foundation of the *absolute equality of rights of all the citizens*—a principle until then unknown in Naples. There had been no gradations in society. There were a few families of extreme opulence, enjoying rank and exclusive privileges, and then came the almost beggared masses, with no incentives to exertion. The enervating climate induced indolence. Life could be maintained with but little clothing, and but little food. The cities and villages swarmed with half-clad multitudes, vegetating in a joyless existence.

Joseph gave his earnest attention to rousing the multitude from this apathy. He thought that one of the most important means to awaken a love of industry was to make these poor people, as far as possible, landed proprietors. The man who owns land, though the portion may be small, is almost resistlessly impelled to cultivate it. His ambition being thus roused, his intellectual and social condition becomes ameliorated, and he is prepared to take part, as a citizen, in the administration of affairs. A new division of territory was created into provinces and districts, in which the prominent men, who were imbued with the spirit of reform, were appointed to the administration of local interests.   Still many of the old nobility struggled hard to maintain their feudal power.   But resolutely Joseph proceeded in laying the foun-dations of a national representation, derived from popular election, which should be the or-gan of the whole nation, to make known to the King the wishes and necessities of the people.

This was an immense stride in the direction of a popular government. It endangered the feudal privilege, which upheld the throne and the castle, in other lands.   Hence it was that the throne and the castle combined to over-throw institutions so republican in their ten-dencies.

The whole system of administration had been awfully corrupt.   Justice was almost un-known.   All the tribunals were concentrated in the city of Naples.   There were tens of thousands of prisoners, very many for political offenses, awaiting trial.   In the provinces of Calabria Joseph appointed judicial commissions to attend to these cases.   In three months about five thousand prisoners had a hearing.   Many of them had been detained over twenty years. Not a few were incarcerated through malicious accusations.   Those guilty of some slight of-fense were imprisoned with assassins, all alike exposed to the damp of dungeons and infected air.

A system of very effective prison reform was immediately established by Joseph. The prisoners were placed in apartments large and well-ventilated. They were separated in accordance with the nature of the offenses of which they were accused. Distinct prisons were appropriated to females. Hospitals were established for the sick of both sexes, with every necessary arrangement for the restoration of health.

A thorough reform was introduced into the finances. Under the old régime, all had been confusion and oppression. The only object of the Government seemed to be to get all it could. In the country the people often were compelled to pay their lords not only money, but also very onerous personal services. This was all remedied by the adoption of an impartial system of taxation. And it was found that the new imposts, honestly collected, were far less oppressive to the people, and more in amount.

The overthrow of the feudal system placed at the disposal of the State a vast amount of land which had been uncultivated. This was divided among a large number of people, who

paid for it an annual sum into the treasury.
Thus the welfare of these individuals was greatly promoted, and the resources of the State increased.

And now Joseph turned his attention to public instruction. The last Government had been opposed to education. It had entered into open warfare against the sciences, prohibiting the introduction of the most important foreign publications. Joseph immediately established schools for primary instruction all over the realm. Normal schools were organized for the education of teachers. In the smallest hamlets teachers were provided to instruct the children in the elements of the Christian religion, and school-mistresses, who, in addition to the same lessons, were to teach the young girls the duties proper to their sex.

This impulse to education spread rapidly through all the provinces. The free schools established in Naples were soon so crowded that it became necessary to add to their number. The university at Naples, frowned upon by the former Government, had fallen into deep decline. Nineteen chairs of professors were vacant. Others were occupied, but their duties quite neglected. The university was

reorganized in accordance with the enlighten-
ment of modern times. New professorships
were endowed in the place of those which had
become useless. Especial efforts were made
to secure learned men for those chairs from
the kingdom of Naples. But education was
at so low an ebb that it was necessary to obtain several professors from abroad. Everywhere a thirst for knowledge seemed to manifest itself.

These reforms were exceedingly popular
with the great majority of the Neapolitans.
But there were not wanting those who opposed
them. There were those of the privileged
class who had been enriched by the ignorance
and debasement of the people. These men
began gradually to develop their opposition.
Joseph had endeavored to employ Neapolitans
as much as possible in the Government. He
employed Frenchmen in the military and civil
service only where he could find no Neapolitans equal to the post. Some of the Neapolitans, jealous of French influence, while also
secretly clinging to ancient abuses, began cau-
tiously the attempt to retard these reforms.
Joseph listened patiently to their objections in
cabinet council, and then said:

"I have carefully followed a discussion which relates so intimately to the public welfare. I had hoped to hear reasons. I have heard only passions. I look in vain for any indications of love of country in the objections to the proposed laws. I must say that I see only the spirit of party."

He then examined, one by one, the objections which had been brought forward, and added, "Do you think, gentlemen, that I am willing to sustain these exclusive privileges? We have not destroyed these Gothic institutions, the remnants of barbarism, in order to reconstruct them under other forms. And can any of you cherish the thought that this resistance, which ought to surprise me, can induce me to retrograde toward institutions condemned by the spirit of the age? No; too long have the people groaned under the weight of intolerable abuses. They shall be delivered from them. If obstacles arise, be assured that I shall know how to remove them."

The fine arts were also languishing, with every thing else, under the execrable régime of the Bourbons of Naples. But the taste for the fine arts survived their decay. The new Government instituted schools of art under the direction of the most skillful masters. Painting, drawing, sculpture, engraving, all received a new impulse.

There were difficulties to be encountered in this attempt to regenerate an utterly depraved state more than can now be easily imagined. He who should attempt to erect a modern mansion upon the ruins of the Castle of Heidelberg would find more difficulty in removing the old foundations than in rearing the new structure. Thus Joseph found ancient abuses, hallowed by time, and oppressive institutions interwoven with the very life of the people, which it was necessary utterly to abolish or greatly to modify. The monastic institution was one of these. The land was filled with gloomy monasteries, crowded with idle, useless, and often dissolute monks. There had been in past ages seasons of persecution, in which the refuge of these sanctuaries was needed, but the spirit of the age no longer required them. They had rendered signal service in times of barbarism, but it was no longer needful for religion to hide in the obscurity of the cloister.

"Altars," said Joseph, "are now erected in the interior of families. The regular clergy respond to the wants of the people. The love

of the arts and of the sciences, widely dif-
fused, and the colonial, commercial, and military spirit constrain all the Governments of
Europe to direct to important objects the genius, activity, and pecuniary resources of their
nations. The support of considerable land
and sea forces involves the necessity of great
reforms in other departments of the general
economy of the State. The first duty of peoples and princes is to place themselves in a
condition of defense against the aggressions of
their enemies. Still we do not forget that we
ought to reconcile these principles with the
respect with which we should cherish those
celebrated places which, in barbaric ages, preserved the sacred fire of reason, and which became the dépôt of human knowledge."

The debates upon this subject in the Council of State were long and animated. The
peasantry, ignorant and superstitious, clung to
their old prejudices, and could not easily throw
aside the shackles of ages. Many of these religious communities were wealthy, the recipi-
ents of immense sums bequeathed to them by
the dying. There was no *legal* right, no right
but that of revolution and the absolute necessities of the State, for wresting this property

from them. But it was manifest to every in-telligent mind that the Neapolitan kingdom could never emerge from the stagnation of semi-barbarism without the entire overthrow of many, and the radical reform of the remain-der of these institutions.

At length a law, very carefully matured, was enacted, suppressing a large number of these religious orders, and introducing essen-tial changes into those which were permitted to survive. The possessions of those which were abolished, generally consisting of large tracts of land, reverted to the State, and were sold at auction in small farms. The money thus raised helped replenish the bankrupt treasury. The poor monks, expelled from their cells, with no habits of industry, and no means of obtaining a support, received a life pension, amounting to a little more than one hundred dollars a year.

The three abbeys of Mount Cassin, Cava, and Monte Verginè contained very consider-able libraries, and were the dépôts of impor-tant records and manuscripts. These were in-trusted to the keeping of a select number of the most intelligent monks. It was their duty to arrange and catalogue the books and manu-

scripts, and to search out those works which
could throw light upon the sciences, the arts,
and the past history of the realm. They retained the buildings, the necessary furniture,
and received a small additional stipend.

There were some passes through the mountains which were perilous in the winter season.
Upon these bleak eminences houses of refuge
were erected, to shelter travellers and to help
them on their way. In each of these twenty-
five monks were placed. Their labors were
arduous, as often all the necessaries of life had
to be brought upon their backs from the plains
below. They received a frugal but comfortable support.

The salaries of the hard-working clergy
were increased. The vases and ornaments
from the suppressed convents were distributed
among those poorer parishes which were in a
state of destitution. The furniture of the convents was transferred to the civil and military
hospitals. The pictures, bas-reliefs, statuary,
and other objects of art were collected for the
national museum which the King wished to
establish. The mendicant friars, who had sufficient education, were intrusted with the instruction of the children.

The number of priests under the old régime had increased to a degree entirely dis-
proportioned to the wants of the community.
They were consequently wretchedly poor. A
fixed salary was assigned to the rectors, that
they might live respectably, and the ordina-
tions in each diocese were so regulated that
there should be but one priest for about one
thousand souls.

It is not to be supposed that such changes
could be effected without much friction. Not
only bigotry opposed them, but there was a
deep-seated, though unintelligent religious sentiment, which remonstrated against them. The
advocates of the old régime availed themselves,
in every possible way, of this sentiment, while
the British fleet, continually hovering around
the coasts, and occasionally landing men at
unguarded points, contributed much toward
keeping the spirit of insurrection alive, and
preventing the tranquillity of the country.

New public works were commenced in the
capital, to employ the idle and starving multitudes there. The country roads, so long infested with robbers, were in a wretched condition. The entire stagnation of all internal commerce had left them unused and almost im-

passable. The old roads were repaired, and new ones vigorously opened. The inhabitants of the provinces, and even the soldiers who could be conveniently spared, were employed in these enterprises. The soldiers, receiving slight additional pay, cheerfully contributed their labors. French officers of engineers, of established ability, superintended these national works.

King Joseph was but the agent of his brother Napoleon. Though himself a man of superior ability, and imbued with an ardent spirit of humanity, in these great enterprises he was carrying out the designs with which the imperial mind of his brother was inspired. Thus the kingdom of Naples, in a few months, under the reign of Joseph, made more progress than had been accomplished in scores of years under the dominion of the Neapolitan Bourbons.

On the 8th of May, 1806, Joseph wrote to Napoleon: "My previous letters have announced to your Majesty that perfect order is restored in the Calabrias. I am not less pleased with the inhabitants of Apulia. They are more enlightened, less passionate, but equally zealous with the Calabrians to withdraw their country from the debasement into which it is plunged. I am particularly satisfied with the priests, the nobles, and the landed proprietors.

"I now fully recognize the justice of the principles which I have so often heard from the lips of your Majesty. And I confess that experience has proved to me how true it is that it is necessary to see to every thing one's self; that not a moment of time must ever be lost; that we can not rely upon the activity of any person, and that every thing is possible, with a determined will on the part of the chief. I say to myself, ten times a day, the Emperor was right.

"I have established in each province a president, or prefect, who is entirely independent of the military commandant. I have decreed the formation in each province of a legion whose organization I will soon send to your Majesty. It is not paid. It is commanded by those men who are the most opulent, the most respectable, and the most attached to the present order of things. In each province I form a company of gendarmerie, composed of Frenchmen and Neapolitans. It is with some pride that I see that all the measures which your Majesty has prescribed to me I have adopted in advance.

9

" Whatever I may say, your Majesty can form no conception of the state of oppression, barbarism, and debasement which existed in this realm. And I can assure your Majesty that the Neapolitan officers returning to their homes become well pleased in witnessing the spirit which animates their fellow-citizens. I derive much advantage from the knowledge I have of the language, the manners, and customs of the country. The inhabitants of the mountains and of the villages resemble closely those of Corsica. And I do not think that I can be mistaken when I assure your Majesty that the people regard themselves as happy in being governed by a man who is so nearly related to your Majesty, and who bears a name which your Majesty rendered illustrious before he became an emperor, and which has for them the advantage of being Italian."

On the 22d of June, 1806, Napoleon wrote to Joseph, " MY BROTHER—the Court of Rome is entirely surrendered to folly. It refuses to recognize you, and I know not what sort of a treaty it wishes to make with me. It thinks that I can not unite profound respect for the spiritual authority of the Pope, and at the same time repel his temporal pretensions. It forgets that Saint Louis, whose piety is well known, was almost always at war with the Pope, and that Charles V., who was a very Christian prince, held Rome besieged for a long time, and seized it, with every Roman state."

On the 28th of February, 1806, M. de Meneval, the Emperor's secretary, had written to Joseph, "The Emperor works prodigiously. He holds three or four councils every day, from eight o'clock in the morning, when he rises, until two or three o'clock in the morning, when he goes to bed."

Napoleon well knew the fickle, unreliable, debased character of the Italian populace. He was sure that Joseph, in the kindness of his heart, was too confiding and unsuspicious. He wrote reiteratedly upon this subject: "Put it in your calculations," said he, "that sooner or later you will have an insurrection. It is an event which always happens in a conquered country. You can never sustain yourself by *opinion* in such a city as Naples. Be sure that you will have a riot or an insurrection. I earnestly desire to aid you by my experience in such matters. Shoot pitilessly the lazzaroni who plunge the dagger. I am greatly surprised that you do not shoot the spies of the

King of Naples. Your administration is too feeble. I can not conceive why you do not execute the laws. Every spy should be shot. Every lazzaroni who plies the dagger should be shot. You attach too much importance to a populace whom two or three battalions and a few pieces of artillery will bring to reason. They will never be submissive until they rise in insurrection, and you make a severe example. The villages which revolt should be surrendered to pillage. It is not only the right of war, but policy requires it. Your government, my brother, is not sufficiently vigorous. You fear too much to indispose people. You are too amiable, and have too much confidence in the Neapolitans. This system of mildness will not avail you. Be sure of that. I truly desire that the mob of Naples should revolt. Until you make an example, you will not be master. With every conquered people a revolt is a necessity. I should regard a revolt in Naples as the father of a family regards the small-pox for his children. Provided it does not weaken the invalid too much, it is a salutary crisis."

Such were the precautions which Napoleon was continually sending to Joseph. His amiable brother did not sufficiently heed them. He fancied that the most ignorant, fanatical, and debased of men could be held in control by kind words and kind deeds alone. But he awoke fearfully to the delusion when a savage insurrection broke out among the peasants and the brigands of the Calabrias, and swept the provinces with flame and blood. Then scenes of woe ensued which can never be described. It became necessary to resort to the severest acts of punishment. Much, if not all of this, might have been saved had the firm government which Napoleon recommended been established at the beginning. It is cruelty, not kindness, to leave the mob to feel that they can inaugurate their reign of terror with impunity.

The following extracts from a letter which Joseph wrote his wife, dated Naples, March 22d, 1806, throw interesting light upon the characters of both the King and the Emperor.

"I repeat it, the Emperor ought not to remain alone in Paris. Providence has made me expressly to serve as his safeguard. Loving repose, and yet able to support activity; despising grandeurs, and yet able to bear their burden with success, whatever may have been the slight differences between him and me, I can truly say that he is the man of all the world whom I love the best. I do not know if a climate and shores very much resembling those which I inhabited with him, have given back to me all my first love for the friend of my childhood; but I can truly say that I often find myself weeping over the affections of twenty years' standing as over those of but a few months.

"If you can not come to me immediately, send Zénaïde.[1] I would give all the empires of the world for one caress of my tall Zénaïde, or for one kiss of my little Lolotte. As for you, you know very well that I love you as their mother, and as I love my wife. If I can unite a dispersed family and live in the bosom of my own, I shall be content; and I will surrender myself to fulfill all the missions which the Emperor may assign to me, provided they can be temporary, and that I may cherish the hope of dying in a country in which I have always wished to live."

[1] Zénaïde and Lolotte (Charlotte), the two daughters of Joseph.

CHAPTER V.

THE CROWN A BURDEN.

THE close of the year 1806 was rendered memorable by the victories of Jena and Auerstadt, and the occupation of Prussia by the armies of Napoleon. The war was wantonly provoked by Prussia. Napoleon wrote to Joseph from St. Cloud, on the 13th of September:

"Prussia makes me a thousand protestations. That does not prevent me from taking my precautions. In a few days she will disarm, or she will be crushed. Austria protests her wish to remain neutral. Russia knows not what she wishes. Her remote position renders her powerless. Thus, in a few words, you have the present aspect of affairs."

A few days after he wrote again to Joseph from St. Cloud: "MY BROTHER,—I have just received the tidings that Mr. Fox is dead. Under present circumstances, he is a man who dies regretted by two nations. The horizon is some·

what clouded in Europe. It is possible that I
may soon come to blows with the King of
Prussia. If matters are not soon arranged, the
Prussians will be so beaten in the first encoun-
ters, that every thing will be finished in a few
days."

Napoleon cautioned his brother against
making the contents of his letters known to
others, saying, "I repeat to you, that if this letter is read by others than yourself, you injure
your own affairs. I am accustomed to think
three or four months in advance of what I do,
and I make arrangements for the worst."

England, Russia, and Prussia entered into a
new alliance to crush the Empire in France.
The armies of Prussia, two hundred thousand
strong, commenced their march by entering
Saxony, one of the allies of Napoleon. Alexander of Russia was hastening to join Prussia, with two hundred thousand men in his
train. England was giving the most energetic
co-operation with her invincible fleet and her
almost inexhaustible gold. Upon the eve of
this terrible conflict, Napoleon, in the following terms, addressed Europe, to which address
no reply was returned but that of shot and
shell.

Napoleon's Address to Europe.

"Why should hostilities arise between France and Russia? Perfectly independent of each other, they are impotent to inflict evil, but all-powerful to communicate benefits. If the Emperor of France exercises a great influence in Italy, the Czar exerts a still greater influence over Turkey and Persia. If the Cabinet of Russia pretends to have a right to affix limits to the power of France, without doubt it is equally disposed to allow the Emperor of the French to prescribe the bounds beyond which Russia is not to pass.

"Russia has partitioned Poland. Can she then complain that France possesses Belgium and the left banks of the Rhine? Russia has seized upon the Crimea, the Caucasus, and the northern provinces of Persia. Can she deny that the right of self-preservation gives France a title to demand an equivalent in Europe. Let every power begin by restoring the conquests which it has made during the last fifty years. Let them re-establish Poland, restore Venice to its Senate, Trinidad to Spain, Ceylon to Holland, the Crimea to the Porte, the Caucasus and Georgia to Persia, the kingdom of Mysore to the sons of Tippoo Saib, and the Mahratta States to their lawful owners, and

then the other powers may have some title to
insist that France shall retire within her ancient limits."

It was important to prevent the union of
these mighty hosts, now combined to overthrow
the new system in France. As Napoleon left
Paris, to strike the Prussian army before it
could be strengthened by the arrival of the
Russians, he wrote to Joseph :

"Give yourself no uneasiness. The present
struggle will be speedily terminated. Prussia
and her allies, be they who they may, will be
crushed. And this time I will settle finally
with Europe. I will put it out of the power
of my enemies to stir for ten years."

In his parting message to the Senate, he
said, "In so just a war, which we have not
provoked by any act, by any pretense, the true
cause of which it would be impossible to assign, and where we only take arms to defend
ourselves, we depend entirely upon the support
of the laws, and upon that of the people, whom
circumstances call upon to give fresh proof of
their devotion and courage."

The Prussian army was overwhelmed at
Jena and Auerstadt, and then Napoleon, pressing on to the north, met the Russians at Fried-

land, and annihilated their forces also. The atrocities perpetrated by the Italian bandits were so terrible, that the exasperated soldiers often retaliated with fearful severity. Joseph, by nature a very humane man, endeavored in every way in his power to mitigate this ferocity. The revolt in Calabria was attended with almost every conceivable act of perfidy and cruelty. The wounded French were butchered in the hospitals; the dwellings of Neapolitans friendly to the new government were burnt, and their families outraged; treachery of the vilest kind was perpetrated by those acting under the mask of friendship. The crisis, which Napoleon had been continually anticipating and warning his brother against, had come. The case demanded rigorous measures. It was necessary to the very existence of the Government that it should prove, by avenging crime, that it was determined to protect the innocent. Still the amiable Joseph was disposed to leniency. Napoleon wrote him:

"The fate of your reign depends upon your conduct when you return to Calabria. There must be no forgiveness. Shoot at least six hundred rebels. They have murdered more soldiers than that. Burn the houses of thirty of the principal persons in the villages, and distribute their property among the soldiers. Take away all arms from the inhabitants, and give up to pillage five or six of the large villages. When Placenza rebelled, I ordered Junot to burn two villages and shoot the chiefs, among whom were six priests. It will be some time before they rebel again."

Where there is this energy to punish crime, the good repose in safety. This apparent inhumanity may be, with a ruler who has millions to protect, the highest degree of humanity. When a lawless mob is rioting through the streets of a city, robbing, burning, murdering, it is not well for the Government affectionately to address them with soothing words. It is far more humane to mow down the insurgents with grape and canister.

The English fleet still menaced and assailed the kingdom of Naples at every available point. It held possession of the island of Capin, near the mouth of the gulf of Naples. There was a Neapolitan, by the name of Vecchioni, who had professed the warmest attachment to the new government, and whom Joseph had appointed as one of his counsellors of state. This man entered into a conspiracy

with the English, to betray to them the King
to whom he had perfidiously sworn allegiance.
His treason was clearly proved. But he was
an old man. His life had hitherto been pure.
The tender heart of Joseph could not bear to
inflict upon him merited punishment. He said
compassionately, " The poor old man has suffered enough already. Let him go." To govern an ignorant, fanatical, and turbulent nation
swarming with brigands, requires a character
of stern mould. But for the energies communicated to Joseph by Napoleon, Joseph could
not long have retained his throne. The Emperor at Saint Helena, speaking of his brother,
said :

"Joseph rendered me no assistance, but he
is a very good man. His wife, Queen Julia,
is the most amiable creature that ever existed.
Joseph and I were always attached to each
other, and kept on good terms. He loves me
sincerely, and I doubt not that he would do
every thing in the world to serve me ; but his
qualities are only suited to private life. He is
of a gentle and kind disposition, possesses talent and information, and is altogether a most
amiable man. In the discharge of the high
duties which I confided to him, he did the best

he could.   His intentions were good, and therefore the principal fault rested not so much with
him as with me, who raised him above his
proper sphere.   When placed in important
circumstances, he found himself unequal to the
task imposed upon him."

On another occasion, the Emperor at Saint
Helena, speaking of the different members of
his family, said, "In their mistaken notions
of independence, the members of my family
sometimes seemed to consider their power as
detached, forgetting that they were merely
parts of a great whole, whose views and interests they should have aided, instead of opposing.   But, after all, they were very young and
inexperienced, and were surrounded by snares,
flatterers, and intriguers with secret and evil
designs.

"And yet, if we judge from analogy, what
family, in similar circumstances, would have
acted better?   Every one is not qualified to
be a statesman.   That requires a combination
of powers that does not often fall to the lot of
one.   In this respect, all my brothers are singularly situated.   They possessed at once too
much and too little talent.   They felt themselves too strong to resign themselves blindly

to a guiding counsellor, and yet too weak to be left entirely to themselves. But, take them all in all, I have certainly good reason to be proud of my family.

"Joseph would have been an ornament to society in any country; and Lucien would have been an honor to any political assembly. Jerome, as he advanced in life, would have developed every qualification requisite in a sovereign. Louis would have been distinguished in every rank and condition in life. My sister Eliza was endowed with masculine powers of mind; she must have proved herself a philosopher in her adverse fortune. Caroline possessed great talents and capacity. Pauline, perhaps the most beautiful woman of her age, has been, and will continue to be to the end of her life, the most amiable creature in the world. As to my mother, she deserves all kind of veneration.

"How seldom is so numerous a family entitled to so much praise? Add to this that, setting aside the jarring of political opinions, we sincerely loved each other. For my part, I never ceased to cherish fraternal affection for them all; and I am convinced that, in their hearts, they felt the same sentiments toward

me, and that, in case of need, they would have
given me proof of it."

The soil of Italy presented widely, upon its
surface, impressive monuments of the past.
The grand memories inspired by these crea-
tions of olden time tended to arouse the slug-
gish spirit of the degenerate moderns.   To promote these ennobling studies, and to increase
the taste for the fine arts, Joseph established
"The Royal Academy of History and Antiq-
uities."   The number of members was fixed
at forty.   The King appointed the first twenty
members, and they nominated, for his appointment, the rest.   A museum was formed for
the collection of antique works of art found in
the excavations.   An annual fund, of about
ten thousand dollars, was appropriated to the
expenses of the institution.   Two grand sessions were to be held each year, at which time
prizes were awarded by the Academy to the
amount of about two thousand dollars for the
most important literary works which had been
produced.   The first sessions were held in the
hall of the palace.   The King wished thus to
manifest his interest in the objects of the
Academy, to co-operate in their labors, and to
avail himself of the advantages of their re-

searches. The clergy, and the medical and legal professions, were alike represented in this learned body.

It is an interesting fact, illustrative of the state of learning at the time, that of the twenty academicians first appointed by the King, eleven were ecclesiastics. Two only were nobles. This class, rioting in sensual indulgence, disdained any intellectual labor. Notwithstanding all these expenses, such system and economy were introduced into the finances, that they were rapidly becoming extricated from the chaos in which they had long been plunged.

In the midst of these incessant and diversified labors, letters were almost daily passing between Joseph and his brother the Emperor. On the first day of the year 1807, Napoleon was, with his heroic and indomitable army, far away amidst the frozen wilds of Poland. Joseph sent a special deputation to his brother, with earnest wishes for "a happy new year." Napoleon thus replied, under the date of Warsaw, January 28, 1807:

"MY BROTHER,—I have not received the letter of your Majesty and his wishes for my happiness without lively emotion. Your destinies and my successes have placed a vast country between us. You touch, on the south, the Mediterranean. I touch the Baltic. But, by the harmony of our measures, we are seeking the same object. Watch over your coasts; shut out the English and their commerce. Their exclusion will secure tranquillity in your states. Your realm is rich and populous. By the aid of God it may become powerful and happy. Receive my most sincere wishes for the prosperity of your reign, and rely at all times upon my fraternal affection. The deputation which your Majesty has sent to me has honorably fulfilled its mission. I have requested it to bear to your Majesty the assurance of my sincere attachment. Whereupon, my brother, I pray that God may ever have you in his holy and worthy keeping."

Some reference was made in one of Joseph's letters to the sufferings which the army in Naples endured. Napoleon replied, "The members of my staff, colonels, officers, have not undressed for two months, and some for four. (I myself have been fifteen days without taking off my boots), in the midst of snow and mud, without bread, without wine, without brandy, eating potatoes and meat; making long marches and counter-marches, without any kind of rest; fighting with the bayonet, and very often under grapeshot: the wounded being borne on sledges in the open air one hundred and fifty miles.

" It is then ill-timed pleasantry to compare us with the Army of Naples, which is making war in the beautiful country of Naples, where they have bread, oil, cloth, bedclothes, society, and even that of the ladies. After having destroyed the Prussian monarchy, we are now contending against the rest of the Prussians, against the Russians, the Cossacks, the Calmucks, and against those tribes of the north which formerly overwhelmed the Roman empire. In the midst of these great fatigues, every body has been more or less sick. As for me, I was never better, and am gaining flesh.

"The Army of Naples has no occasion to complain. Let them inquire of General Berthier. He will tell them that their Emperor has for fifteen days eaten nothing but potatoes and meat, whilst bivouacking in the midst of the snows of Poland. Judge from that what must be the condition of the officers. They have nothing but meat."

On the 26th of March, 1807, Joseph wrote, in a letter to his brother Napoleon, urging the promotion of Colonel Destrees, who, by his probity, had won the affections of the people.

"Here, sire, an honest man is worth more to me than a man of ability. When I find both qualities united in the same person, I esteem him of more value than a regiment. It is for this reason that I value so highly Reynier, Partouneaux, Donzelot, Lamarque, Jourdan, Saligny, and Mathieu; it is this which leads me to prize so highly Roederer and Dumas."

Again he wrote to his brother on the 29th of March: "Sire, as I see more of men and become better acquainted with them, I recognize more and more the truth of what I have heard from your Majesty during the whole of my life. The experience of government has confirmed the truth of that which your Majesty has so often said to me. I hope your Majesty will not regard this as flattery. But it is true; and I never cease to repeat, and particularly to myself, that you have been born with a superiority of reason truly astonishing, and now I recognize fully that men are what you have always told me that they were. How many abuses, which I confess still astonish me, have I encountered, in the journey which I have just made. A prince confiding and amiable is a great scourge from heaven. I am instructed, sire, and I hope ere long to be a better ruler by not giving the majority of men the credit for that spirit of justice and humanity which I hope your Majesty recognizes in me. I have assembled the notables of this province. How docile these people are! but they are very badly governed. I have dismissed the prefect, the sub-prefect, the general, the commandant, a set of rascals who were here the instruments and the agents of an honest prince. This province, the most tranquil in the realm, had become, in the opinion of notables, the most disaffected and the most ready to desire the arrival of the enemy. I journeyed from village to village, and speedily repaired the evil. These people have so much vivacity of spirit and ardor of soul, that both good and evil operate easily upon them. Their inconstancy is not so much the result of their character as of their topographical and military position.

"I am aware, sire, that I have not, as your Majesty has, the art of employing all kinds of

men. I need honest men, in whom I can repose some confidence. Sire, I am in that mood
of mind, which your Majesty recognizes in
me, in which I love to say whatever I think
right. Your Majesty ought to make peace at
whatever price. Your Majesty is victorious,
triumphant everywhere. You ought to recoil
before the blood of your people. It is for the
prince to hold back the hero. No extent of
country, be it more or less, should restrain you.
All the concessions you may make will be
glorious, because they will be useful to your
peoples, whose purest blood now flows; and
victorious and invincible as you are, by the ad-
mission of all, no condition can be supposed to
be prescribed to you by an enemy whom you
have vanquished.

"Sire, it is the love which I bear for a
brother who has become a father to me, and
the love which I owe to France and to the
people whom you have given me, which dic-
tates these words of truth. As for me, sire, I
shall be happy to do whatever may be in my
power to secure that end."

This strain of remark must have been not a
little annoying to the Emperor. While Joseph did not deny that the Emperor was wa-

ging war solely in self-defense, he assumed that
he was now so powerful that he could make
peace at any time upon his own terms. But
dynastic Europe was allying itself, coalition
after coalition, in an interminable series, with
the avowed object of driving Napoleon from
the throne, reinstating the Bourbons, re-establishing the old feudal despotisms, and of then
overthrowing the regenerated kingdoms of
Italy and of Naples, and all the other popular
governments established under the protection
of Napoleon. Against these foes the Emperor
was contending, not for France alone, but for
the rights of humanity throughout Europe and
the world. As Napoleon left Paris for the
campaigns of Jena and Auerstadt, he said to
the Senate,

"In so just a war, which we have not provoked by any act, by any pretense, the true
cause to which it would be impossible to assign, and where we only take up arms to defend ourselves, we depend entirely upon the
support of the laws and of the people."

No man could deny the truth of this statement. Napoleon was driven to all the rigors
of a winter's campaign in the wilds of Poland.
To have received, by the side of his bleak bi-

vouac, whilst thus struggling to defend the rights of humanity throughout Europe, a letter from his amiable brother, written in such a strain of implied reproach, must have been extremely annoying. One would look for an outburst of indignation in response. We turn to the Emperor's reply. It was as follows :

"MY BROTHER,—I have received your letter of the 29th of March, and I thank you for all that you have said. Peace is a marriage which depends upon a union of wills. If it be necessary still to wage war, I am in a condition to do so. You will see, by my message to the Senate, that I am about to raise additional troops."

Joseph had expressed the opinion that the Neapolitans truly loved him. Napoleon, in his reply, said,

"I am not of the opinion that the Neapolitans love you. It is all resolved to this. If there were not a French soldier in Naples, could you raise there thirty thousand men to defend you against the English and the partisans of the Queen? As the contrary is evident to me, I can not think as you do. Your people will love you undoubtedly, but it will be after eight or ten years, when they will tru-

ly know you, and you will know them. To
love, with the people, means to esteem; and
they esteem their prince when he is feared by
the bad, and when the good have such confidence in him that he can, under all circumstances, rely upon their fidelity and their aid."

In a letter to Joseph, written a few days before this, the Emperor made the following
striking remarks: "Since you wish me to
speak freely of what is done at Naples, I will
say to you that I was not just pleased with
the preamble to the supression of the convents.
In referring to religion, the language should
be in the spirit of religion, and not in that of
philosophy. Why do you speak of the services rendered to the arts and the sciences by
the religious orders? It is not that which has
rendered them commendable; it is the administration of the consolations of religion. The
preamble is entirely philosophical, and I think
that it should not be so. It ought to have
been said that the great number of the monks
rendered their support difficult; that the dignity of the State required that they should be
maintained in a condition of respectability:
hence the necessity for reform, that a portion
of the clergy must be retained for the admin-

istration of the sacraments, that others must
be dismissed. I give this as a general principle."

Joseph was well aware how difficult it is
for truth to reach the steps of the throne. In
his tour through the provinces, he often, on
foot, penetrated the crowd which surrounded
him, and conversed with any one whose intelligence attracted his attention. He listened to
every well-founded complaint, and avowed
himself deeply moved in view of the oppression which the people had suffered even from
his own agents. But for this personal observation, he would have remained in ignorance of
these wrongs which he promptly and vigorously repressed. Joseph was a man of the
purest morals, and, as a husband and father,
was a model of excellence. While engaged in
these labors at Naples, his wife, Julie, who was
in delicate health, remained in Paris, occupy-
ing the palace of the Luxembourg. They ex-
changed *daily* letters. The following extract
from one of Joseph's letters, written on the
26th of April, 1807, will give the reader some
insight to the nature of this correspondence,
and to the heart of Joseph.

"MY DEAR JULIE,—I have received no let-

JOSEPH ON HIS NEAPOLITAN TOUR.

ter from you to-day. I pray you not to fail to write to me. I can not but feel anxious when I receive no letter, since your correspondence is otherwise regular. I wrote you yesterday of the rumors which malevolence had set in circulation, but that facts will gradually destroy them. I can give you the positive assurance that you need have no solicitude upon that point.

"I have come to pass Sunday here. It is somewhat remarkable that *fête* days are the seasons which I choose for a little recreation. This shows with what constancy I am employed on other days in the labors of the Cabinet. Moreover, the response to every accusation is the result which has already been attained here. Notes upon the Bank of Naples, which were twenty-five per cent. below par when I came here, are now at par. I have, with my own resources, conducted the war and the siege of Gaëta, which has cost six millions of francs ($1,200,000); I have found the means to support and pay ninety thousand men, for I have, besides sixty thousand land soldiers, thirty thousand men as marines, invalids, pensioners of the ancient army, coast guards, shore gunners; and I have fifteen hundred leagues of coast, all beset, blockaded, and often attacked by the enemy.

"With all this, I have not so much increased the taxes as to excite the discontent of the landed proprietors and the people. There is so little dissatisfaction that I can travel almost anywhere alone without imprudence; that Naples is as tranquil as Paris; that I can borrow here whatever one has to lend; that I have not a single class of society discontented; and it is generally admitted that if I do not do better it is not my fault; that I set the example of moderation, of economy; that I indulge in no luxuries; that I make no expenses for myself; that I have neither mistresses, minions, nor favorites; that no person leads me, and, indeed, that every thing is so well ordered here that the officers and other Frenchmen whom I am compelled to send away complain, when they are absent, that they can not remain in Naples.

"Read this, my good Julie, to mamma and to Caroline, since they are anxious, and say to them that if they knew me better, they would feel less solicitude. Say to them that one does not change at my age; remind mamma that at every period of my life, an obscure citizen, cultivator, magistrate, I have always sacrificed with pleasure my time to my duties. It surely is not I, who prize grandeurs so little, who can fall asleep in their bosom. I see in them only duties, never privileges.

"I work for the kingdom of Naples with the same good faith and the same self-renunciation with which, at the death of my father, I labored for his young family, whom I never ceased to bear in my heart, and all sacrifices were for me enjoyments. I say this with pride, because it is the truth. I live only to be just; and justice requires that I should render this people as happy as the scourge of war will render possible. I venture to say, notwithstanding their situation, that the people of Naples are perhaps more happy than any other people.

"Be tranquil, then, my love, and be assured that these sentiments are as unchanging in my soul as the immortal attachment which I bear for you and for my children; if there be any sacrifice which they cost me, it is being separated from you. Ambition certainly would not have led me away two steps if I could have remained tranquil. But honor and the sentiment of my duty induce me, three times a year, to make the tour of my realm to solace the unhappy.

Reforms.

"Under these circumstances, I thank Heaven for having given me health and ability to bear the burden of affairs, and moderation which does not permit me to be dazzled by grandeur, and energy which does not allow me to slumber at my post; and a good conscience and a good wife to pronounce judgment upon what I ought to do. I embrace you all tenderly."

It was clear that the statesmanship of Napoleon was the controlling influence in Joseph's administration, for in reading the details of his interior policy, we find that the institutions of regenerated France were taken as the models. To invest with honor the profession of a soldier, no one who had been condemned for crime was permitted to enter the army. Degrading punishments were abolished; distinctions and rewards were accorded to eminent merit. Promotion depended no longer upon the accident of birth, but upon services rendered, so that every office of honor or emolument was alike within the reach of all. Joseph, in his tour through the provinces, received very touching proofs of the affections of the people. It was indeed manifest to all that a new era of prosperity had dawned upon Naples. Still no devotion to the interests of the people can save a ruler from enemies. Two assassins attempted the life of the King. They were arrested, tried, condemned, and executed.'

On the 14th of May, 1807, Joseph set out on a tour through the provinces of the Abruzzes, a mountainous region traversed by the Apennines. He found the government admirably administered under the authority of the French General, Guvion Saint Cyr. The people were everywhere prosperous and happy. The region, abounding in precipitous crags and gloomy defiles, with communications often rendered impracticable by the rains and the melting snows cutting gullies through the soil of sand and clay, had become quite isolated.

The inhabitants spontaneously arose to celebrate the arrival of the King by constructing durable roads. Joseph promptly lent the en-

---

[1] "The entrance of Joseph to Cosenza, the capital of hither Calabria, on the 11th of April, was as a national fête. Guards of honor, chosen from among the most distinguished families, all the clergy, all the population were at the gates to receive him. He was accompanied into the city with shouts of joy, the streets being ornamented with triumphal arches. One would have thought that he was a sovereign returning after a long absence to the midst of a people by whom he was idolized."—*Memoires et Correspondence Politique et Militaire, du Roi Joseph*, p. 127.

terprise his royal support. He appointed a
committee of able men, selected from each of
the capitals of the three provinces, with three
road engineers, to secure the judicious expen-
diture of the money and the labor ; and offered
rewards to those communes which should push
the improvements with the greatest vigor. A
system of irrigation and drainage was also
adopted which contributed immensely to the
prosperity of the region, checking emigration
by opening wide fields to agricultural industry.

During all this time Joseph kept up almost
a daily correspondence with his brother. The
letters of Napoleon were written hurriedly, in
the midst of overwhelming cares, intended to
be entirely private, with no idea that their un-
studied expressions, in which each varying
emotion of his soul, of hope, of disappointment, of irritation, found utterance, would be
exposed to the malignant comments of his foes.
The friends of Napoleon appeal triumphantly
to this unmutilated correspondence, running
through the period of many long and eventful
years, to prove that Napoleon was animated by
a high ambition to promote the interests of
humanity ; that he was one of the most philanthropic as well as one of the greatest of men.

Joseph himself, whose upright character no intelligent man has yet questioned, says, in his autobiography, written at Point Breeze, New Jersey, when sixty-two years of age:

"Having attained a somewhat advanced age, and enjoying good health, disabused of many of the illusions which enable me to bear the storms of life, and replacing those illusions by that tranquillity of soul which results from a good conscience, and from the security which is afforded by a country admirably constituted, I regard myself as having reached the port. Before disembarking upon the shores of eternity, I wish to render an account to myself of the long voyage, and to search out the causes which have borne so high, in the ranks of society, my family, and which have terminated in depriving us of that which appertains to the humblest individual— a country which was dear to us, and which we have served with good faith and devotion.

"It is neither an apology nor a satire which I write. I render an account to myself of events, and I wish to place upon paper the recollections which they have left behind. There are some transactions which I now condemn, after having formerly approved of them; there are others of which I to-day approve, after having formerly condemned them. Such is the feebleness of our nature, dependent always upon the circumstances which surround us, and which frequently govern us—a thought which ought to lead every true and reflective man to charity.

" I venture to affirm that it is the love of truth which leads me to undertake this writing. *It is a sentiment of justice which I owe to the man who was my friend, and whom human feebleness has disfigured in a manner so unworthy. Napoleon was, above all, a friend of the people, and he was a just and good man, even more than he was a great warrior and administrator. It is my duty, as his elder brother, and one who has not always shared in his political opinions, to speak of that which I know, and to express convictions which I profoundly cherish.* I am now in a better situation to appreciate what were the causes foreign to his nature, which forced him to assume a factitious character—a character which made him feared by the instruments which he had to employ, in order to sustain against Europe the war which the oligarchy had declared against the principles of the revolution, and which the British Cabinet waged against that

France whose supremacy it could prevent only by exciting against her Continental wars and civil dissensions, and those despotic principles of government which no longer belonged to the nation or the age in which we lived."

CHAPTER VI.

THE SPANISH PRINCES.

TOWARD the close of the year 1807 brigandage was entirely suppressed, all traces
of insurrection had disappeared, and tranquillity and prosperity reigned throughout the kingdom of Naples. In July Joseph wrote from
Capo di Monte to Queen Julie, who was then
at Mortfontaine, as follows:

"MY DEAR JULIE,—I have received your
letter of the 15th from Mortfontaine. The
sentiment which you have experienced in returning to that beautiful place, where we have
been so happy for so long a time, and at so little expense, needs not the explanation of any
supernatural causes. You perceive that there
you have been happier than you are now, than
you will be for a long time. The happiness
which you have there enjoyed is sure as the
past; that which is destined for you here is as
uncertain as the future. Life at Mortfontaine
is that of innocence and peace; it is that of the

patriarchs. The life at Naples is that of kings. It is a voyage over a sea, often calm, but some-times stormy. The life at Mortfontaine was a promenade as placid as its waters. It flowed noiselessly like the light skiff which a slight effort of the oars of Zénaïde[1] sufficed to push forward around the isle of Molton.[2]

"But after all these regrets of a good heart, gentle and reasonable, there come the results of the reflections of a strong mind and an ele-vated soul which owes itself entirely to the will of Providence, manifested by the spontane-ous coming, and not desired by us, of grand-eurs which point us to other duties. I con-sole myself, in this new career, by seeing it traversed by my wife and my children. The most unpleasant part of the voyage is over, that which I have taken without them. Now peace will reunite us. And if you do not find here your own country, our reunion will give us the illusion of it. As we shall be the same to each other, I believe that, come what may, you will find Mortfontaine, where you see me hap-py in the love of my family, and in the happi-ness which I shall be able to confer, and in that

[1] Daughter of the king.
[2] An island in the lake of Mortfontaine.

still greater happiness of which I shall dream.
Adieu, my dear Julie. I embrace you tenderly."

The victories of the Emperor, the peace of
Tilsit, the Russian alliance, had greatly diminished the influence of the British Cabinet upon
the Continent, and, in the same proportion, had
increased that of France. Still the Cabinet of
St. James was unrelenting in opposition to Napoleon. The British cruisers ran along the
coast of Italy, landing here and there Sicilian
or Calabrian brigands, who were under the pay
of Ferdinand and Caroline. It was also proved
that assassins were in the employ of Ferdinand
and his queen.

Toward the end of November Napoleon visited Venice, and, by appointment, met his brother Joseph there. It has generally been affirm-
ed that there was a *secret* article in the treaty
of Tilsit authorizing Napoleon to dethrone the
Bourbons of Spain, who had treacherously endeavored to strike him in the back when, in
the campaigns of Jena, Auerstadt, and Austerlitz, he was contending against England, France,
and Russia. But that secret article, if there
were such, has been kept so secret, that no
sufficient evidence has yet been adduced that

it existed. Joseph, however, wrote, when an exile in America:

"At the time of my interview with the Emperor at Venice, he spoke to me of troubles in the royal family of Spain as probably leading to events which he dreaded. 'I have enough work marked out,' he said. 'The troubles in Spain will only aid the English to impair the resources, which I find in this alliance, to continue the war against them.'"

On the 16th of December Joseph returned to Naples, and the next day presided at the council of ministers. He did not make any communication of importance. "It is only known," writes the Count of Melito, "that he sent one of his aides on a mission to the Emperor Alexander. It was hence concluded that arrangements of some nature had been entered into at Venice in harmony with the views of the Emperor of Russia." Joseph, however, writes, in reference to this mission, "General Marie took letters to Russia and congratulations, and brought me back letters, affectionate even, from the Emperor Alexander, and his compliments; that was all."

Lucien Bonaparte, a very independent and impulsive young man, was not disposed to submit to the dictation of his elder brother Napoleon. He had entered into a second marriage, which displeased Napoleon, as it very seriously interfered with his plans of forming a dynasty. Joseph was sent to meet the refractory brother at Modena, and to endeavor to promote reconciliation. The following letter from Eliza, written to her brother Lucien upon this subject will be read with interest. It was dated Marlia, June 20th, 1807 :

"MY DEAR LUCIEN,—I have received your letter. Permit, to my friendship, a few reflections upon the present state of things. I hope that you will not be annoyed by my observations.

"Propositions were made to you, a year ago, which you should have found seasonable, and which you should immediately have accepted, for the happiness of your family and of your wife. You now refuse them. Do you not see, my dear friend, that the only means of placing obstacles in the way of adoption is, that his Majesty should have a family of which he can dispose? In remaining near Napoleon, or in receiving from him a throne, you will be useful to him. He will marry your daughters;

and so long as he can find, in the members of his family, the instruments for executing his projects and his policy, he will not choose strangers. We must not treat with the master of the world as with an equal. Nature made us the children of the same father, and his prodigies have rendered us his subjects. Although sovereigns, we hold every thing from him. It is a noble pride to acknowledge this; and it seems to me that our only glory should be to prove by our manner of governing that we are worthy of him and of our family.

"Reflect then anew upon the propositions which are made to you. Mamma and we all should be so happy to be reunited, and to make only one political family. Dear Lucien, do that for us, who love you, for the people whom my brother has given for you to govern, and to whom you will bring happiness.

"Adieu. I embrace you. Do not feel unkindly to me for this; and believe that my tenderness will always be the same for you. Embrace your wife and your amiable family. Chevalier Angelino, who has come to see me, has often spoken to me of you and of your wife. My little one is charming. I have weaned her.

I shall be very happy if she is soon able to play with all the family. Adieu.

"Your sister and friend,   ELIZA."

The letters of the Emperor were sometimes severe in reproof of the policy of his brother. It is evident that Joseph was, at times, quite wounded by these reproaches. At the conclusion of a long letter, written on the 19th of October, 1807, Joseph says:

"I am far from complaining of any one. The people and the enemy are what they must be.   But it would be pleasant to me, could your Majesty truly know my position, and render some justice to the efforts and to the privations of every kind which I impose upon myself to do the best I can. Although the present state of affairs may not be good, still I hope for better times.   No person desires it more than I do.   When I have a thousand ducats I give them; and I can assure your Majesty that I have never in my life, which has been composed of so many different shades, found less opportunity to gratify my private inclinations. I have no expenses but for the public wants. I occupy myself day and night in the administration.   I think the administration as good as possible; but it has no more the power than have I to correct the times, and to create that which does not exist and can not exist, except where there is interior tranquillity and external peace."

On the 13th of August, 1806, Joseph wrote to his brother, "I remain here till your Majesty's birthday, on which I wish you joy. I hope that you may receive with some little pleasure this expression of my affection. The glorious Emperor will never replace to me the Napoleon whom I so much loved, and whom I hope to find again, as I knew him twenty years ago, if we are to meet in the Elysian Fields."

Napoleon replied from Rambouillet, on the 23d of August,

"MY BROTHER,—I have received your letter of the 13th of August. I am sorry that you think that you will find your brother again only in the Elysian Fields. It is natural that at forty he should not feel toward you as he did at twelve. But his feelings toward you are more true and strong. His friendship has the features of his mind."

In December Napoleon had a personal interview with Lucien, and he gives the follow-

ing account of it, in a letter to Joseph, dated
Mantua, 17th December, 1807:

"My Brother,—I have seen Lucien at Mantua. I talked with him several hours. He
undoubtedly will inform you of the disposition
in which he left. His thoughts and his language are so different from mine that I found it
difficult to get an idea of what he wished. I
think that he told me that he wished to send
his eldest daughter to Paris, to be near her
grandmother. If he continue in that disposition, I desire to be immediately informed of it.
And it is necessary that that young person
should be in Paris in the course of January,
either accompanied by Lucien, or intrusted by
him to the charge of a governess, who will convey her to Madame.[1] Lucien seems to be agitated by contrary sentiments, and not to have
sufficient strength to come to a decision.

"I have exhausted all the means in my
power to recall Lucien, who is still in his early
youth, to the employment of his talents for
me and for the country. If he wish to send
his daughter, she should leave without delay,
and he should send a declaration by which he
places her entirely at my disposal, for there is

[1] Madame Letitia, Napoleon's mother.

not a moment to be lost; events hurry onward, and I must accomplish my destiny. If he has changed his opinion, let me immediately be informed of it, for then I must make other arrangements.

"Say to Lucien that his grief and the parting sentiments which he manifested moved me; that I regret the more that he will not be reasonable, and contribute to his own repose and to mine. I await with impatience a reply clear and decisive, particularly in that which relates to Charlotte."

On the 31st of January, 1808, a fiend-like attempt was made to blow up the palace of Salicetti, Joseph's minister of police. About one o'clock in the morning, just as the minister was entering his chamber, there was a terrific explosion. An infernal machine had been placed in the cellar. The whole palace was shattered and rent, while large portions were thrown into utter ruin. Salicetti, severely wounded, heard the shrieks of his daughter, the Duchess of Lavello, and rushed to her aid. He found her buried five or six feet deep in the débris which had been thrown upon her. It was more than a quarter of an hour before her agonized father, aided by the domestics, could succeed in extricating her. Though alive, she was sadly maimed. Two of the inmates of the palace were killed, and others were severely injured.

Napoleon, when informed of the event, wrote to Joseph, under date of February 11th, 1808: "The terrible misfortune which has happened to Salicetti seems to me to have been the result of over-indulgence. When were traitors ever before allowed to live free in a capital—wretches who had plotted against the State? Their lives ought not to be spared; but if that is done, at least you ought to send them sixty leagues from the capital or shut them up in a fortress. Any other conduct is madness."

Napoleon, having gained a glorious peace upon the plains of Poland, which disarmed the nations of the north, now turned his special attention to the south—to Portugal, Spain, Italy, Rome, and Naples. The possession of the kingdom of Naples, instead of being a source of profit to the Emperor, occasioned him continued and heavy expense. Joseph was ever calling for money to meet the innumerable demands involved in carrying on war with the English, and in urging forward those reforms which were essential to the regeneration of a realm which former misgovernment had plunged to a very low abyss of poverty and ruin. The Emperor, bearing the burden of the exhaustive wars ever waged against him, while continually aiding Joseph, still often and severely reproached him with the manner in which his finances were conducted. On the 11th of February, 1808, he wrote:

"MY BROTHER,—The administration of the realm of Naples is very bad. Roederer makes brilliant projects, ruins the country, and pays no money into your treasury. This is the opinion of all the French who come from Naples. Roederer is upright, and has good intentions, but he has no experience."

Again, on the 26th of February, he wrote: "Roederer is of the race of men who always ruin those to whom they are attached. Is it want of tact, is it misfortune? No matter which; there is not one of your friends who does not detest Roederer. He is at Naples as at Paris, without credit with any party; a man of no sagacity, of no tact, whom, however, I esteem for many good qualities, but whom, as a statesman, I can make nothing of."

Joseph, however, earnestly defended his

12

financial agent as an able and an honest man, who made enemies only of those who wished to plunder the treasury. This led Joseph, whose constant effort it was to promote the happiness of his people, to whose interests he was entirely devoted, to order a minute statement to be drawn up of the condition of the realm in all respects. This remarkable document was written by Count Melito, the Minister of the Interior. It gave an accurate narrative of all the ameliorations which had been introduced by Joseph, and will ever remain a monument of his goodness and tireless energies as a sovereign. As none of the statements could be doubted, the document at the time produced a profound impression throughout Europe.

Queen Julie now came to Naples with her children to join her husband. She was received with great enthusiasm. There has seldom been found, in the history of the world, a worse woman than Caroline, the wife of Ferdinand, the former King of Naples. And history records the name perhaps of no better woman than Julie, the wife of Joseph. The King met the Queen on the 4th of April at Saint Lucie, and conducted her, greeted by the.

acclamations of their rejoicing subjects, into their beautiful capital.

The treachery of the Court of Spain, which, like an assassin, endeavored to strike the Empire of France stealthily, with a poisoned dagger, in the back, was known throughout Europe. These proud dynasties regarded Napoleon, because he was an *elected*, not a *legitimate* sovereign, as an outlaw, with whom no treaties were binding, and whom they could betray, entrap, and shoot at pleasure.

When Napoleon was far away, in his winter campaign, bivouacking upon the cold summit of the Landgräfenberg, the evening before the battle of Jena he received information that the Bourbons of Spain, then professing friendship, and bound to him by a treaty of alliance, were secretly entering into a contract with England to assail him in the rear. Napoleon had neither done nor meditated aught to injure Spain. His crime was that he had accepted the crown from the people, and was ruling in behalf of their interests, and not in the interests of the nobles alone.

"A convention," says Alison, "was secretly concluded at Madrid between the Spanish Government and the Russian ambassador, to

which the Court of Lisbon was also a party,
by which it was agreed that, as soon as the
favorable opportunity was arrived, by the
French armies being far advanced on their
road to Berlin, the Spanish Government should
commence hostilities in the Pyrenees, and in-
vite the English to co-operate."

Napoleon, by his camp-fire, upon the eve of
a terrible battle, read the account of this perfidy. As he folded the dispatches, he said
calmly, but firmly, " The Bourbons of Spain
shall be replaced by princes of my own family."

" The Spanish Bourbons," says Napier,
" could never have been sincere friends to
France while Bonaparte held the sceptre; and
the moment that the fear of his power ceased
to operate, it was quite certain that their apparent friendship would change to active hostility."

" When I made peace on the Niemen," said
Napoleon, " I stipulated that if England did
not accept the mediation of Alexander, Russia
should unite her arms with ours, and compel
that power to peace. I should be indeed weak
if, having obtained that single advantage from
those whom I have vanquished, I should per-

mit the Spaniards to embroil me afresh on my
weak side. Should I permit Spain to form an
alliance with England, it would give that hostile power greater advantages than it has lost
by the rupture with Russia. I wish, above
all things, to avoid war with Spain. Such a
contest would be a species of sacrilege. If I
can not arrange with either the father or the
son, I will make a clean sweep of them both."

Rumor was busy throughout Europe in dis-
cussing the plans of Napoleon. The report
soon became general that the crown of Spain
was to be offered to Joseph. His kindness of
heart, his nobleness of character, and the immense benefits which he had conferred upon
the Neapolitan realm, had secured for him almost universal respect and affection. The Neapolitans were greatly alarmed from fears that
he would be transferred to Spain.

"The King," writes his very able biographer, A. du Casse, "was universally beloved,
because he began to be appreciated at his true
value. His good qualities, the love with which
he cherished his subjects, had won all hearts.
His departure was dreaded. Joseph, however,
did not slacken the reins of government. The
Councils of State and the ministers, presided

over by him, continued their labors to amelio-
rate the administration of the realm, to embellish Naples, to encourage discoveries, to unite
the learned in a literary corps. The King
wished that, even after his departure, the impulse which he had given should continue uninterrupted."

It was at Naples, under the encouragement
of Joseph, that the art of lithography was discovered. On the 23d of May, 1808, the King,
by the request of Napoleon, left Naples for
France. He left his family behind him, and
hastened through Turin and Lyons to meet
his brother at Bayonne. His departure caused
great anxiety and sadness throughout the kingdom of Naples. Who would wear the crown
about to be vacated? Would the Two Sicilies
be annexed to the kingdom of Italy under Eugene? Would Louis, Lucien, or one of Napoleon's marshals succeed Joseph?

On the journey Joseph met the Bishop of
Grenoble, formerly the abbé Simon, his ancient
professor of mathematics and philosophy in
the College of Autun. Joseph had ever cherished the memory of his teacher with great
affection, and, upon meeting, threw his arms
around him in a tender embrace. As the

bishop complimented him upon his high destiny, and congratulated him upon the probability of his immediate elevation to the throne
of Spain, Joseph replied sadly,[1]

"May your felicitations, Monsieur the Bishop, prove of happy augury to your former pupil. May your prayers avert the calamities
which I foresee. As for me, ambition does
not blind me. The joys of the crown of Spain
do not dazzle my eyes. I leave a country in
which I think that I have done some good,
where I flatter myself to have been beloved,
and that I leave behind me some regrets.
Will it be the same in the new realm which
awaits me?

"The Neapolitans have, so to speak, never
known nationality. By turns conquered by
the Normans, the Spaniards, the French, it was
little matter to them who their masters were,
provided that these masters left them their
blue skies, their azure sea, their spot in the
sunshine, and a few pence for their macaroni.

"Arriving among them, I found every
thing to do. I stimulated their natural apathy, gave nerve to the administration, intro-

[1] We are indebted, for the report of this conversation, to
M. Simon, of Nantes, a nephew of the bishop.

duced some order everywhere. They were pleased with my good intentions, with my efforts. They loved me with the same fervor with which they hated the King of Sicily and his odious ministers. In Spain, on the contrary, I shall labor in vain ; I can not so completely lay aside my title of a foreigner that I can escape the hatred of a people proud and sensitive upon the point of honor; of a people who have known no other wars but wars of independence, and who abhor, above all things, the French name.

" The Peninsula contains at this moment, under arms, nearly one hundred thousand national soldiers, who will excite, at the same time, against my government, the monks, the clergy, the friends (and they are still numerous) of legitimacy, the ancient and faithful servants of old Charles IV., the gold and the intrigues of England. Every thing will prove an obstacle to my plans of amelioration. They will be misrepresented, calumniated, disowned.

" In view of the insurrection of which the Prince of Asturias has recently given an example against his own father, in the midst of license and anarchy, the natural consequence of long demoralization and the disorders of a

dissolute court, of a dynasty used up, will not
all wise and well-moderated liberty be regarded as the equal of tyranny? Monsieur the
Bishop, I see a horizon charged with very
black clouds. They contain in their bosom a
future which terrifies me. The star of my
brother, will it always shine luminous and brilliant in the skies? I do not know; but sad
presentiments oppress me in spite of myself.
They besiege me; they govern me. I greatly
fear that, in giving me a crown more illustrious than that which I lay aside, the Emperor
will place upon my brow a burden heavier
than it can bear. Pity me, then, my dear
teacher, pity me; do not felicitate me."

The brigands in the kingdom of Naples, and
the eternal and natural enemies of repose
which are to be found in all countries, availing themselves of the absence of King Joseph,
and encouraged by the presence of the British
fleet and the gold of the British Cabinet, redoubled their efforts in local insurrections, and
committed cowardly assassinations. The bandits would land here and there, and perpetrate
the most atrocious crimes, burning, plundering,
murdering.

Joseph was anxious, before leaving Naples,

to establish *institutions of liberty* which might be permanent. On the 21st of July, the Council of State received from the King a constitution, which he had drawn up with the aid of his ministers. It contained the clear announcement of the principles which had animated him during his reign, and was founded upon the constitutions in France and in the kingdom of Italy. Though the constitution was not perfect—for the world is ever making progress—-it was greatly in advance of any thing which had been known in the kingdom of Sicily before, and conferred immense advantages upon the realm. There was but one legislative body. It consisted of five sections, equal in number: the clergy, the nobility, the landed proprietors, the philosophers, and the merchants. The Council of State chose five of the most distinguished persons, of the various classes, to convey to Joseph their thanks for the constitution he had conferred upon the realm.

On the 6th of July, Queen Julie, with her children, left Naples to join her husband in Spain. A numerous cortége escorted her from the city with every testimonial of regret. On the 8th Joseph abdicated the crown, which

QUEEN JULIE LEAVING NAPLES.

was subsequently transferred to the brow of Napoleon's cavalry leader, Murat, who had married Caroline Bonaparte.

"Here terminates," writes M. Casse, "our task relative to the short reign of Joseph in Naples. That prince had rendered to that beautiful country services which, long after his departure, conferred blessings upon the realm, which had been surrendered until then to the sad régime of a feudalism crushing to the people. His successor found the ground clear, war extinct almost everywhere, the conquest assured, tranquillity established, abuses reformed, civil administration organized, the monks suppressed, the finances restored, credit consolidated, public instruction and legislation founded upon liberal bases, and wisely adapted to the manners of the inhabitants.

"The army was formed under the shade of the flag of France; the marine commenced to be regenerated. The sciences and the arts, encouraged, were beginning to diffuse themselves; brigandage was breathing its last sigh. There remained for Murat only to reap the fruits of the wise and paternal conduct of the older brother of the Emperor. He inherited a country of rich and fertile soil, with a delight-

ful climate, inhabited by a population blessing
the guardian hand which had delivered them
from the ignorance into which the ancient Government seemed to have plunged them by design. The task of the new sovereign seemed
to be only to complete the work of the phil-
osophic King."

It was the implacable hostility of the British Government, ever ready to avail itself of
the treachery of Spain, which in the view of
Napoleon rendered it necessary for him, as an
act of self-preservation, to place the government of the Spanish Peninsula in friendly
hands. On the 18th of April, 1808, Napoleon
had written to Joseph,

"England begins to suffer. Peace with that
power alone will enable me to sheathe the
sword and restore tranquillity to Europe."

Before we accompany Joseph to Spain, let
us briefly review the condition of Europe at
this time. By the peace of Tilsit, the Emper-
or Alexander had recognized all the changes
which the sword of Napoleon had effected upon
the Continent of Europe. The Czar was on
terms of personal friendship with Napoleon, and
it was understood that he had given his consent
to Napoleon's design to dethrone the Bour-

Condition of Europe.

bons of Spain. The infamous British expedition to Copenhagen, with the bombardment of the city and the destruction of the Danish fleet, had created general indignation throughout the European world. England had but one single ally left, the half-mad King of Sweden. The ships of England, excluded from every port upon the Continent, wandered idly over the seas.

Austria, humiliated by the treaty of Presburg, was sullen and silent, watching for an opportunity to regain its former ascendency and military prestige. In Prussia the House of Brandenburg had been terribly punished. Though it still reigned, it was with diminished territory, with its military strength nearly destroyed, and with all its strong places held by French troops. The Cabinet at Berlin could not venture in any way to oppose the will of Napoleon. All the kings and princes of the Confederation of the Rhine were united to France by the closest alliance.

Jerome, Napoleon's youngest brother, was king of Westphalia. Louis reigned in Holland. French influence was supreme in Switzerland. The Emperor Napoleon was king of Italy, and Joseph, reigning at Naples, was about to be transferred to Spain. Turkey was allied with France, seeking from the Emperor protection from the encroachments of Russia. Consequently England was at war with the Porte.

Spain occupied a peculiar position. The King, Charles IV., a near relative of Louis XVI., had united with allied Europe in the war against the French Republic. Terribly punished by the French armies, Spain had made peace at the treaty of Basle in July, 1795. Soon after, the two powers entered into an alliance, offensive and defensive, engaging to assist each other with both land and sea forces.

This brought down upon Spain the vengeance of the British Government, which, with its invincible fleet, swept all seas. Spanish commerce at once became the prey of English privateers. Cadiz was bombarded, and the Spanish naval fleet encountered very severe loss. The peace of Amiens, to which the British Government had been very reluctantly compelled to assent by the pressure of English public opinion, gave peace to Spain. But when the Court of Saint James, by the rupture of the peace of Amiens, renewed its assault upon France, the Spanish Court, anxious to avoid a war with England, proposed to Napoleon that, instead of aiding him directly by fleet and army, according to the terms of the alliance, Spain should pay France an annual subsidy of six million francs. The proposition was accepted.

The English minister, ascertaining this, *without any declaration of war*, seized every thing belonging to Spain which could be found afloat. As Spain, supposing that her assumed neutrality would be respected, had her fleet and merchandise everywhere exposed, her loss was very severe.

When the Bourbons of Spain saw that the British Government had succeeded in forming a new alliance against Napoleon, which would compel the French Emperor to take his armies hundreds of leagues north to struggle against the united armies of Prussia and Russia, it was thought that Napoleon must inevitably fall. Spain decided again to make common cause with the Allies, as we have before mentioned. A vehement proclamation was issued, calling the Spaniards to arms. The utter crushing of Prussia on the fields of Jena and Auerstadt literally frightened Spain out of her wits. She sent an ambassador extraordinary to *congratu-*

*late Napoleon upon his victory, and to assure him
of the continued friendship of the Spanish Government.* Napoleon concealed his just resentment.
The time to rectify the wrong had not yet
come.

Queen Caroline, the wife of Charles IV. of
Spain, was one of the most infamous of women;
still she could not be worse than her husband.
There was a very handsome young fellow in
the body-guard, named Godoy. Caroline fell
in love with him, made him her intimate friend,
lavished upon him titles and wealth and posts
of responsibility. He was called the Prince of
Peace, in consequence of the agency he had in
effecting the treaty of Basle. He was in all
respects a very weak and worthless creature;
but he had become in reality the sovereign of
Spain, governing with unlimited power. This
man, in his anxiety to disarm the anger of Napoleon, sent an ambassador to the Emperor to
renew his pledges of friendship, and to give assurance of his entire submission in all things
to Napoleon's will. A secret treaty was accordingly made on the 27th of October, 1807,
which enabled Napoleon, among other concessions, to station large bodies of French troops
within the Spanish territory.

The King's eldest son, Ferdinand, the heir to the throne, was then twenty-five years of age, and bore the title of the Prince of Asturias. His mother had truly characterized him as having "a mule's head and a tiger's heart." He hated Godoy, and was accused of attempting to poison his father and mother, that he might get the crown. His arrest and threatened execution by his father roused the masses of Madrid to a fury of insurrection. Much as they detested Ferdinand, they hated still more implacably the King and Queen, and the Queen's infamous paramour, Godoy. A raging insurrection swept the streets of Madrid. The King was terror-stricken, and implored help from Napoleon. He wrote:

"SIRE, MY BROTHER,—I have discovered with horror that my eldest son, the heir presumptive to the throne, has not only formed the design to dethrone me, but even to attempt the life of myself and his mother. Such an atrocious attempt merits the most exemplary punishment. I pray your Majesty to aid me by your light and council."

Ferdinand also appealed to the Emperor. He wrote, "The world more and more daily admires the greatness and goodness of Napoleon. Rest assured that the Emperor shall ever find in Ferdinand the most faithful and devoted son. Ferdinand implores, therefore, his powerful protection, and prays that he will grant him the honor of an alliance with some august princess of his family."

Thus Napoleon suddenly and unexpectedly found the King of Spain, Godoy, and the Ferdinands, all kneeling at his feet. Speaking upon this subject at Saint Helena, he said :

"The fact is, that had it not been for their broils and quarrels among themselves, I should never have thought of dispossessing them. When I saw those imbeciles quarrelling and trying to dethrone each other, I thought I might as well take advantage of it, and dispossess an inimical family. Had I known at first that the transaction would have given me so much trouble, or that even it would have cost the lives of two hundred men, I would never have attempted it. But being once embarked, it was necessary to go forward."

JOSEPH RRCEIVING THE ADDRESSES OF THE SPANISH SENATE.

Abdication of Charles IV.

CHAPTER VII.

JOSEPH KING OF SPAIN.

AFTER a series of the wildest, most tumultuous, and frantic scenes of which even Spanish history gives any account, Charles IV. abdicated in favor of his son Ferdinand. On the 20th of March, 1808, the new King, Ferdinand VII., was saluted by the acclamations of the people and the soldiers, and received the homage of the Court. One of his first acts was to arrest the hated Manuel Godoy. Murat was then in command of the French troops in Spain, and was about entering Madrid. Junot, with a French army, had taken possession of Portugal. Spain was nominally in alliance with France. England was consequently waging war against Spain. The French troops were, in Spain to protect the kingdom from the English.

The young King Ferdinand immediately dispatched the Duke of Pargue to convey assurances of friendship to Murat, and to sound his intentions. At the same time he sent three of the grandees of Spain to announce his accession to the throne to Napoleon, and to give him renewed pledges of his friendship and devotion. On the 23d of April Murat took military possession of Madrid. The next day Ferdinand made his triumphal entrance into the metropolis. He was received with boundless exultation, so greatly were the people rejoiced to be delivered from the detestable Godoy. Thus far Napoleon did not recognize the accession of Ferdinand. He however sent the Duke of Rovigo to Madrid to ascertain the circumstances of the abdication. In the mean time the old King, who had retired with the Queen to Aranjuez, wrote a letter to the Emperor, in which he said that he had been forced to abdicate in favor of his son by the clamors of the people and the insurrection of the soldiers, threatening him with instant death if he refused.

"I protest and declare," he said, "that my decree of the 19th of March, in which I abdicated the crown in favor of my son, is an act to which I have been forced to prevent the greatest misfortunes and the effusion of the blood of my well-beloved subjects. It ought consequently to be regarded as of no value."

Measures of Murat.

The Queen also wrote to Murat, entreating him, in the most supplicating terms, to rescue her paramour Godoy from prison, and stating that they had abdicated only to save their lives. While Charles IV. and Caroline were making these secret protestations to Napoleon and Murat, the abdicated King, to lull the suspicions of Ferdinand, was reiterating the public declaration that the abdication was free and unconstrained, and that never in his life had he performed an act more agreeable to his inclinations.

Murat took the old King and Queen under his protection, provided them with a suitable guard, and demanded the liberation of Godoy. Ferdinand, convinced that he could not maintain the throne without the support of Napoleon, sent his younger brother, Don Carlos, to intercede with the Emperor in his favor. While these scenes were transpiring, Savary, Duke of Rovigo, arrived at Madrid. He assured Ferdinand that it was the Emperor's desire to unite France and Spain in the closest alliance. He proposed that Ferdinand should visit Napoleon, that in a personal interview they might the better mutually understand each other. The counsellors of Ferdinand urged the adoption of this measure, as one which would secure the confidence of the Emperor, and which might induce him to give a princess of his family to Ferdinand. Such was the condition of affairs in April, 1808. The great object of Napoleon was to secure a government in Spain whose treachery he need not fear, and upon whose friendly co-operation he could rely. Charles IV., the weakest of weak men, enslaved by long habit, was the obsequious tool of his stronger-minded wife. The Queen, Caroline, sought, at whatever price, to save her lover Godoy. Ferdinand wished to crush Godoy, his implacable foe.

Ferdinand decided to visit the Emperor, and on the 10th of April left Madrid for that purpose. When he reached his frontiers he wrote a very suppliant letter to Napoleon, entreating the recognition of his right to the throne, and pledging his friendship. Napoleon replied that he was ready to recognize the Prince of Asturias as King of Spain if it should appear that Charles IV. had not been compelled to abdicate through fear of his life. By this extraordinary concurrence of circumstances Napoleon became the judge between the father and the son, both of whom had appealed to his decision.

Ferdinand, with his suite, crossing the frontiers, hastened to Bayonne, and entered the city on the morning of the 20th of April. He was received by the Emperor with distinguished marks of attention and kindness, but not with regal honors. The Prince of Peace, whose liberation Murat had secured, came hurrying on to Bayonne, to plead his cause before the Emperor; and he was followed, in a few hours, by Charles IV. and the Queen. Thus the whole family was assembled at Bayonne. The result of several stormy interviews, in which the King, the Queen, and their son exhausted upon each other the language of vituperation, and in which the enraged old King was with difficulty restrained from a violent personal attack upon his son, the parties all agreed to cede to Napoleon the crown of Spain. Ferdinand first renounced his rights in favor of his father, and Charles IV. transferred the sceptre to Napoleon. The imperial palace of Campiegne, its parks and forests, were placed at the disposition of Charles IV. for himself, his Queen, and Godoy, during his life, with an annual pension of thirty million reals. He was also given the *proprietorship* of the chateau of Chambord, with its parks, forests, and farms, to dispose of as he pleased. Upon the death of the King, the Queen was to receive a pension of two million reals. The two princes, Ferdinand and Don Carlos, were assigned to the castle of Valençay, its park, forests, and farms, with an income amounting to about half a million dollars.

It is said that Napoleon obtained at Bayonne such developments of the character of Ferdinand that he saw that it was utterly in vain to attempt to make a respectable king of him; one upon whom he could repose the slightest reliance ; and he could no longer think of sacrificing the daughter of Lucien to so worthless a creature. Speaking upon this subject at Saint Helena, Napoleon said to Las Casas:

"Ferdinand offered, on his own account, to govern entirely at my devotion, as much so as the Prince of Peace had done in the name of Charles IV. And I must admit that if I had fallen into their views I should have acted much more prudently than I have actually done. When I had them all assembled at Bayonne, I found myself in command of much more than I could have ventured to hope for. The same occurred there, as in many other events of my life, which have been ascribed to my policy, but in fact were owing to my good-fortune.

"Here I found the Gordian knot before me.

Proclamation of Charles IV.

I cut it. I proposed to Charles IV. and the Queen that they should cede to me their rights to the throne. They at once agreed to it, I had almost said voluntarily; so deeply were their hearts ulcerated toward their son, and so desirous had they and their favorite now become of security and repose. The Prince of Asturias did not make any extraordinary resistance. Neither violence nor menaces were employed against him. And if fear decided him, which I well believe was the case, it concerns him alone."

On the 8th of May Charles IV. issued a proclamation to the Spanish nation, informing them that he had ceded the crown to Napoleon, and enjoining it upon them to transfer their homage to him. "We have," said he, "ceded all our rights over Spain to our ally and friend the Emperor of the French, by a treaty signed and ratified, stipulating the integrity and independence of Spain and the preservation of our holy religion, not only as dominant, but as alone tolerated in Spain."

As the throne was thus transferred without any action of the people whatever, Napoleon felt the necessity of obtaining something like a national sanction of the deed, and an expres-

sion of the national will in respect to the sovereign who should be placed over them. Murat, at Madrid, announced to the council-gen-
eral of Castile, to the junta or council of the
Government, and to the municipality, that the
Emperor desired to know their opinion in reference to the choice of a sovereign from the
princes of his own family. All these three
bodies united in the expression of the wish
that the choice should fall upon Prince Joseph,
King of Naples. A deputation of distinguished men was sent to convey this wish to the
Emperor. Fortified by these documents, Napoleon, on the 6th of June, proclaimed that
the crown of Spain was transferred to his
brother Joseph.

Joseph was at that time on the road to Bayonne, not yet knowing the decision of his brother, and in heart very reluctant to assume the
crown of Spain. Napoleon rode out from
Bayonne to meet Joseph, whom he sincerely
loved, and who was so ready to sacrifice his inclinations and his happiness to aid the Emperor in his gigantic plans. The Emperor made
the following statement to Joseph as they rode
back together to Bayonne:

"The passions of the princes of the House

of Spain have precipitated a crisis which has arrived too soon. They could no more agree together at Bayonne than they could in Spain. Charles IV. preferred to retire to France upon certain conditions, rather than go back to Spain without the Prince of Peace. The Queen also preferred to see a stranger ascend the throne rather than Ferdinand. Neither Ferdinand nor any other Spaniard wished for Charles IV. if the reign of Godoy were to be recommenced; they preferred a stranger to him. I am fully satisfied," said the Emperor, "that it would require greater efforts to sustain Charles and the Prince of Peace than to change the dynasty. Ferdinand has shown himself so moderate in ability, and so unreliable in character, that it would be inconsistent for me to commit myself for him in sustaining a son who has dethroned his father. This dynasty is no longer suitable for Spain. With it no regeneration is possible. The most prominent personages of the monarchy, in rank, in intelligence, and in character, assembled at Bayonne in a national junta, are, in general, convinced of this truth. Since destiny has so ordered it, and since it is in my power now to do that which I had no wish to undertake, I

have designed to regenerate Spain by placing
over it my brother, the King of Naples, who is
agreeable to the junta, and who will be also so
to the nation.   Ferdinand has, for a long time,
sought one of my nieces in marriage.   But
since the interview at Bayonne, knowing
more intimately the character of the prince,
I can not think it proper to accede to his demands.

"The Spanish princes have already left for
France.   They have ceded their rights to the
crown.   I wish to transfer the crown to my
brother, the King of Naples.   It is important
that he should not hesitate.   The Spaniards,
as also foreign sovereigns, will think that I
wish to place that crown upon my head, as I
have done with that of Lombardy when Joseph refused to accept it.   The tranquillity of
Spain, of Europe, the reconciliation of all the
members of the family[1] depend upon the decision which Joseph now makes.   I will not
cherish the thought that the regret to leave a
beautiful country, where there are no longer
any dangers to be encountered, can induce
Joseph to refuse a throne, where there are

[1] Napoleon then contemplated making Lucien King of
Naples.

great obstacles to be overcome, and much good
to be accomplished."

When they reached Bayonne, Joseph found
all the members of the Junta assembled in the
chateau of Marrac. He responded vaguely to
the address of congratulation the Junta made
to him, wishing first to converse with each individual member of that body. The Spanish
princes left for Valençay, and Charles IV. had
no partisans whatever. The Duke of Infantado and M. Cevallos had been considered the
warmest advocates of Ferdinand. They both
called upon Joseph, and held a long interview
with him. The duke offered him his services,
saying that he had possessions in the kingdom
of Naples, and that his agents there had informed him of the wonders which Joseph had
wrought. "If Joseph," said he, "can be in
Spain what he has been in Naples, there is no
doubt that the entire nation will rally around
him." M. Cevallos expressed the same views.
Joseph then saw every member of the Junta
individually, nearly one hundred in number.
They all, without exception, described the
wretchedness into which Spain had fallen, and
the apparent facility with which it could be
regenerated. Upon one point they all agreed:

14

that it would be impossible to live in peace under either the father or the son ; that Joseph alone, sacrificing the throne of Naples that he might ascend that of Spain, would meet the wishes of all parties, and bring back prosperity to the distracted realm.

These assurances, which were given to Joseph by all the members of the Spanish Junta assembled at Bayonne, that his acceptance of the throne would calm all troubles, assure the independence of the monarchy, the integrity of its territory, its liberty, and its happiness, roused his generous enthusiasm. "He yielded," writes his biographer, "sacrificing his dearest interests to the hope of doing good to a greater number of people, and decided to accept the crown which was offered him. He considered it his duty to occupy the most dangerous post. Virtue, not ambition, led Joseph to Spain."

The Emperor wished to introduce into Spain the same advanced principles of popular liberty which Joseph, by the Constitution, had conferred upon Naples. With that object he convoked at Bayonne, on the 15th of June, a Spanish assembly, called the *Constitutional Junta.* This Congress was to consist of one hundred and fifty persons of the most distinguished orders in the state, though but about one hundred were actually convened. A large number had already assembled when Joseph reached Bayonne. They hastened to welcome him. Many of them, however, afterward proved his most inveterate enemies. The Duke of Infantado, addressing him in the name of the grandees of Spain, said,

"Sire, the Spaniards expect, from the reign of your Majesty, all their happiness. They ardently desire your presence in Spain to fix ideas, to conciliate all interests, and to establish that order so necessary for the regeneration of the country. Sire, the grandees of Spain have always been distinguished by their fidelity to their sovereigns. Your Majesty will experience this, as also our personal affection. Receive, sire, these testimonies of our loyalty with that kindliness so well known by your people of Naples, the renown of which has reached even to us."

The deputation of the Royal Council of Castile said to the new King: "Sire, your Majesty is a branch of a family destined by Heaven to reign. May Heaven grant that our prayers may be heard, and that your Majesty may become the most happy King in the universe, as we desire for him in the name of the supreme tribunal of which we are the deputies."

Even the Inquisitor, Don Raymond Estenhard, organ of the councils of the Inquisition, declared in their name "that they were full of fidelity and of affection; that they offered their prayers for Joseph, who was charged to govern the country, that he might find happiness in his own heart by contributing to the happiness of his subjects, and that he might elevate them to that degree of prosperity which might be expected from him, particularly when aided by the genius and power of his august brother, Napoleon the Great."

The Duke of Pargue, at the head of a deputation representing the army, gave the same assurances of homage and support. Even Ferdinand wrote Joseph a letter of congratulation, dated Valençay, June 22. It was as follows:

"Sire,—Permit me, in the name of my brother and of my uncle,[1] as well as in my own, to testify to your Majesty the part which we have taken in his induction to the throne of Spain. The object of all our desires having ever been the happiness of the generous nation which he

[1] Don Carlos and Don Antonio.

is called to govern, that happiness is now complete, in view of the accession to the throne of
Spain of a prince whose virtues have rendered
him so dear to the Neapolitans. We hope
your Majesty will accept our prayers for his
happiness, to which is united that of our country, and that he will grant to us his friendship, to which we are entitled, for the friendship which we feel for your Majesty. I pray
your Catholic Majesty to receive the oath
which I owe him as King of Spain, and also
the oath of the Spaniards who are now with
me. From your Catholic Majesty's affectionate brother."

The Constitutional Junta of Spain commenced its session at Bayonne on the 15th of
June. Ninety-one members were present. A
constitution was presented very much resembling that which had been conferred upon Naples. It was discussed and voted upon with
perfect freedom. Finally, on the 7th of July,
it was accepted as amended by the signature
of all the members; "considering," as the act
said, "that we are convinced that under the
régime which the Constitution establishes, and
under the government of a prince as just as the
one whom we have the happiness to possess,

Spain and all its possessions will be as happy
as we can desire it to be."

The Constitution being accepted, Joseph appointed his ministry and constituted his court;
placing all the important offices in the hands
of distinguished Spaniards. On the 9th of
July Joseph left Bayonne and entered Spain,
accompanied by the members of the Junta,
many grandees of Spain, his ministers, and the
officers of his household.

Many have reproached Joseph for having
accepted the crown. But it should be remembered that when he arrived at Bayonne, the
treaty of abdication by the Spanish princes had
already been signed. An assemblage of Spanish notables met him there, and entreated him
to accept the crown, to rescue Spain from ruin.
There seemed to be no dissent from the opinion
that his presence would be the signal of peace
and harmony, that it would calm agitation, and
unite all parties. In a word, they declared
that it was the only way to rescue the country
from anarchy, and from those calamities which
menaced its entire ruin. The intelligence of
the nation exulted in the change, as promising
a new era of equality and prosperity.

On the 20th of July Joseph arrived in Ma

drid. There were about eighty thousand French troops in Spain. Much to Joseph's surprise and disappointment, he found, all over the kingdom, in the provinces, insurrection rising against him. These scattered bands soon amounted, it was estimated, to one hundred and fifty thousand men. The fanatic monks, alarmed in view of the changes which had been effected in Naples, were very active in rousing the peasantry to resistance. The British Government, which was then at war with Spain because it was the ally of Napoleon, instantly espoused the cause of the insurgents, and contributed all its energies of fleet and army and money to drive Joseph out of Spain.

The new sovereign had entered Madrid without being greeted with any signal demonstrations of enthusiasm. In accordance with the established etiquette of the realm, he was received at the foot of the grand stairs of the palace by the nobility of the country, and was proclaimed king in the public squares and principal streets of Madrid with the accustomed ceremonies upon the advent of a new sovereign. Intensely occupied with the cares of his new government, Joseph did not, for some time, fully comprehend the perils which menaced him.

Step by step he was led on, as he quelled here
and there a popular insurrection, until he found
himself involved in a stern war with the great
mass of the Spanish peasantry, with all the
priesthood fanning the flames of opposition, and
the British Government energetically co-opera-
ting with purse and sword. It would require
volumes to describe, with any degree of mi-
nuteness, the tremendous struggle. Napier has
performed that task in his immortal work upon
the Peninsular War.

Joseph soon awoke to a full realization of
the peril of his position. On the 13th of July
he wrote to the Emperor from Burgos at three
o'clock in the morning, "It seems to me that
no person has been willing to tell the exact
truth to your Majesty. I ought not to conceal it. The task undertaken is very great.
To accomplish it with honor will require immense resources. Fear does not make me see
double.

"In leaving Naples, I have indeed yielded
my life to the most hazardous events. My life
is of but little consequence. I surrender it to
you. But in order not to live with the shame
attached to failure, great resources are requisite in men and money. I am not alarmed, in

view of my position. But it is unique in history. I have not here a single partisan."

Again, on the 19th, he wrote, "It is evident that we have not the soil, since all the provinces are in insurrection or occupied by considerable armies of the enemy."

On the 28th of July he wrote, "I have no need to inform your Majesty that one hundred thousand men are necessary to conquer Spain. I repeat it, that we have not a partisan, and the entire nation is exasperated, and decided to sustain with arms the part which it has embraced."

"All my Spanish officers except five or six have abandoned me. The disposition of the nation is unanimous against that which has been done at Bayonne."

On the 6th of August he wrote, "Your Majesty recommends me to be happy. Never have I been so tranquil and so well, and so indefatigable; and if I have occasion to envy in your Majesty a superior genius which has always enabled him to command victory, I have that in common with all the world. But I have no need to envy any person for composure and tranquillity of soul. And I must avow that I find that adversity enables me to experience a sentiment which is not without a certain charm; it is to be above adversity."

The Emperor endeavored to cheer his despondent brother with hopeful words. On the 19th of July he wrote him, "I see with pain that you are troubled. It is the only misfortune which I fear. You have a great many partisans in Spain, but they are intimidated. They are all the honest people. I do not the less admit that your task is great and glorious. You ought not to consider it extraordinary that you have to conquer your kingdom. Philip V. and Henry IV. were obliged to conquer theirs. Be happy. Do not permit yourself to be easily affected, and do not doubt for an instant that every thing will end sooner and more happily than you think."

Again, on the 1st of August, Napoleon wrote, "Whatever reverses fortune may have in store for you, do not be uneasy; in a short time you will have more than one hundred thousand men. All is in motion, but it must have time. You will reign. You will have conquered your subjects, in order to become their father. The best of kings have passed through this school. Above all, health to you and happiness, that is to say, strength of mind."

Capitulation of Junot.

On the 3d of August the Emperor again wrote, "You can not think, my friend, how much pain the idea gives me, that you are struggling with events as much above what you are accustomed to, as they are beneath your natural character. . . . Tell me that you are well, in good spirits, and are becoming accustomed to the soldier's trade. You have a fine opportunity to study it."

General Junot, with a small French force, at that time held possession of Portugal. The Cabinet of Saint James offered to the Spanish Junta at Seville to send an army of about thirty thousand men to co-operate with the Spaniards in their struggle against the French. For some unknown reason the offer was declined, and the troops were sent to Portugal. These British troops, acting in vigorous co-operation with the Portuguese, greatly outnumbered the French, and, after a severe battle at Torrès Vedras, Junot capitulated at the Convention of Cintra, and his army re-embarked, and was transported to France. This event added greatly to the embarrassment of Joseph. Junot had afforded him much moral and even material support. Now Junot was driven from the Peninsula, and a British army of over thirty thousand men, under the ablest officers, and flushed with victory, was on the frontiers of Spain, ready in every way to co-operate with the Spaniards.

This roused Napoleon. He was the last man to recoil before difficulties. He had the honor of his arms to avenge, and his policy to justify by success. Never before, in the history of the world, was there such a display of energy, sagacity, and power. He well knew that all dynastic Europe was hostile to those principles of popular liberty which were represented by his name, and that, notwithstanding the obligations of treaties, they were ever ready to spring to arms against him whenever they should see an opportunity to strike him a fatal blow.

Napoleon at once ordered eighty thousand veteran troops of the grand army from the north to assemble at Bayonne. He hastened to Erfurt to hold an interview with Alexander to strengthen their alliance, and to prevent, if possible, a new coalition from being formed against him while absent with his troops in Spain. The Spanish insurgents, as they were called—for they had no established government —were everywhere triumphant. The French army was driven out of Madrid, and, in a state of great destitution, was standing on the defensive. Joseph and all his generals were thoroughly disheartened, and were only anxious to devise some honorable way by which they could abandon the enterprise. The priests, with a crucifix in one hand and a dagger in the other, had traversed the realms of Spain and Portugal, rousing the religious fanaticism of the unenlightened masses almost to frenzy. Charles IV., his Queen, and Ferdinand had all been intensely devoted to the interests of the Church. The French were represented as infidels, and as the foes of the Church. The whole nation was roused against them. Even the women took an active part in the conflict, perilling their own lives upon the field, and inspiring the men with the courage of desperation. The English, victorious in Portugal, were now welcomed into Spain. They lavished their gold in paying the Spanish armies. Their fleet was busy in transporting supplies. To all Europe the position of Joseph seemed utterly hopeless.

On the 25th of October, Napoleon, on the eve of leaving Paris for Spain, said, at the opening of the Legislative Corps:

" A part of my troops are marching against the armies which England has formed or disembarked in Spain. It is an especial favor of Providence, which has constantly protected our arms, that passion has so blinded the counsels of the English, that they have renounced the protection of the seas, and at length present their armies on the Continent.

" I leave in a few days, to place myself at the head of my army, and, with the aid of God, to crown in Madrid the King of Spain, and to plant my eagles upon the forts of Lisbon.

" The Emperor of Russia and I have met at Erfurt. Our first thought has been of peace. We have even resolved to make many sacrifices that, if possible, the hundred millions of men whom we represent may enjoy the benefits of maritime commerce. We are in perfect harmony, and unchangeably united for peace as for war."

In the mean time Joseph, struggling heroically against adversity, and exceedingly embarrassed by the false position in which he found himself placed, received many consoling messages of confidence and affection from prominent men in the Spanish nation. We present the following extract from a letter ad-

The marvellous Energy of Napoleon.

dressed to him on the 2d of September, 1808,
by M. M. Azanza and Urquijo, as a specimen
of many others which might be quoted:

" We do not doubt that your Majesty con-
templates, with deepest grief, the disasters with
which Spain is menaced, by the obstinacy of
those people who will not know the true interests of the realm. But at least no one is ignorant that your Majesty has done and is doing every thing which is humanly possible to
avoid such calamities for his subjects. The
day will come when they will recognize the
benevolent intentions and paternal kindness
of your Majesty; and they will respond to it
by testimonies of gratitude and of fidelity
which will fill with contentment the noble
heart of your Majesty."

The almost supernatural power of the Emperor was never more conspicuously displayed
than in the brief, triumphant, overwhelming
campaign which ensued. He wrote to Joseph
from Erfurt, " I leave to-morrow for Paris, and
within a month shall be at Bayonne. Send
me the exact position of the army, that I may
form a definite organization by making as little displacement as possible. In the present
state of affairs, we may conclude that the pre-

sumption of the enemy will lead him to remain in the positions which he now occupies. The nearer he remains to us the better it will be. The war can be terminated in a single blow by a skillfully-combined manœuvre, and for that it is necessary that I should be there."

The single blow Napoleon contemplated would unquestionably have annihilated his foes, but for an inopportune movement of Marshal Lefebre. As it was, it required three or four blows, which were delivered with stunning and bewildering power and rapidity. On the 29th of October Napoleon took his carriage for Bayonne. Madrid was distant from Paris about seven hundred miles. The rains of approaching winter had deluged the roads. He soon abandoned his carriage, and mounted his horse. Apparently insensible to exposure or fatigue, he pressed forward by night and by day, until, at two o'clock in the morning of the 3d of November, he reached Bayonne. He found that his orders had not been obeyed, and that the troops, instead of being concentrated, had been dispersed. Instantly, at the very hour of his arrival, new life was infused into every thing. He seemed by instinct to comprehend the posture of affairs, and to know just what was to be done. Orders were issued with amazing rapidity; couriers flew in all directions. Barracks were erected; the troops were reviewed; unexecuted contracts were thrown up; agents were sent in every direction to purchase all the cloths in the south of France; hundreds of hands were busy in cutting and making garments; and at the close of a day of such work as few mortals have ever accomplished, Napoleon leaped into his saddle and galloped sixty miles over the mountains to Tolosa, on the Spanish side of the Pyrenees. Here he indulged in an hour or two of rest, and then galloped on thirty miles farther to Vittoria. He encamped with the Imperial Guard outside of the city.

The Spaniards have always been accused of a tendency to vainglorious boasting. The trivial successes which they had attained, in alliance with the English, quite intoxicated them. "We have conquered," they said, "the armies of the great Napoleon. We will soon trample all his hosts in the dust. With an army of five hundred thousand indignant Spaniards we will march upon Paris, and sack the city. The powers of Russia, Austria, and Prussia have fallen before Napoleon; but

Spanish peasants, headed by the priests and the monks, will roll back the tide of victory." Such was the insane boasting.

Napoleon was, at the same time, the boldest and the most cautious of generals. He ever made provision for every possible reverse. Stationing two strong forces to guard his flanks, he took fifty thousand of the *élite* of his army, and plunged upon the centre of the Spanish troops. Such an onset none but veterans could withstand. There was scarcely the semblance of a battle. The Spaniards fled, throwing down their arms, and leaping like goats amidst the crags of the mountains. Pressing resistlessly forward, Napoleon reached Burgos on the night of the 11th. Here the Spaniards attempted another stand upon some strongly intrenched heights. A brief conflict scattered them in the wildest confusion, defeated, disbanded, leaving cannon, muskets, flags, and munitions of war.

Onward he swept, without a check, without delay, crushing, overwhelming, scattering his foes, over the intrenched heights of Espinosa, through the smouldering streets of the town, across the bridge of Trueba, choked with terrified fugitives, through the pass of Somosierra, in one of the most astounding achievements which war has ever witnessed, till he led his victorious troops, with no foe within his reach, into the streets of Madrid. He commenced the campaign at Vittoria on the 9th of November, and on the 4th of December his army was encamped in the squares of the Spanish metropolis. Europe gazed upon this meteoric phenomenon with astonishment and alarm.

The Spanish populace had been roused mainly by the priests. In their frenzy, burning and assassinating, they overawed all who were in favor of regenerating Spain by a change of dynasty. It is the undisputed testimony that the proprietors, the merchants, the inhabitants generally who were rich, or in easy circumstances, and even the magistrates and military chiefs, were quite disposed to listen to the propositions of the Emperor. But overawed by the populace, who threatened to carry things to the last extremity, they dared not manifest their sentiments.

As the French army took possession of the city, order was immediately restored. The theatres were re-opened, the shops displayed their wares, the tides of business and pleasure flowed unobstructed along the streets. Numerous deputations, embracing the most wealthy and respectable inhabitants of Madrid, waited upon the Emperor with their congratulations, and renewed their protestations of fidelity to Joseph. The Emperor then issued a proclamation to the Spanish nation, in which he said,

"I have declared, in a proclamation of the 2d of June, that I wished to be the regenerator of Spain. To the rights which the princes of the ancient dynasties have ceded to me, you have wished that I should add the rights of conquest. That, however, shall not change my inclination to serve you. I wish to encourage every thing that is noble in your exertions. All that is opposed to your prosperity and your grandeur I wish to destroy. The shackles which have enslaved the people I have broken. I have given you a liberal constitution, and, in the place of an absolute monarchy, a monarchy mild and limited. It depends upon yourselves whether that constitution shall still be your law."

CHAPTER VIII.

THE SPANISH CAMPAIGN OF NAPOLEON.

IN less than five weeks from the time when Napoleon first placed his foot upon the soil of Spain he was master of more than half the kingdom. Sir John Moore, with an army of about 30,000 Englishmen, was marching rapidly from Portugal, to form a junction with another English army of about 10,000 men under Sir David Baird, who were advancing from Corunna. It was supposed in England that the co-operation of these highly-disciplined troops with the masses of the Spaniards who had already fought so valiantly, would speedily secure the overthrow of the French.

But when Sir John Moore and Sir David Baird learned that Napoleon himself was in Spain, that he had scattered the Spanish armies before him as the tornado drives the withered leaves of the forest, that he was already in possession of Madrid, and would soon be ready to direct all his energies against them, they were both greatly alarmed, and, turning about, fled precipitately back to their ships. A deputation of about twelve hundred of the notables of Spain called upon Napoleon, to confer with him respecting the affairs of the kingdom. He informed them very fully of the benefits he wished to confer upon Spain by rescuing the people from the dominion of the old feudal lords, and bringing them into harmony with the more enlightened views of modern times. He closed his remarks to them by saying,

"The present generation will differ in opinion respecting me. Too many passions have been called into exercise. But your posterity will be grateful to me as their regenerator. They will place in the number of memorable days those in which I have appeared among you. From those days will be dated the prosperity of Spain. These are my sentiments. Go consult your fellow-citizens. Choose your part, but do it frankly, and exhibit only true colors."

General Moore was retreating toward Corunna. An English fleet had repaired to that port to receive the troops on board. On the 22d of December Napoleon left Madrid, with 40,000 men, to pursue the flying foe. The Spaniards, instead of rallying to the support of the English, whom they never loved, dispersed in all directions, leaving them to their fate. " The

Spanish insurgents," says Napier," were conscious that they were fighting the battles of
England. To restore Spain to Ferdinand, England expended one hundred millions sterling
($500,000,000) on her own operations. She
subsidized Spain and Portugal besides, and
with her supply of clothing, arms, and ammunition, maintained the armies of both, even to
the guerrillas."[1]

By forced marches the Imperial troops rushed along, threading the defiles of the mountains of Gaudarrama in mid-winter, through
drifts and storms of snow. Napoleon climbed
the mountains on foot, sharing all the toil and
peril of his troops. Such a leader any army
would follow with enthusiasm. In one of the
wildest passes of the mountains he passed a
night in a miserable hut. Savary, who was
with him, writes:

"The single mule which carried his bag-
gage was brought to this wretched house. He
was provided with a good fire, a tolerable supper, and a bed. On those occasions the Emperor was not selfish. He was quite unmind-
ful of the next day's wants when he alone was
concerned. He shared his supper and his fire

[1] Napier, vol. iii. p. 78, vol. iv. p. 438.

with all who had been able to keep up with him, and even compelled those to eat whose reserve kept them back."

General Moore was straining every nerve to escape. The weather was frightful, and the miry roads almost impassable. The advance-guard of Napoleon was soon within a day's march of the foe. General Moore, as he fled, blew up the bridges behind him, and reckless-ly plundered the wretched inhabitants. His troops became exceedingly exasperated against the Spaniards for their cowardly desertion, and reproached them with ingratitude.

"We ungrateful!" the Spaniards replied; "you came here to serve your own interests, and now you are running away without de-fending us."

So bitter was the hostility which thus arose between the English and the Spaniards, and the brutality of the drunken English soldiers was so insupportable, that the Spaniards often welcomed the French troops, who were under far better discipline, as their deliverers. Sir Archibald Alison, in his account of these scenes, says:

"The native and uneradicable vice of north-ern climates, drunkenness, here appeared in frightful colors. The great wine-vaults of Bembibre proved more fatal than the sword of the enemy. And when the gallant rear-guard, which preserved its ranks unbroken, closed up the array, they had to force their way through a motley crowd of English and Spanish soldiers, stragglers and marauders, who reeled out of the houses in disgusting crowds, or lay stretched upon the roadside, an easy prey to the enemy's cavalry, which thundered in close pursuit.

"The condition of the army became daily more deplorable; the frost had been succeeded by the thaw; rain and sleet fell in torrents; the roads were almost broken up; the horses foundered at every step; the few artillery-wagons which had kept up fell, one by one, to the rear; and being immediately blown up to prevent their falling into the hands of the enemy, gave melancholy tokens, by the sound of their explosions, of the work of destruction which was going on."

On the 2d of January Napoleon's advance-guard had reached Astorga. Notwithstanding the condition of the roads, and all the efforts of the retreating foe, an army of forty thousand men had marched two hundred miles in ten

days. It was a cold and stormy winter morning when Napoleon left Astorga, in continu-
ance of the pursuit. He had proceeded but a
few miles on horseback, when he was overta-
ken by a courier from France, bearing important dispatches. The Emperor alighted by the
roadside, and, standing by a fire which his at-
tendants kindled, read the documents. His officers gathered anxiously around him, watching
the expression of his countenance as he read.

The dispatches informed Napoleon that
Austria had entered into a new alliance with
England to attack him on the north, and that
the probability was, that Turkey, exasperated
by Napoleon's alliance with Russia, would also
be drawn into the coalition. It was also
stated that, though Alexander personally was
strong in his friendship for Napoleon, the Russian nobles, hostile to the principle of equal
rights, inscribed upon the French banners, were
raising an opposition of such daily increasing
strength, that it was feared the Czar also might
be compelled to join in the new crusade against
France.

To conduct the war in Spain, Napoleon had
withdrawn one hundred thousand of his best
troops from the Rhine. His frontiers were

thus greatly exposed. For a moment it was
said that Napoleon was staggered by the blow.
The vision of another European war, France
struggling single-handed against all the combined powers of the Continent, appalled him.
Slowly, sadly he rode back to Astorga, deeply
pondering the awful question. There was
clearly but one of two courses before him. He
must either ignobly abandon the conflict in favor of equality of rights, and allow the chains
of the old feudal despotism to be again riveted
upon France, and all the new governments in
sympathy with France, or he must struggle
manfully to the end. All around him were
impressed with the utter absorption of his
mind in these thoughts. As he rode back
with his retinue, not a word was spoken. Napoleon seldom asked advice.

Soon his decision was formed, and all dejection and hesitation disappeared. It was
necessary for him immediately to direct all his
energies toward the Rhine. He consequently
relinquished the personal pursuit of the English; and commissioning Marshal Soult to
press them with all vigor, he prepared to return
to France. Rapidly retracing his steps to Valladolid, he spent five days in giving the most

minute directions for the movements of the army, and for the administration of affairs in Spain.   In those few days he performed an amount of labor which seems incredible.   He had armies in France, Spain, Italy, and Germany, and he guided all their movements, even to the minute details.

On the first day of the year Joseph had written to Napoleon, and, in the expression of those kindly sympathies which the advent of a new year awakens, had said, " I pray your Majesty to accept my wishes that, in the course of this year, Europe, pacified by your efforts, may render justice to your intentions."

Napoleon replied, " I thank you for what you say relative to the new year.   I do not hope that Europe can this year be pacified. So little do I hope it, that I have just issued a decree for levying one hundred thousand men. The rancor of England, the events of Constantinople, every thing, in short, indicates that the hour of rest and quiet is not arrived."

The Emperor, having finished his dispatches at Valladolid, mounted his horse, and set out for Paris.   Mr. J. T. Headley thus describes this marvellous ride:

" In the first five hours he rode the aston-

ıshing distance of eighty-five miles, or seventeen miles the hour. This wild gallop was long
remembered by the inhabitants of the towns
through which the smoking cavalcade of the
Emperor passed. Relays of horses had been
provided on the road; and no sooner did he arrive at one post, than he flung himself on a fresh
horse, and, sinking his spurs in his flanks, dash-
ed away in headlong speed. Few who saw
that short figure, surmounted with a plain cha-
peau, sweep by on that day, ever forgot it.
His pale face was calm as marble, but his lips
were compressed, and his brow knit like iron;
while his flashing eye, as he leaned forward,
still jerking impatiently at the bridle as if to
accelerate his speed, seemed to devour the distance. No one spoke, but the whole suite
strained forward in the breathless race. The
gallant chasseurs had never had so long and so
wild a ride before."

Napoleon had acted a very noble part
toward his brother. The masses of the Spanish people were very ignorant and fanatical.
The priests, wielding over them supernatural
terrors, controlled them at will. There were
certain reforms which were essential to the regeneration of Spain. But these reforms would

exasperate the priests, and, through them, the people. Napoleon, anxious to save his brother from the odium of these necessary measures, took the responsibility of them upon himself. He issued a series of decrees when he entered Madrid as a conqueror, and by virtue of the acknowledged rights of conquest, in which, after proclaiming pardon for all political offenses, he introduced the following reforms.

The execrable institution of the Inquisition was abolished. The number of convents, which had been thronged with indolent monks, was reduced one-half. One-half of the property of these abolished convents was appropriated to the payment of the salary of the laboring clergy. The other half was set apart to the payment of the public debt. The custom-houses between the several provinces of the kingdom, which had been a great source of national embarrassment, were removed, and imposts were collected only on the frontiers. All feudal privileges were annulled.

These measures, of course, exasperated the priests and the nobles. Unfortunately the people were too ignorant to appreciate their full value. As Joseph returned to Madrid, under the protection of the arms of his imperial brother, though the bells rang merrily, and pealing cannon uttered their voices of welcome, and though the most respectable portion of the middle class received him with satisfaction, there was no enthusiasm among the populace, and the clergy and the nobility received him with suspicion and dislike. The Emperor, upon his departure, had confided to Joseph the command of the army in Spain. But the great generals of Napoleon, ever ready to bow to the will of the Emperor, whose superiority they all recognized, yielded a reluctant obedience to Joseph, whom they did not consider their superior in the art of war.

Sir John Moore continued his precipitate flight, vigorously pursued by Marshal Soult. "There was never," says Napier, "so complete an example of a disastrous retreat. Abandoning their wagons, blowing up their ammunition, and strewing their path with the débris of an utterly routed army, they finally, with torn, bleeding, and greatly-diminished columns, escaped to their ships."

The new coalition in Germany against Napoleon rendering it necessary for him to withdraw a large part of his troops from Spain, greatly encouraged the foes of the new régime. The British Government, animated by its success in inducing Austria again to co-operate in an attack upon France, and sanguine in the hope of drawing Russia and Turkey into the coalition, which would surely bring the armies of Prussia into the same line of battle, redoubled its efforts in Spain and Portugal. Emissaries were sent everywhere to rouse the populace. Gold was lavished, and arms and ammunition were transmitted by the British fleet to important points.

A central junta was assembled at Seville. It issued a proclamation, calling upon the people everywhere to rise in guerrilla bands. The whole male population was summoned to the field. Death was the penalty denounced upon all those who, by word or deed, favored the French. Twenty thousand troops in Portugal were taken under British pay, and placed under British officers, so that, while nominally it was a Portuguese army, it was in reality but a British force of mercenaries. Numerous transports conveyed a large body of troops from England under Sir Arthur Wellesley, which was landed in Lisbon.

Where the French army had control, there seemed to be a disposition, especially among the most intelligent and opulent portion of the people, to accept the new régime of Joseph. The bitterest foe of Joseph will not deny that the reforms which he was endeavoring to introduce were admirable, and absolutely essential to the regeneration of Spain. The British Government wished to restore the old régime under Ferdinand; for that Government was in sympathy with the British rule of aristocratic privilege. The French Government wished to maintain the new régime under Joseph, because that Government would bring Spain into sympathy with France, in her defensive struggle against the combined despotisms of Europe. Popular opinion in Spain seemed now to be upon one side, and again upon the other, according to the presence of the different armies.

"At Madrid," says Alison, "Joseph reigned with the apparent consent of the nation. Registers having been open for the inscription of those who were favorable to his government, no less than twenty-eight thousand heads of families in a few days enrolled themselves. And deputations from the Municipal Council, the Council of the Indies, and all the incorporations, waited upon him at Valladolid, to entreat that he would return to the capital and reassume the royal functions, to which he at length complied."

At Saragossa, on the other hand, Joseph was opposed with persistence and bravery, which has rendered the siege of Saragossa one of the most memorable events in the annals of war. A very determined leader, Parafox, with about thirty thousand men, threw himself into that city. A proclamation was issued, declaring that no mercy would be shown to those who manifested any sympathy for the reign of Joseph. Suspicion was sufficient to doom one to mob violence and a cruel death.

"Terror," says Alison, "was summoned to the aid of loyalty. And the fearful engines of popular power, the scaffold and the gallows, were erected on the public square, where some unhappy wretches, suspected of a leaning to the enemy, were indignantly executed.

"The passions of the people were roused to the very highest pitch by the dread of treason, or any accommodation with the enemy. And popular vehemence, overwhelming all restraints of law or order, sacrificed almost every night persons to the blind suspicions of the multitude, who were found hanging in the morning on the gallows erected in the Corso and market-place."

The priests summoned the peasants from all the region around, so that soon there were fifty thousand armed men within the walls, inspired by as determined a spirit of resistance as ever possessed the human heart. The siege was commenced about the middle of December with thirty-five thousand men, according to the statement of Napier. It is generally understood in warfare that one man, acting upon the defensive within a fortress, is equal to at least five men making the assault from the outside. But in the memorable siege of Saragossa, the besieged had a third more men than the besiegers. Alison thinks Napier incorrect, and makes the besieging force forty-three thousand. This gives the besieged a superiority of seven thousand men. It surely speaks volumes for the courage and skill of the French army, that under such circumstances the siege could have been conducted to a successful issue, especially when the determination and bravery of the people of Saragossa are represented as almost without a parallel.

The scenes of woe which ensued within the walls of Saragossa no pen can describe, no imagination can conceive. In addition to the garrison of fifty thousand men, the city was

crowded with women and children, the aged
and the infirm. For fifty days the storm of
war raged, with scarcely a moment's intermis-
sion. Thirty-three thousand cannon shots and
sixteen thousand bombs were thrown into the
thronged streets. Fifty-four thousand human
beings perished in the city during these fifty
days—more than a thousand a day. Many
perished of famine and of pestilence. When
the French marched into the town, there were
six thousand dead still unburied. There were
sixteen thousand helplessly sick, and many of
them dying. Only twelve thousand of the garrison remained, pale, emaciate, skeleton men,
who, as captives of war, were conveyed to
France. When we reflect that all this heroism and bravery were displayed, and all these
unspeakable woes endured, to re-introduce the
reign of as despicable a monarch as ever sat
upon a throne, and to rivet the chains of despotism upon an ignorant, debased, and enslaved
people, one can not but mourn over the sad
lot of humanity.

The rank and file of armies is never composed of men of affectionate, humane, and an-
gelic natures. It is the tiger in the man which
makes the reckless soldier. Familiarity with

crime, outrage, misery, renders the soul callous. There is no rigor of army discipline which can prevent atrocities that should cause even fiends to blush. The story of the sweep of armies never can be truly told.

As all the physical strength of the region for leagues around Saragossa had been gathered in that city, its fall secured the submission of the surrounding country. Lannes was called to join the grand army in Germany. Junot, who was left in command of the troops at Saragossa, prepared for an expedition against Valencia. City after city passed, with scarcely any resistance, into the hands of the French. The campaign in Germany rendered it necessary for Napoleon to withdraw all his best troops, leaving Joseph to maintain his position in Spain, with a motley group of Italians, Swiss, and Germans, who were by no means inspired either with the political intelligence or the martial enthusiasm of the French.

The Spanish peasants, depressed by failure, and inspired, not by intelligent conviction, but by momentary religious fanaticism, threw down their arms and returned to their homes. There was but little integrity or sense of honor to be found in Spain, long demoralized by a

wretched government; and the immense supplies which England furnished were embez-
zled or misapplied.   The Spaniards are not
cowards.   The feeble resistance they often
made proved that they took but little interest
in the issues of the war.   Ferdinand had done
nothing to win their regard.   But he was a
Spanish prince, in the regular line of descent
from their ancient kings.   Joseph Bonaparte
was a stranger, a foreigner, about to be imposed upon them by the aid of foreign arms.
It was easy, under these circumstances, to rouse
a transient impulse for Ferdinand, but not an
abiding devotion.

General Duhesme was in Barcelona with a
few thousand troops, cut off from communication with his friends by the English fleet, and
a large army of Spanish peasants which was
collected to secure his capture.   General St.
Cyr, with about sixteen thousand infantry and
cavalry, marched to his relief.   In a narrow
defile, amidst rocks and forests, he encountered
a Spanish force forty thousand strong, drawn
up in a most favorable position to arrest his
progress.   St. Cyr formed his troops in one
solid mass, and charging headlong, without firing a shot, in half an hour dispersed the foe,

killing five hundred, wounding two thousand, and capturing all their artillery and ammunition. The next day St. Cyr entered Barcelona. The Spaniards were so utterly dispersed that not ten thousand men could be re-assembled two days after the battle.

But the English fleet was upon the coast, with encouragement and abundant supplies. After a little while, another Spanish army, twenty thousand strong, was rendezvoused at Molinas del Rey. St. Cyr again fell upon these troops. They fled so precipitately that but few were hurt. Their supplies, which the British had furnished them, were left upon the field. St. Cyr gathered up fifty pieces of cannon, three million cartridges, sixty thousand pounds of powder, and a magazine containing thirty thousand stand of English arms. Lord Collingwood, who commanded the British fleet, declared that all the elements of resistance in the province were dissolved. These events took place just before the fall of Saragossa.

In the middle of February of this year, 1809, St. Cyr had twenty-three thousand men concentrated at Villa Franca. Forty thousand Spaniards were collected to attack him. Almost contemptuously, he took eleven thousand of his troops, surprised the Spaniards, and scattered them in the wildest flight. He pursued the fugitives, and wherever they made a stand dispersed them with but little effort or loss upon his own side. There was no longer any regular resistance in Catalonia, though guerrilla bands still prowled about the country.

Thus the wretched, desolating warfare raged, month after month. Nothing of importance toward securing the abiding triumph of either party was gained. Whenever the French army withdrew from any section of country, British officers entered, to re-organize, with the aid of the Spanish priests, the peasants to renewed opposition, and British gold was lavished in paying the soldiers. Junot was taken sick, and Suchet, whom Napoleon characterized at Saint Helena as the first of his generals, was placed in command. We have not space to describe the numerous battles which were fought, and the patience of our readers would be exhausted by the dreary narration. The siege of Gerona by St. Cyr occupied seven months.

Joseph was still in Madrid. As we have said, the more intelligent and opulent classes rallied around him. Sir Archibald Alison, ever the advocate of aristocratic privilege, while admitting the fact of Joseph's apparent popularity in Madrid, in the following strain of remark endeavors to explain that fact:

"Addresses had been forwarded to Joseph Bonaparte at Valladolid from all the incorporations and influential bodies at Madrid, inviting him to return to the capital and resume the reins of government. Registers had been opened in different parts of the city for those citizens to inscribe their names who were favorable to his cause. In a few days thirty thousand signatures, chiefly of the more opulent classes, had been inscribed on the lists. In obedience to these flattering invitations, the intrusive King had entered the capital with great pomp, amidst the discharge of a hundred pieces of cannon, and numerous, if not heartfelt, demonstrations of public satisfaction; a memorable example of the effect of the acquisition of wealth, and the enjoyments of luxury, in enervating the minds of their possessors, and of the difference between the patriotic energy of those classes who, having little to lose, yield to ardent sentiments without reflection, and those in whom the suggestions of interest and the habits of indulgence have stifled the generous emotions of nature."

The great defect in Joseph's character as an

executive officer, under the circumstances in which he was placed, was his apparent inability fully to comprehend the grandeur of Napoleon's conceptions. Instead of looking upon Spain as an essential part of the majestic whole, and which, by its money and its armies, must aid in sustaining the new principle of equal rights for all, he forgot the general cause, and sought only to promote the interests of his own kingdom. Napoleon, having secured the reign of the new régime of equality in France, in antagonism to the old régime of privilege, immediately found all Europe banded against him. France could not stand alone against such antagonism. Hence it became essential that alliances should be formed for mutual protection. The genius of Napoleon was of necessity the controlling element in these alliances.

In that view, he had enlarged and strengthened the boundaries of France. He had created the kingdoms of Italy and Naples. He had, impelled by the instinct of self-preservation, bought out the treacherous Bourbons of Spain, and was endeavoring to lift up the Spaniards from ages of depressing despotism, that Spain, under an enlightened ruler, rejoicing in the intelligence and prosperity which existed under all the new governments, might contribute its support to the system of equal rights throughout Europe.

England, Russia, Prussia, Austria, and the aristocratic party throughout all Europe, were in deadly hostility to the principle of abolishing privileged classes, and instituting equal rights for all. They were ever ready to squander blood and treasure, to violate treaties, to form open or secret coalitions, in resisting these new ideas. Regarding Napoleon as the great champion of popular rights, and conscious that there was no one of his marshals who, upon Napoleon's downfall, could take his place, all their energies were directed against him personally.

Thus we have the singular spectacle, never before witnessed in the history of the world, never again to be witnessed, of the combined monarchs of more than a hundred millions of men waging warfare against one single man. And therefore Napoleon called upon all the regenerated nations in sympathy with his views to rally around him. He regarded them as wings of the great army of which France was the centre. In combating the coalition, he was fighting battles for them all. They stood or

fell together.   In the terrific struggle which
deluged all Europe in blood, Napoleon was the
commander-in-chief of the whole army of reform.   He was such by the power of circumstances.   He was such by innate ability.   He
was such by universal recognition.

When therefore Napoleon regarded the sovereigns appointed over the nations whom his
genius had rescued from despotism but as the
generals of his armies, who were to co-operate
at his bidding in defense of the general system
of dynastic oppression, it was not arrogance,
it was wisdom and necessity that inspired his
conduct.   Louis in Holland, Jerome in Westphalia, Eugene in Italy, Murat in Naples, Joseph in Spain, all were bound, under the lead-
ership of Napoleon, to contribute their portion
to the general defense.

Very strangely, Joseph seemed never to be
able fully to comprehend this idea.   He was a
man of great intelligence, of high culture, and
a more kindly, generous heart never throbbed
in a human bosom; and yet, notwithstanding
all Napoleon's arguments, it seemed impossible
for him to comprehend why he should not be
as independent as the King of Spain, as Napoleon was in the sovereignty of France.   Fully

recognizing the immeasurable superiority of his brother to any other man, and loving him with a devotion which has seldom if ever been exceeded, he was still disposed to regard himself as placed in Spain only to promote the happiness of the Spanish people, without regard to the interests of the general cause. Instead of being ready to contribute of men and money from Spain to maintain the conflict against coalesced Europe, he was continually writing to his brother to send him money to carry on his own Government, and to excuse him from making any exactions from the people. He was exceedingly reluctant to deal with severity, or to quell the outrages of brigands with the necessary punishment. His letters to the Emperor are often filled with complaints. He deplores the sad destiny which has made him a king. He longs to return, with his wife and children, to the quiet retreat of Mortfontaine.

Napoleon dealt tenderly with his brother. He fully understood his virtues; he fully comprehended his defects. Occasionally an expression of impatience escaped his pen, though frequently he made no allusion, in his reply, to Joseph's repinings.

The Duke of Wellington is reported to have

said that "a man of refined Christian sensi-
bilities has no right to enter into the profession of a soldier." A successful warrior must
often perform deeds at which humanity shud-
ders. Joseph was, by the confession of all, one
of the most calm and brave of men upon the
field of battle. Still, he was too modest a man,
and had too little confidence in himself to perform those hazardous and heroic deeds of arms
which war often requires. Napoleon, conscious
that his brother was not by nature a warrior, and
also wishing to save him from the unpopularity
of military acts in crushing sedition, left him
as much as possible to the administration of
civil affairs in Madrid. His statesmanship and
amiability of character could here have full
scope.

To his war-scarred veterans, Junot, Soult,
Jourdan, Suchet, the Emperor mainly intrusted the military expeditions. Still, to save Joseph from a sense of humiliation, the Emperor
acted as far as possible through his brother, in
giving commands to the army. But the marshals, obedient as children to the commands of
Napoleon, whose superior genius not one of
them ever thought of calling in question, often
manifested reluctance in executing operations

directed by Joseph. At times they could not
conceal from him that they considered their
knowledge of the art of war superior to his.
Joseph was king of Spain, and was often humiliated by the impression forced upon him that
he was something like a tool in the hands of
others.

During the year 1809 Joseph remained
most of the time in Madrid. There were innumerable conflicts during the year, from petty
skirmishes to pretty severe battles, none of
which are worthy of record in this brief sketch.

The latter part of April the Duke of Wellington landed in Portugal, with English re-enforcements of thirty thousand men. With
these, aided by such forces as he could raise
in Portugal and rally around him in Spain, he
was to advance against the French. Napoleon
had been compelled to withdraw all of the Imperial Guard, and all of his choicest troops, to
meet the war on the plains of Germany. Marshal Soult was on the march for Oporto.
With about twenty thousand troops he laid
siege to the city. The feebleness of the defense of the Portuguese may be inferred from
the fact that the city was protected by two
hundred pieces of cannon, and by a force of

regular troops and armed peasants amounting
to about seventy thousand men. Soult, having made all his preparations for the assault,
and confident that the city could not resist his
attack, wrote a very earnest letter to the
magistrates, urging that by capitulation they
should save the city from the horrors of being
carried by storm. No reply was returned to
the summons except a continued fire.

The attack was made. The Portuguese
peasants had tortured, mangled, killed all the
French prisoners that had fallen into their
hands. Both parties were in a state of extreme exasperation. The battle was short.
When the French troops burst through the
barriers, a general panic seized the Portuguese
troops, and they rushed in wild confusion
through the streets toward the Douro. The
French cavalry pursued the terrified fugitives,
and, with keen sabres, hewed them down till
their arms were weary with the slaughter.

A bridge crossed the river. Crowded with
the frenzied multitude, it sank under their
weight, and the stream was black with the
bodies of drowning men. Those in the rear,
by thousands, pressed those before them into
the yawning gulf. Boats pushed out from the

banks to rescue them, but the light artillery of the French was already upon the water's edge, discharging volleys of grape upon the helpless, compact mass. Before the city surrendered, four thousand of these unhappy victims of war, torn with shot, and suffocated by the waves, were swept down the stream. Though the marshal exerted himself to the utmost to preserve discipline, no mortal man could restrain the passions of an army in such an hour. The wretched city experienced all the horrors of a town taken by storm. The number of the slain, according to the report of Marshal Soult, was more than eighteen thousand, not including those who were engulfed in the Douro. Multitudes of the wounded fled to the woods, where they perished miserably of exposure and starvation. But two hundred and fifty prisoners were taken. The French took two hundred thousand pounds of powder, a vast amount of stores, and tents for the accommodation of fifty thousand men. They captured also in the port thirty English vessels loaded with wine. The loss of the French in capturing Oporto, according to the report of the general-in-chief, was but eighty killed, and three hundred and fifty wounded.

17

Continued Scenes of Carnage.

It is heart-sickening to proceed with the recital of these horrors. Similar scenes took place in Tarancon, where General Victor destroyed the remains of the regular Spanish army with terrible slaughter. A band of about twelve thousand men were cut to pieces by General Sebastiani. Again the Spaniards met with a fearful repulse upon the plains of Estremadura. The Spanish general, Cuesta, with twenty thousand infantry and four thousand horse, was attacked by General Victor with fifteen thousand foot and three thousand horse. As usual, the French cut to pieces their despised foes, capturing all their artillery, inflicting upon them a loss in killed, wounded, and prisoners, of ten thousand men, while the French lost but about one thousand.

While these scenes were transpiring, Joseph, at Madrid, not only occupied himself with the general direction of the war, so far as the instructions which he perpetually received from Paris enabled him to do, but labored incessantly, as he had done in Naples, in promoting all needful reforms, and in forming and executing plans for the happiness of his subjects. He caused a constitution, which had been formed at Bayonne, to be published and widely circulated, that the Spaniards might be convinced that it was his desire to reign over them as a father rather than as a sovereign.

Napoleon, speaking of his brother Joseph to Dr. O'Meara at Saint Helena, said:

"Joseph is a very excellent man. His virtues and his talents are appropriate to private life. Nature destined him for that. He is too amiable to be a great man. He has no ambition. He resembles me in person, but he is much better than I. He is extremely well educated."

"I have always observed," O'Meara remarks, "that he spoke of his brother Joseph with the most ardent affection."

The fickleness of the multitude was very conspicuous during all these stormy scenes. Joseph made a short visit to the southern provinces. Everywhere he was received with the greatest enthusiasm, the people crowding around him, and greeting him with shouts of "*Vive le Roi.*" Deputations from the cities and villages hastened to meet him with protestations of homage and fidelity. Joseph responded, in those convincing accents which the honesty of his heart inspired, that he wished to forget all the past, to maintain the salutary

institutions of religion, and to confer upon
Spain that constitutional liberty which would
secure its prosperity. Joseph and the friends
who accompanied him were so much impressed with the apparent cordiality of their greeting that they were sanguine in the hope that
the nation would rally around the new dynasty. On the 4th of March the King entered
Malaga. The enthusiasm of his reception
could scarcely have been exceeded. The
streets through which he passed were strewn
with flowers, and the windows filled with the
smiling faces of ladies. He remained there for
eight days, receiving every token of regard
which affection and confidence could confer.

But in other parts of the country where Joseph was not present it seemed as if the whole
population, without a dissenting voice, was rising against him. His embarrassments became
extreme. He not only had no wish to impose
himself upon a reluctant people, but no earthly consideration could induce him to do so. It
was his sincere and earnest desire to lift up
Spain from its degradation, and make it great
and prosperous. The emissaries of Great
Britain were everywhere busy recruiting the
Spanish armies, lavishing gold in payment,

JOSEPH ENTERING MALAGA.

supplying the troops abundantly with clothing and all the munitions of war, and giving them English officers. Guerrilla bands were organized, with the privilege of plundering and destroying all who were in favor of the new régime. The friends of the new régime dared not openly avow their attachment to the government of Joseph, unless protected by French troops. It was thus extremely difficult to ascertain the real wishes of the nation.

The Duke of Wellington was upon the frontiers, with an army of seventy thousand English and Portuguese. If Joseph remained in Spain, it was clear that he had a long and bloody struggle before him. If he threw down the crown and abandoned the enterprise, it was surrendering Spain to England, to be forced inevitably into the coalition against France. Thus the existence of the new régime in France seemed to depend upon the result of the struggle in Spain. Joseph could not abandon the enterprise without being apparently false to his brother, to his own country, and to the principle of equal rights for all throughout Europe.

CHAPTER IX.
The War in Spain Continued.

IN July of 1809 Joseph was in Madrid, with
an army of about forty thousand men.
The rest of the French army was widely dispersed. The Duke of Wellington thought this
a favorable opportunity to make a rapid march
and seize the Spanish capital. Collecting a
force of eighty-five thousand troops, he pressed
rapidly forward to Talavera, within two days'
march of Madrid. Joseph, being informed of
the approach of this formidable allied army,
and that they were expecting still very considerable re-enforcements, resolved to advance
and attack them before those new troops
should arrive. By great exertions he collected about forty-five thousand veterans, and on
the 27th of July found himself facing his vast-
ly-outnumbering foes, very formidably posted
among the groves and hills of Talavera. For
two days the battle raged. It was fearfully
destructive. The allied army lost between six

and seven thousand men. The French between eight and nine thousand. The tall grass took fire, and, sweeping along like a prairie conflagration, fearfully burned many of the wounded. The Spaniards . and Portuguese were easily dispersed. They seemed to care but little for the conflict, regarding themselves as the paid soldiers of England, fighting the battles of England. But the British troops fought with the determination and bravery which has ever characterized the men of that race.

At the close of the second day's fight the French troops drew off in good order, and encamped about three miles in the rear. Though unable to disperse the army of Wellington, Joseph had accomplished his purpose in so crippling the enemy as to arrest his farther advance, and thus to save Madrid. Joseph waited in his encampment for the arrival of Soult, Ney, and Mortier, who were hastening to his aid. Wellington, finding that he could place but very little reliance upon his Portuguese and Spanish allies, decided to retreat, abandoning his wounded to the protection of some Spanish troops whom he left as a rearguard, who in turn abandoned the sufferers entirely and returned to Portugal.

The British complained bitterly of the luke-
warmness and even treachery of their Spanish
allies. Alison gives utterance to these complaints in saying:

"From the moment the English troops entered Spain, they had experienced the wide
difference between the promises and the per-
formance of the Spanish authorities. We have
the authority of Wellington for the assertion
that if the Junta of Truxillo had kept their
contract for furnishing two hundred and forty
thousand rations, the Allies would, on the night
of the 27th of July, have slept in Madrid.
But for the month which followed the battle of Talavera their distresses in this respect
had indeed been excessive, and had reached
a height which was altogether insupportable.
Notwithstanding the most energetic remon-
strances from Wellington, he had got hardly
any supplies from the Spanish generals or authorities from the time of his entering Spain.
Cuesta had refused to lend him ninety mules
to draw his artillery, though at the time he had
several hundred in his army doing nothing.
The troops of all arms were literally starving.
During the month which followed the junction
of the two armies, on the 22d of July, they

had not received ten days' bread. On many days they got only a little meat without salt, on others nothing at all. The cavalry and artillery horses had not received, in the same time, three deliveries of forage, and in consequence a thousand had died, and seven hundred were on the sick list.

"These privations were the more exasperating that, during the greater part of the time, the Spanish troops received their rations regularly, both for men and horses. The composition of the Spanish troops, and their conduct at Talavera and upon other occasions, was not such as to inspire the least confidence in their capability of resisting the attack of the French armies. The men, badly disciplined and without uniform, dispersed the moment they experienced any reverse, and permitted the whole weight of the contest to fall on the English soldiers, who had no similar means of escape. These causes had gradually produced an estrangement, and at length a positive animosity between the privates and officers of the two armies. An angry correspondence took place between their respective generals, which widened the breach."

A few skirmishes ensued between the con-

tending parties until the 3d of November, when
Joseph, with thirty thousand men, encountered fifty-five thousand Spaniards.   The odds
in favor of the Spaniards was so great that
they rushed vigorously upon the French.   A
battle of four hours ensued.   The Spanish army
was broken to pieces, dispersed, trampled under
foot.   Twenty thousand prisoners, fifty-five
pieces of cannon, and the whole ammunition
of the army were captured by the French.

"Wearied with collecting prisoners," says
Alison, "the French at length merely took the
arms from the fugitives, desiring them to go
home, telling them that war was a trade which
they were not fit for."

From this conflict Joseph returned in triumph to his capital.   It seemed for a time that
no more resistance could be offered, and that
his government was firmly established.   Wellington was driven back into Portugal, and
loudly proclaimed that he could place no reliance upon the promises or the arms of the
Spaniards or the Portuguese.

Napoleon had returned from the triumphant campaign of Wagram.   Again he had shattered the coalition in the north, and was upon
the pinnacle of his greatness.   The total failure

of Wellington's campaign had greatly disappointed the British people. The Common Council of London petitioned Parliament for an inquiry into the circumstances connected with this failure.

"Admitting the valor of Lord Wellington," they said in their address, "the petitioners can see no reason why any recompense should be bestowed on him for his military conduct. After a useless display of British valor, and a frightful carnage, that army, like the preceding one, was compelled to seek safety in a precipitous flight before an enemy who we were told had been conquered, abandoning many thousands of our wounded countrymen into the hands of the French. That calamity, like the others, has passed without any inquiry, and, as if their long-experienced impunity had put the servants of the Crown above the reach of justice, ministers have actually gone the length of advising your majesty to confer honorable distinctions on a general who has thus exhibited, with equal rashness and ostentation, nothing but a useless valor."

Still, after an angry debate, in which there was very strong opposition presented against carrying on the war in Spain, it was finally decided to prosecute hostilities against Napoleon in the Peninsula with renewed vigor. The advocates of the measure urged that there was no other point in Europe where they could gain a foothold to attack Napoleon, and that by protracting the war there, and drawing down the French armies, they might afford an opportunity for the Northern powers again to rise in a coalition against the new régime. These views were very strenuously urged in the House of Lords by Lord Wellesley, Lord Castlereagh, and Lord Liverpool. The vote stood sixty-five for the war, thirty-three against it. It was resolved to concentrate the whole force of England for a new campaign in the Peninsula. One hundred millions of dollars were voted to the navy, one hundred and five millions to the army, and twenty-five millions for the ordnance. The British navy engaged in the enterprise consisted of a thousand and nineteen vessels of war. In addition to these forces, the English were to raise all the troops they could from Spain and Portugal, offering them the most liberal pay, and encouraging them to all those acts of guerrilla warfare for which they were remarkably adapted, and which might prove most annoying to the French communications.

Napoleon, to meet the emergency, had in the Peninsula an army of two hundred and eighty thousand men ready for service. Slowly the months of the year 1810 rolled away over that wretched land. There were battles on the plains and among the hills, sieges, bombardments, conflicts hand to hand in the blood-stained streets, outrages innumerable, pestilence, famine, conflagration, misery, death. The causes of the conflict were clearly defined and distinctly understood by the leading men on each side. Never was there a more momentous question to be decided by the fate of armies. England was fighting to perpetuate in England and on the Continent the old régime of *aristocratic privilege.* France was fighting to defend and maintain in France and among the other regenerated nations of Europe, the new régime of *equal rights for all men.* The intelligent community everywhere distinctly comprehended the nature of the conflict, and chose their sides. The unintelligent masses, often blinded by ignorance, deluded by 'fanaticism, or controlled by power, were bewildered, and swayed to and fro, as controlled by circumstances.

The year 1811 opened sadly upon this war-

deluged land.   It would only lacerate the heart
of the reader to give an honest recital of the
miseries which were endured.   No one can
read with pleasure the account of these scenes
of blood, misery, and death.   Equal bravery
and equal determination were displayed by the
French and by the English, and, alas for man,
there was probably much conscientiousness
on both sides.   There were religious men in
each army, men who went from their knees in
prayer into the battle.   There were men who
honestly believed that the interests of humanity required that the government of the nations
should be in the hands of the rich and the noble.   There were others who as truly believed
that the old feudal system was a curse to the
nations, and that a new era of reform was demanded, at whatever expense of treasure and
blood.   And thus these children of a common
father, during the twelve long months of another year, contended with each other in the death-
struggle upon more battle-fields than history
can record.

Joseph, in view of this slaughter and this
misery, was at times extremely wretched.   He
knew not what to do.   Nothing can exceed the
sadness of some of his letters to his brother.

To abandon the conflict seemed like cowardice, and might prove the destruction of the popular cause all over Europe. To persevere was to perpetuate blood and misery. Seldom has any man been placed in a position of greater difficulty, but the integrity, the conscientiousness, and the humanity of the man were manifest in every word he uttered, in every deed he performed.

"My first duties," said Joseph, "are for Spain. I love France as my family, Spain as my religion. I am attached to the one by the affections of my heart, and to the other by my conscience."

Napoleon, wearied with these incessant wars, which were draining the treasure and the blood of France, thought that if he could connect himself by marriage with one of the ancient dynasties, he could thus bring himself into the acknowledged family of kings, and secure such an alliance as would prevent these incessant coalitions of all dynastic Europe against France. In March, 1810, the Emperor, having committed the greatest mistake of his life in the divorce of Josephine—a sin against God's law, though with him, at the time, a sin of ignorance and of good intentions—a mistake

18

which he afterward bitterly deplored as the ultimate cause of his ruin—married Maria Louisa, the daughter of the Emperor of Austria. This union seemed to unite Austria with France in a permanent alliance, and for a time gave promise of securing the great blessing which Napoleon hoped to attain by it. On the 20th of March, 1811, Napoleon wrote to Joseph:

"MONSIEUR MON FRERE,—I hasten to announce to your Majesty that the Empress, my dear wife, has just been safely delivered of a prince, who at his birth received the title of the King of Rome. Your Majesty's constant affection towards me convinces me that you will share in the satisfaction which I feel at an event of such importance to my family and to the welfare of my subjects.

"This conviction is very agreeable to me. Your Majesty is aware of my attachment, and can not doubt the pleasure with which I seize this opportunity of repeating the assurance of the sincere esteem and tender friendship with which I am," etc.

On the same day, a few hours later, he wrote again to his brother giving a minute account of the accouchement, which was very severe. He closed this letter by saying:

" The babe is perfectly well. The Empress is as comfortable as could be expected. This evening, at eight o'clock, the infant will be privately baptized. As I do not intend the public christening to take place for the next six weeks, I shall intrust General Defrance, my equerry, who will be the bearer of this letter, with another in which I shall ask you to stand godfather to your nephew."

In May, Joseph, accompanied by a small retinue, visited Paris, to have a personal conference with his brother upon the affairs of Spain. He was much dissatisfied that the French marshals there were so independent of him in the conduct of their military operations. The result of the conversations which he held with his brother was, that he returned to Spain apparently satisfied. He entered Madrid on the 15th of July, in the midst of an immense concourse of people. The principal inhabitants of the city, in a long train of carriages, came out to meet him, a triumphal arch was constructed across the road, and joy seemed to beam from every countenance. He immediately consecrated himself with new ardor to the administration of the internal affairs of his realm.

There was very strong opposition manifested by the people of England against the Spanish war. There were many indications that the British Government might be forced, by the voice of the people, to relinquish the conflict. Animated by these hopes, Joseph announced his intention of calling a Spanish congress, in which the people should be fully represented, to confer upon the national interests. Wellington was thoroughly disheartened. His dispatches were full of bitter complaints against the incapacity of the British Government. Napoleon, in his address to the legislative body on the 18th of June, 1811, in the following terms alluded to the war in Spain:

"Since 1809 the greater part of the strong places in Spain have been taken, after memorable sieges, and the insurgents have been beaten in a great number of pitched battles. England has felt that the war is approaching a termination, and that intrigues and gold are no longer sufficient to nourish it. She has found herself, therefore, obliged to alter the nature of her assistance, and from an auxiliary she has become a principal. All her troops of the line have been sent to the Peninsula.

"English blood has, at length, flowed in

Grandeur of Napoleon.

torrents in several actions glorious to the French arms. This conflict with Carthage, which seemed as if it would be decided on fields of battle on the ocean or beyond the seas, will henceforth be decided on the plains of Spain. When England shall be exhausted, when she shall at last have felt the evils which for twenty years she has with so much cruelty poured upon the Continent, when half her families shall be in mourning, then shall a peal of thunder put an end to the affairs of the Peninsula, the destinies of her armies, and avenge Europe and Asia by finishing this second Punic War."[1]

At the close of the year 1811 Napoleon stood upon the highest pinnacle of his power. Coalition after coalition had been shattered by his armies, and now he had not an avowed foe upon the Continent. The Emperor of Russia was allied to him by the ties of friendship ; the Emperor of Austria by the ties of relationship. Other hostile nations had been too thoroughly vanquished to attempt to arise against him, or, by political regeneration, had been brought into sympathy with the new régime in France.

The English, aided by their resistless fleet,

[1] Moniteur, Jan. 11, 1811.

still held important positions in Portugal.
They however had no foothold in Spain ex-
cepting at Cadiz, situated upon the island of
Leon, upon the extreme southern point of the
Peninsula. The usual population of the city
of Cadiz was one hundred and fifty thousand.
But this number had been increased by a
hundred thousand strangers, who had thrown
themselves into the place. About fifty thousand troops under Marmont were besieging the
city. The garrison defending Cadiz consisted
of about twenty thousand men, five thousand
of whom were English soldiers. The British
fleet was also in its harbor, with encouragement
and supplies. Here and there predatory bands
occasionally appeared, but this was nearly all
the serious opposition which was then presented to the reign of Joseph. The French lines
encompassing the city were thirty miles in
length, extending from sea to sea.

To the great chagrin of England, the Spanish leaders in Cadiz convened a Congress, which
formed a constitution, called the Constitution
of 1812, far more radically democratic than
even Napoleon could advocate for Spain.
Wellington was exceedingly vexed, and complained bitterly of this conduct on the part of

the men whose battle he assumed to be fighting.   "The British Government were well
aware," says Alison, "while democratic frenzy
was thus reigning triumphant at Cadiz, from
the dispatches of their ambassador there, the
Honorable H. Wellesley, as well as from Wellington's information of the dangerous nature
of the spirit which had been thus evolved,
that they had a task of no ordinary difficulty
to encounter in any attempt to moderate its
transports."[1]

Joseph grew more and more disheartened.
All his plans for the pacification of the country
were baffled.   On the 23d of March, 1812, he
wrote to his brother from Madrid as follows:

"SIRE,—When a year ago I sought the advice of your Majesty before coming back to
Spain, you urged me to return.   It is therefore that I am here.   You had the kindness to
say to me that I should always have the privilege of leaving the country if the hopes we
had conceived should not be realized.   In that
case your Majesty assured me of an asylum in
the south of the Empire, between which and
Mortfontaine I could divide my residence.

"Events have disappointed my hopes.   I

[1] Alison, vol. iii. p. 407.

have done no good, and I have no longer any hopes of doing any. I entreat, then, your Majesty to permit me to resign to his hands the crown of Spain, which he condescended to transmit to me four years ago. In accepting the crown of this country, I never had any other object in view than the happiness of this vast monarchy. It has not been in my power to accomplish it. I pray your Majesty to receive me as one of his subjects, and to believe that he will never have a more faithful servant than the friend whom nature has given him."

The resignation was not then accepted, and circumstances soon became such that Joseph felt that he could not with honor withdraw from the post he occupied.

The Spaniards looked with great distrust upon the Duke of Wellington, who was the embodiment of the principles of aristocracy, the more to be feared in consequence of his inflexible will. The English deemed the re-enthronement of Ferdinand VII. and his despotic sway essential to the success of their cause. The uncrowned King and his brother Don Carlos were living very sumptuously and contentedly, chasing foxes and hares at Valençay, and cut-

ting down the park to build bonfires in cele-
bration of Napoleon's victories.

The British Government, alarmed in view
of the democratic spirit unexpectedly developed
by a portion of the Spanish allies, sent a secret
agent, Baron Rolli, a man of great sagacity,
address, and intrepidity, to persuade Ferdinand
to violate his pledge of honor, to escape from
Valençay, and place himself at the head of the
Spaniards who were in opposition to Joseph.
It was hoped that this would awaken new enthusiasm on the part of the Church and the advocates of the old régime, and that it would
check the spirit of ultra democracy which was
threatening to sweep every thing before it.

The nearest approach to an honorable deed
to which Ferdinand ever came, was in the
very questionable act of revealing the plot to
the French Government. Rolli was arrested
and sent to Vincennes. The democratic leaders in Cadiz were so incensed against what
Alison calls "the orderly spirit of aristocratic
rule in England," that, burying their animosity
against the French invasion, they almost welcomed those foreign armies, who bore everywhere upon their banners "Equal Rights for
all Men." They opened secret negotiations

with Joseph, offering to surrender Cadiz to the
French troops, and to secure the entire submission of the whole peninsula to the government of Joseph if he would accept the radical Constitution of 1812 in place of the more
moderate Republicanism of the Constitution of
Bayonne.   The hostility of the Spanish generals and soldiers to Wellington and the English troops was bitter and undisguised.[1]

But more bloody scenes soon ensued.   Napoleon, deeming the war in Spain virtually end-
ed, had been induced to withdraw large numbers of his troops, and to embark in his fatal
campaign to Moscow.   Thus Russia became allied to England, and a new opportunity, under
more favorable auspices, was afforded to renew
the war in Spain.   England concentrated her
mightiest energies upon the Peninsula against
the remnants of the French army which Napoleon had left there.   The Emperor, with all his
chosen troops, composing an army of over five
hundred thousand men, was on the march thousands of miles toward the north.   On the 9th
of May, 1812, the Emperor left Paris, to place
himself at the head of his troops in Dresden.
The war in Spain was now urged by the Brit-

Napier, v. 406, 407.

ish Government with renovated fury. The mind is wearied and the heart is sickened, in reading the recital of sieges, and battles, and outrages which make a humane man to exclaim, in anguish of spirit, "O Lord, how long! how long!" Equal ferocity was upon both sides. French, English, Spanish, and Portuguese sol- diers, maddened by passion and inflamed with intoxicating drinks, perpetrated deeds which fiends could scarcely exceed. Tortosa, Tarra- gona, Manresa, Saguntum, Valencia, Badajoz, Ciudad Rodrigo, and a score of other places, testified to the bravery, often the tiger-like ferocity, of the contending parties, and to the misery which man can inflict upon his brother- man.

Physical bravery is the cheapest and most vulgar of all earthly virtues. The vilest rab- ble gathered from the gutters of any city can, by a few months of military discipline and ex- perience in the horrors of war, become so reck- less of danger that bullets, shells, and grape- shot are as little regarded as snowflakes. Rob- ber bands and piratic hordes will often fight with ferocity and desperation which can not be surpassed. It is the cause alone which can ennoble the heroism of the battle-field. In

these terrific conflicts, especially when the
French and the British troops were brought
into contact, there often were exhibited all the
energy and desperation of which human nature
is capable.

As the Emperor set out on the Russian
campaign, he invested Joseph with the command of the armies in Spain. These troops
were widely dispersed, to protect different points
in the kingdom. But few could be promptly
rallied upon any one field of battle. The Em
peror, burdened with the expense of his immense army, and far away amidst the wilds of
Russia, could give but little attention to the affairs of Spain, and could send neither money
nor supplies to his brother, who was so uneasi-
ly settled upon an impoverished throne. As
days of darkness gathered around the Emperor,
a sense of honor prevented Joseph from abandoning his post. His troops were everywhere
in a state of great destitution and suffering.
His humane heart would not allow him to wrest
supplies from the people, who were often in a
still greater state of poverty and want.

Marshal Massena had entered Portugal with
an army of seventy-five thousand men. Reduced by sickness and destitution, he was com-

SACK OF CIUDAD RODRIGO.

Ciudad Rodrigo.

pelled to withdraw with but thirty-five thousand men. Thus the English army, no longer held in check, occupied Ciudad Rodrigo and Badajoz.[1]

Three thousand men were left in garrison at Ciudad Rodrigo. Forty thousand men under Wellington besieged it. After opening two practicable breaches, Wellington summoned a surrender. The French general, Barrie, replied :

"His Majesty, the Emperor, has intrusted me with the command of Ciudad Rodrigo. I and my garrison are resolved to bury ourselves beneath the ruins."

The place was taken by assault, the British troops rushing into the breaches with courage which could not have been surpassed. The French, after losing half their number, were overpowered. The victorious British soldiers, forgetting that the inhabitants of the city were their allies, pillaged the houses and the shops, and committed every conceivable outrage upon the inhabitants. Sir Archibald Alison thus describes the scene:

"The churches were ransacked, the wine and spirit cellars pillaged, and brutal intoxica-

[1] Encyclopædia Americana, article Joseph Bonaparte.

tion spread in every direction. Soon flames were seen bursting in several quarters. Some houses were burned to the ground, others already ignited. By degrees, however, the drunken men dropped down from excess of liquor, or fell asleep; and before morning a degree of order was restored."

Advancing from Ciudad Rodrigo, Wellington, at the head of a force then numbering sixty thousand men, laid siege to Badajoz, crossing the Guadiarra above and below the city. The garrison in the city consisted of but forty-five hundred combatants. The trenches were opened upon the night between the 17th and 18th of March. There was no more desperate fighting during all the wars of Napoleon than was witnessed within and around the walls of Badajoz. The British lost five thousand officers and men ere the city was captured. Again had the Spaniards bitter cause to mourn over the victory of those who called themselves their allies. As the British troops rushed into the streets of this Spanish city which they had professedly come to rescue from the government of Joseph Bonaparte, Alison says:

"Disorders and excesses of every sort prevailed, and the British soldiery showed, by their conduct after the storm, that they inherited their full share of the sins as well as the virtues of the children of Adam. The disgraceful national vice of intemperance, in particular, broke forth in its most frightful colors. All the wine shops and vaults were broken open and plundered. Pillage was universal. Every house was ransacked for valuables, spirits, or wine; and crowds of drunken soldiers for two days and nights thronged the streets, while the breaking open of doors and windows, the report of casual muskets, and the screams of despoiled citizens resounded on all sides."

The throne of Joseph was now enveloped in gloom. To add to his trouble and anguish of spirit, a dreadful famine afflicted Spain. But the British fleet, in undisputed command of the seas, could convey ample supplies to the army of Wellington, and British gold was lavished in keeping alive the flames of insurrection. Troops were landed at various points, and resistance to the French was encouraged by every means in the power of the British Government. At Madrid every morning there were found in the streets many dead bodies of those who had perished during the night. The

French in the capital, animated by the benevolent spirit of Joseph, imposed upon themselves the severest sacrifices to succor the perishing. The situation of Joseph had become deplorable. The best troops were withdrawn for the Russian campaign. Those which remained were starving, and without means of transport. A new government, under the protection of the English, was organized at Cadiz, and guerrilla bands were springing up in all directions.

Joseph had but about twenty thousand troops in the vicinity of Cadiz, with which force he could be but little more than a spectator of events as they should occur. Wellington had a highly-disciplined army of sixty thousand men, independent of the guerrilla bands whom he could summon to his aid.

CHAPTER X.

THE EXPULSION FROM SPAIN.

JOSEPH was much embarrassed. Should he leave his scattered forces in the south of Spain, there was danger that they would be attacked and destroyed piecemeal by Wellington. Should he withdraw them, and concentrate his forces in the north, the whole south of Spain would be instantly overrun by the English, and Joseph would lose one-half of his kingdom. His total force in Spain, garrisoning the forts and composing his detached bands in the south, the centre, the north, and the west, amounted to a little over two hundred and thirty thousand men.

In the early part of May of this year, 1812, the English, having taken the defenses which were erected for the fortification of the Tagus, became dominant in that region. Disaster followed disaster. The King's couriers were captured, so that his orders did not reach the marshals. It is hard to be amiable in seasons of

adversity, and the marshals reproached each
other. Supplies and communications were cut
off, and women and children were dying of
famine. The deadly warfare of guerrilla bands
increased rapidly. The most atrocious acts of
vengeance and atrocity were multiplied, and
Joseph had no power to prevent them. As
Marmont was in danger of being cut off by
Wellington, Joseph, leaving a small garrison
behind him, took all the troops that could be
spared, and marched rapidly to the relief of
the marshal. Leaving the Escurial on the 23d
of July, he reached Peneranda on the 25th,
where he learned that Marmont had attacked
Wellington on the 23d at Arapiles, and, after
a desperate conflict, had been repulsed. Marmont was severely censured for not awaiting
the arrival of Joseph, whom he knew to be at
hand. He was accused, perhaps without reason, of precipitating the conflict from fear that
Joseph might take the command and gain the
renown. Marmont reported his total loss in
the battle to have been about six thousand
men and nine guns, which were left because
their carriages were knocked to pieces. Wellington reported his own loss at five thousand
two hundred and twenty.

Marmont retreated to Valladolid, to meet re-enforcements which would join him there. Joseph returned to Madrid, entering the city on the 2d of August. As the English approached, Joseph, with two thousand horse, met their advance-guard, and, with the courage of despair, drove them back in the wildest confusion. He then, at the head of but twelve thousand troops, commenced his retreat toward Valence. Twenty thousand Spaniards, men and women, dreading the vengeance of their enemies, followed, in his retreat, the King whom they had much cause to love. It was a mournful spectacle. Nobles of the highest rank, and the most intelligent and opulent of the city, toiled along in their weary march, the women and the children often unable to restrain their tears and sobs. The partisans of the English, who crowded into the city, received Wellington and his troops with every demonstration of joy. The friends of the new régime who remained behind, crushed in all their hopes, closed the shutters of their houses, retired to the remote apartments, and buried their griefs in silence.

Into whatever city the English or the French entered, they were alike received with unbounded enthusiasm. In every large city there is a throng ready to shout hosanna to the conqueror, whoever he may be. When Wellington and his squadrons entered a Spanish city, the friends of the old régime gathered around them. And so it was with the French and their friends when they were the victors. Thus at Valence, where Joseph arrived on the 31st of August, he was received with all the honors which could be conferred upon the most beloved sovereign. An immense crowd thronged the streets, and lavished upon him every demonstration of gratitude. The devout King, much moved by this exhibition of popular affection in these dark hours of defeat and humiliation, repaired at once to the cathedral, and in a solemn *Te Deum* gave expression to his gratitude to God.

Joseph's first care was for the unhappy fugitives who, dreading the vengeance of the foe, had abandoned home and all, to accompany him in his flight. He had neither money, food, nor shelter to give them. He therefore sent this sorrow-stricken band, counting over twenty thousand, under an escort across the Pyrenees into France, where they would be protected and provided for.

At Valence Joseph concentrated his scattered forces, and early in November commenced
his march back to Madrid. It is very difficult
to ascertain the precise number of the forces
on each side. Wellington's army was estimated at ninety-two thousand men. Joseph had
collected superior numbers, and marched eagerly to attack him. Wellington rapidly retreated toward Ciudad Rodrigo, and on the 3d
of December Joseph entered Madrid again in
triumph.

Conciliation, kindness, deference to the wishes of others are not characteristic virtues of the
English. They had long assumed, and with
no little semblance of reason, that in wealth,
power, arts, and arms they were the leading
nation upon the globe. This assumption has
made them unpopular as a people. They are
so honest and plain-spoken that they never
attempt to disguise their contempt for other
nations. The victorious soldiers of Wellington particularly despised the Spaniards. This
contempt neither officers nor soldiers attempted to conceal.

It is just the reverse with the French. The
characteristic politeness of the nation leads
them to compliment others, and to pay them

especial deference. They conceal the sense of
superiority which they may perhaps cherish.
It is frequently said, as characteristic of the two
nations, that the stranger in London gets the
impression that every Englishman he meets
has taken a special dislike to him personally;
in Paris, on the other hand, he receives the
impression that every Frenchman with whom
he is brought into contact has a special fancy
for him, perceiving in him virtues and excel-
lences which he never supposed that he possessed.

The Duke of Wellington himself was a
haughty, overbearing man. No soldier loved
him, but all bowed submissive to his inflexible will. The deportment of the British troops
in the Spanish capital was such as to alienate
those who at first welcomed them, and they
soon became universally disliked. The Spaniards are proud, proverbially proud; and they
could not endure this contemptuous assumption of superiority. So great became the dissatisfaction that many of the Spanish generals
proposed to unite their troops with those of
King Joseph if he would grant them independent commands.

Exultantly the English on the Peninsula

heard the tidings of the terrible disasters Napoleon was encountering in ·Russia. They could scarcely exaggerate them. It was manifest that for a long time, at least, Joseph could receive no assistance from France; on the contrary, many regiments of infantry and cavalry, and a number of companies of artillery, received orders immediately to leave Spain, and to hasten to the aid of the Emperor. Joseph, thus hopelessly crippled, was directed by the Emperor to concentrate his enfeebled forces upon the line of the Douro. Leaving a garrison of ten thousand men in Madrid, Joseph, with the remainder of his troops, retired toward the north.

In Wellington's retreat from Madrid, his troops committed all imaginable outrages. In his dispatch to his officers commanding his divisions and brigades, he said:

"From the moment the troops commenced their retreat from the neighborhood of Madrid on the one hand, and Burgos on the other, the officers lost all command over the men. Irregularities and outrages of all descriptions were committed with impunity, and losses have been sustained which ought never to have occurred. The discipline of every army, after a long and

active campaign, becomes in some degree re-
laxed ; but I am concerned to observe that the
army under my command has fallen off in this
respect, in the late campaign, *to a greater degree
than any army with which I have ever been, or of
which I have ever read.*"[1]

Thus terminated the year 1812. The disappointment of the British Government, in view
of the discomfiture and retreat of Wellington,
was very great, and the indignation of that portion of the English people who were opposed
to this interminable warfare against the new
régime in France knew no bounds. That the
English army had, through a long line of disastrous retreat, according to the testimony of
its commander, inflicted outrages upon the
Spanish people, its allies, *greater than that commander had ever read of in history*, keenly
wounded the national pride.

As fresh tidings arose of the disasters which
had befallen Napoleon in the north, the British Government renewed their zeal to assail
him from the south. Large re-enforcements
were sent out during the winter with such
abundant supplies as to enable Wellington to

[1] Wellington to Officers commanding Divisions and Brigades, ix. 574, 575.

commence the spring campaign with every assurance of success. The Cortes in Cadiz, with
ever-varying policy, much to the disgust of
many of the Spanish generals, invested the
British duke with the supreme command. The
opposition, however, was so great that the
duke's brother, Mr. Henry Wellesley, who was
then British ambassador at Cadiz, advised him
not to accept the office. But the energetic
duke was confident that, by combining the
whole military strength of the Peninsula with
the army and fleet of England, he could drive
the feeble remnants of the French from the
kingdom. He therefore undertook the command.

The Cortes was led to this decisive measure
from the fact that there was a strong and increasing party of their own number in favor
of rallying to the support of Joseph. Their
only choice lay between Joseph or Ferdinand,
or the experiment of a democratic republic. Wellington's visit to Cadiz, says Alison,
" brought forcibly under his notice the miserable state of the Government at that place, ruled
by a furious democratic faction, intimidated by
an ungovernable press, and alternately the prey
of aristocratic intrigue and democratic fury.

He did not fail to report to the Government this deplorable state of things."

In the beginning of May Wellington was prepared to take the field with an allied army of two hundred thousand men. The navy of England actively co-operated with this immense force, conveying supplies and protecting the extreme flanks of the line, which stretched across the kingdom. The storm of war burst forth again in all its fury. Manfully Joseph contended to the last. In the vicinity of Valladolid he had concentrated fifty thousand men, and hoped to be able there to give battle. But Wellington came upon him with an army one hundred thousand strong, which was reported to be one hundred and ninety thousand.

The French on the 14th of June retreated to Vittoria. The garrison in Madrid and the civil authorities now abandoned the capital and took refuge with the army. Here a short but terrible battle ensued. The English had eighty thousand combatants on the field; the French, according to their statement, had but half as many. Alison states their force at sixty-five thousand. It was an awful battle. Both parties fought desperately. The loss of the French was six thousand nine hundred and sixty; that

of the English five thousand one hundred and
eighty.[1] The French army was impoverished
after weary months of warfare, in a land stricken
by famine, and wasted by the sweep of armies
and the plundering of banditti. It was with
very great difficulty that Joseph could support
his destitute troops. Yet Alison, in that strain
of exaggeration which sullies his often eloquent
pages, writes:

"Independent of private booty, no less than
five millions and a half of dollars in the military chest of the army were taken; and of private wealth the amount was so prodigious that
for miles together the combatants may almost
be said to have marched upon gold and silver,
without stooping to pick it up."

In the hour of victory Wellington seemed
to have no control over his soldiers, whom his
pen describes as drunken and brutal. Reeling
in intoxication, they wandered at will. Wellington states that three weeks after the battle above twelve thousand of his soldiers had
abandoned their colors. "I am convinced," he

[1] King Joseph, writing to Clarke, under date of July 6,
1813, says: "Our army at Vittoria was but thirty-five thousand. That fact can not be contested. The enemy had certainly seventy thousand combatants. I can not be deceived
when I say that his force was double of ours."

says in a dispatch to Lord Bathurst, " that we have out of our ranks doubled our loss in the battle, and have lost more men in the pursuit than the enemy have."

The retreat of the French was conducted with the firmness and admirable discipline characteristic of French soldiers. As the troops slowly and sullenly retired toward the French frontier, pressed by superior numbers, they turned occasionally upon their pursuers, and the advance-guard of the foe encountered several very bloody repulses.

We have not space to allude to these various conflicts, which only checked for a moment the onrolling tide of the victorious allied army. Wellington's troops took the town of San Sebastian by storm. This was a beautiful Spanish city, through which the French retreated, and where they made a short and desperate stand. We will leave it to Mr. Alison to describe the conduct of Lord Wellington's troops.

"And now commenced," writes Alison, "a scene which has affixed as lasting a stain on the character of the English and Portuguese troops, as the heroic valor they displayed in the assault has given them enduring and ex-alted fame. The long endurance of the assault had wrought the soldiers up to perfect madness. The soldiers wreaked their vengeance with fearful violence on the unhappy inhabitants. Some of the houses adjoining the breaches had taken fire from the effects of the explosion. The flames, fanned by an awful tempest which burst on the town, soon spread with frightful rapidity. The wretched inhabitants, driven from house to house as the conflagration devoured their dwellings, were soon huddled together in one quarter, where they fell a prey to the unbridled passions of the soldiery.

" Attempts were at first made by the British officers to extinguish the flames, but they proved vain among the general confusion which prevailed. The soldiers broke into the burning houses, pillaged them of the most valuable articles they contained, and rolling numerous casks of spirits into the streets, with frantic shouts, emptied them of their contents, till vast numbers of them sank down like savages, motionless, some lifeless, from the excess.

" Carpets, tapestry, beds, silks and satins, wearing apparel, jewelry, watches, and every thing valuable, were scattered about upon the bloody pavements, while fresh bundles of them

were thrown from the windows above to avoid
the flames, and caught with demoniac yells by
the drunken crowds beneath. Amidst these
scenes of disgraceful violence and unutterable
woe, nine-tenths of the once happy, smiling
town of St. Sebastian were reduced to ashes.
And what has affixed a yet darker blot on the
character of the victors, deeds of violence and
cruelty were perpetrated hitherto rare in the
British army, and which causes the historian
to blush, not merely for his country, but for his
species."

The account which is given by Spanish historians of these transactions is even far more
dreadful than the above; so revolting that we
can not pain our readers by transcribing it
upon these pages. A document issued by
the Constitutional Junta, after describing
crimes as awful as even fiends could commit,
adds:

" Other crimes more horrible still, which our
pen refuses to record, were committed in that
awful night, and the disorders continued for
some days after without any efficient steps
being taken to arrest them. Of above six
hundred houses, of which St. Sebastian consisted on the morning of the assault, there

remained at the end of three days only thirty-six."[1]

The Duke of Wellington, in his dispatch to the Spanish Minister of War, said, in reference to these excesses, that it was impossible for him to restrain the passions of his soldiers, that he and his officers did their utmost to stop the fire and to avoid the disorders, but that all their efforts were ineffectual.

Joseph, in his retreat, threw three thousand men into the citadel of St. Sebastian. They held back the British army sixty days. Their skill and valor extorted the commendation of their foes. The siege cost the allied army three thousand eight hundred men, and delayed for three months the invasion of the southern provinces of France.

Joseph slowly retreated, fighting his way, step by step, across the Pyrenees into France, pursued by the victors. On the 12th of April, Joseph, having crossed the mountains, and being thus driven from his kingdom, had no longer any legitimate power. The command of the French army devolved upon Soult. Utterly weary of the cares and harassments of

[1] Manifeste par la Junte Constitutionale, et les habitans de St. Sebastien.

royalty, for which Joseph never had any inclination, he joined his wife and children at his
estate at Mortfontaine. England had wrested
the crown of Spain from Joseph Bonaparte,
one of the best men whom a crown has ever
adorned, and soon, with the aid of allied Europe, placed that crown upon the brow of Ferdinand VII., one of the worst men who has
ever disgraced a throne. The result was that
Spain was consigned to another half-century
of shame, debasement, and misery.

Joseph had scarcely re-united himself with
his wife and children in their much-loved home
at Mortfontaine, when the allied armies, numbering more than a million and a half of bayonets, came crowding upon France from the
north, from the east, and from the south; while
the fleet of England, mistress of all the seas,
lent its majestic co-operation on the west.
Then ensued the sublimest conflict of which
history gives us any account. Never before,
in all Napoleon's world-renowned campaigns,
had he displayed such vigor as in the masterly
blows with which he struck one after another
of his thronging assailants, and drove them,
staggered and bleeding, before him.

France was exhausted. All Europe had

combined to crush the Republican Empire, and restore the despotism of the old régime. Through an almost uninterrupted series of victories, Napoleon lost his crown. When in any one direction he was driving his foes headlong before him, from all other points they were rushing on, till France and Paris were well-nigh whelmed in the mighty inundation. In these hours of disaster, Joseph offered life, property, all to the service of his brother. They held a few hurried interviews in Paris, and then separated, each to fulfill his appointed task in the terrible drama.

The Emperor confided to Joseph the defense of Paris, and the protection of his son and of the Empress. On the 16th of March, 1814, the Emperor wrote to his brother from Reims:

"In accordance with the verbal instructions which I gave you, and with the spirit of all my letters, you must not allow, happen what may, the Empress and the King of Rome to fall into the hands of the enemy. The manœuvres I am about to make may possibly prevent your hearing from me for several days. If the enemy should march on Paris with so strong a force as to render resistance impossible, send

off toward the Loire the Regent, my son, the
great dignitaries, the ministers, the senators.
the President of the Conseil d'Etat, the chief
officers of the crown, and Baron de la Bouil-
lerie, with the money which is in my treasury.
Never lose sight of my son, and remember that
I would rather know that he was in the Seine,
than that he was in the hands of the enemies
of France.   The fate of Astyanax, prisoner to
the Greeks, has always seemed to me the most
lamentable in history."

Faithfully, energetically, wisely, Joseph fulfilled the mission intrusted to him.   In every
possible way he endeavored to aid the Emper-
or in his heroic efforts; recruiting troops, arm-
ing them, and hurrying them off to the points
where they were most needed.   It was not
till the allied forces were upon the heights
of Montmartre, and where further resistance
would but have exposed the capital to the horrors of a bombardment, that he consented to a
surrender.   All the arms in the city had been
given out to the new levies, as they had been
sent to the seat of war, and none remained to
place in the hands of the populace, even were
it judged best to summon them to the defense
of the metropolis.   A grand council was call-

ed on the 29th of March. The ministers, the grand dignitaries, the presidents of the sections, of the Council of State, and the President of the Senate were present.

The majority of the council were in favor of defending the city to the last possible moment. There were at hand the two corps of the dukes of Ragusa and Trévise, consisting of about seventeen thousand combatants, a few thousand of the National Guard, poorly armed, a few batteries served by the students of the schools and by the Invalides, and a few hundred recruits not yet organized. It was urged that the Empress, like another Maria Theresa, should remain with her son in the city, to assure the populace by her presence, and embolden the defense. She was to show herself to the people at the Hotel de Ville, with her son in her arms. Should the Empress leave the city, it would so discourage the people that all attempts at defense would be hopeless. Should she remain, the danger was very great that both she and her son might be captured; and unless she should immediately escape, all egress might be cut off, as the Allies were rapidly surrounding the city.

Toward the close of the discussion, the Em-

peror's letter to Joseph of the 16th of March
was presented and read. In this it will be remembered that he said:

"You must not allow, happen what may,
the Empress and the King of Rome to fall into
the hands of the enemy. Never lose sight of
my son, and remember that I would rather
know that he was in the Seine, than that he
was in the hands of the enemies of France.
The fate of Astyanax, prisoner to the Greeks,
has always seemed to me the most lamentable
in history."

This settled the question. The situation of
affairs was so desperate that for the Empress
to remain in Paris would be extremely perilous. It was therefore decided that she, with
the Government, should retire to Chartres, and
thence to the Loire. But Joseph stated that
it was important to ascertain the real force of
the hostile army, which was driving before
them the two marshals, Marmont and Mortier.
He therefore offered to remain in the city,
making all possible arrangements for its defense, till that fact should be ascertained.
Should it be found that resistance was quite
impossible, he would rejoin the Government
upon the Loire.

It is very evident that Joseph and the assembled Senate, and that Napoleon himself, hoped that Maria Louisa, from her own inward impulse, would soar to the heights of a heroine. Napoleon could not ask her to come thus to his defense. At St. Helena the Emperor allowed the regret to escape his lips that Maria Louisa was not able to rise to the sublimity of the occasion. The Empress, however, was but an ordinary woman, incapable of a grand action, and it is to be remembered that she must have been embarrassed by the thought that, in striving to arouse France for the defense of her husband, she was arraying the empire against her own father. Maria Louisa, as regent, presided over this private council. The session was prolonged until after midnight. Joseph and the arch-chancellor accompanied the Empress to her home. It is evident, even then, that Joseph hoped that the Empress would assume the responsibility of a heroic act. M. Meneval, the secretary of the Empress, who was present at this interview, says:

"After the exchange of a few words upon the disastrous consequences of abandoning Paris, Joseph and the arch-chancellor ventured to say that the Empress alone could decide what course it was her duty to pursue. The Empress replied ' that they were her appointed advisers, and that she could not undertake any course unless she was advised to do it by them, over their own seal and signature.' Both declined to assume this responsibility."

The departure of the Empress was fixed at eight o'clock the next morning. Joseph had already passed the barriers, to proceed to the advance posts of the army to reconnoitre the foe. The day had not yet dawned, when the saloons of the palace were filled with those who were to accompany the Empress in her flight. Anxiety sat upon every countenance, and the solemnity of the occasion caused every voice to be hushed, so that impressive silence reigned. Early as was the hour, the alarming rumor that the Empress was to abandon Paris had reached the ears of the National Guard. Suddenly the officers of the guard who were stationed at the palace, with several others who had joined them, precipitately entered, and, by their earnest request, were conducted to the Empress. They entreated her not to leave Paris, promising to defend her to the last possible extremity.

ANGUISH OF MARIA LOUISA.

The Empress was moved to tears by their devotion, but alleged the order of the Emperor. Nevertheless, conscious of the discouraging effect of her departure, she delayed hour after hour, hoping without venturing to avow it, that some chance might arise which would enable her to remain. M. Clarke, the Minister of War, alarmed at the danger that soon all egress would be impossible, sent an officer to the Empress to represent to her the necessity of an immediate departure. Thus urged by some to go, by others to remain, the Empress was agitated by the most distracting embarrassment. She returned to her chamber, threw her hat upon her bed, seated herself in a chair, buried her face in her hands, and burst into an uncontrollable flood of tears. "O my God," she was heard to exclaim, "let them decide this question among themselves, and put an end to this my agony."

About ten o'clock the Minister of War sent again to her a message stating that she had not one moment to lose, and that unless she left immediately she was in danger of falling into the hands of the Cossacks. As Joseph was now absent, and she could receive no further counsel from him, she hastened her departure.

It was indeed true that the delay of a few
hours would have rendered her escape impossible, for that very day the banners of the Allies presented themselves before the walls of
the metropolis.

Joseph had returned rapidly to the city, to
make as determined a defense as possible. The
National Guard hastened to the posts assigned
them. Volunteers, many of them armed with
shot-guns, advanced to operate as skirmishers
against the foe. The students of the Polytech-
nic School served the artillery confided to their
"young and brilliant" valor. The thunders
of the cannonade were soon heard, rousing the
populace to a frenzy of courage. They rushed
through the streets demanding arms, but there
were none to be given them. The arsenals
were all empty.

The allied troops came pouring on like the
raging tides of the sea. Their numbers in advance and in the rear far exceeded a million
of bayonets. It was all dynastic Europe ar-
rayed against one man. Distinctly the allied
kings had declared to the world that they
were not fighting against France, but against
Napoleon.

The next day, the 30th, Joseph received a

note from General Marmont, written in pencil, from the midst of the conflict, stating that it would be impossible to prolong the resistance beyond a few hours, and that measures must immediately be adopted to save Paris from the horrors of being carried by storm. Joseph instantly convoked a council, and the opinion was unanimous that a capitulation was inevitable. Accordingly Joseph at once sent General Stroltz, his aide-de-camp, to Marshals Marmont and Mortier, authorizing them to enter into a conference with the enemy, while they were to continue their resistance as persistently as possible.

All hope of defending Paris was now abandoned. In accordance with the instructions of the Emperor, it was the duty of Joseph to join himself to the Empress and her son. At four o'clock he crossed the Seine. A few moments after the bridges were seized by the enemy. Napoleon had retired to Fontainebleau. Passing through Versailles, where he ordered the cavalry in that city to follow him, Joseph proceeded to Chartres, where he joined the Empress and her son, and with them advanced to Blois. He hoped to join his brother at Fontainebleau, there to confer with him upon the

measures to be adopted in these hours of disaster. With this intention he set out from
Blois, but squadrons of hostile cavalry were
sweeping in all directions, and his communication beyond Orleans was cut off. He was
therefore compelled to return to Blois. There
he was in the greatest peril, for the Cossacks
were in his immediate vicinity. He could
neither reach the Emperor nor communicate
with him. Neither could he ascertain the result of the negotiation entered into at Paris
with the foe.

Almost immediately the news came of the
Emperor's abdication. The Cossacks escorted
Maria Louisa and the King of Rome to Rambouillet, where they were placed under the
care of her father, the Emperor of Austria.
The Emperor was sent to Elba. Joseph, who
was still wealthy, purchased the estate of Pran-
gins, on the border of the lake of Geneva.
Here he had a brief respite from the terrible
storms of life, with his wife and children, in
that retirement which he loved so well.

CHAPTER XI.

LIFE IN EXILE.

WHILE Joseph was enjoying his peaceful residence upon the shores of Europe's most beautiful lake, Madame de Staël hastened to inform him of a plot which had been revealed to her for the assassination of the Emperor at Elba. The evidence was conclusive. Joseph was at breakfast with the celebrated tragedian Talma. Both Talma and Madame de Staël were anxious to hasten to Elba to inform the Emperor of his danger. But Joseph sent a personal friend, and two of the assassins were arrested.[1]

At Prangin, in 1815, Joseph learned that Napoleon had landed in France, had advanced as far as Lyons, and was desirous of seeing him

---

[1] "I thanked them for their generous offer, but preferred to charge with that difficult commission M. Boisneau, whose patriotism and personal attachment to Napoleon I had known at the siege of Toulon. You know with what success he fulfilled his commission." — Memoires du Roi Joseph, tome dixième, p. 342.

in Paris as soon as possible. Joseph's wife, Julie, was then in Paris, having been drawn there by the sickness and death of the mother, Madame Clary. He immediately left his cha-teau, after having buried all his valuable pa-pers in a box in the forest, setting out secretly at ten o'clock at night, accompanied by the two princesses, his daughters. A few hours after his departure, an armed band, sent by the influence of the Allies, arrived at the cha-teau to arrest him. Joseph upon his arrival in France, immediately, with characteristic devo-tion, placed himself entirely at the disposition of the brother he loved so well.

As Joseph traversed France, he was every-where met with great enthusiasm, the people shouting, "Napoleon the Emperor of our choice;" "The nation desires him alone;" "No aristocracy;" "Away with the old régime."

Before the departure of the Emperor for Waterloo, many distinguished persons, among others Benjamin Constant, who assisted in drawing up the celebrated Additional Act, were introduced to him by Joseph. One day he conducted to the Tuileries the son of Madame de Staël, who bore a letter from his mother to the Emperor, in which, speaking of the *Addi-*

tional Act, she said, "It is every thing which France can now need; nothing but what it needs, nothing more than it needs."

In speaking of the "*Acte Additionel,*" Mr. Alison says, " It excited unbounded opposition in both the parties which now divided the nation, and left the Emperor in reality no support but in the soldiers of the army." A few paragraphs later, when stating that the " *Acte* " was submitted to the people to be adopted or rejected by popular suffrage, he says truthfully, though in manifest contradiction to his former statement:

" The ' *Acte Additionel* ' was approved by an immense majority of the electors; the numbers being fifteen hundred thousand to five hundred."

After the disaster at Waterloo, Joseph was the constant companion of his brother during those few days of anguish in which he remained in Paris. On the 29th of June he left the metropolis to join his brother, who had preceded him, at Rochefort, where the two intended to embark for America in two different ships, the *Saale* and the *Medusa.* After several days of necessary delay, at four o'clock in the afternoon of July 8th Napoleon was rowed out

to the *Saale*, which was anchored at a distance from the quay.   But the Bourbons and
the Allies were now in power in France, and
British guard-ships were doubled along the
French coast.   No vessel was allowed to leave.

Joseph, who had received letters from his
wife informing him of all that had transpired
in Paris, proposed that the Emperor should return to land, place himself at the head of the
Army of the Loire, summon the population of
France to rise *en masse*, and again appeal to
the fortunes of war.   But the Emperor could
not be persuaded to resort to a measure which
would enkindle the flames of civil war in
France, and which might also expose the kingdom to dismemberment, since the Allies already
held a considerable portion of its territory.

Joseph then urged his brother to embark
in a small American vessel which chanced to
be in the port, while Joseph, personating Napoleon, whom he strongly resembled, should surrender himself as the Emperor.   It was thought
that the British cruisers, thus deceived, would
allow the American vessel to sail without a
very rigid search.   But the Emperor declined
the offer to escape at the hazard of his brother's
captivity.   Neither would his pride of charac-

ter allow him to seek flight in the garb of disguise. He therefore urged Joseph to leave him
to his destiny, and to provide immediately for
his own safety.

During the whole of Napoleon's career there
were always multitudes ready to lay down their
lives at any time for his protection. The captain of the *Medusa*, a sixty-gun frigate, offered
to grapple the English frigate *Bellerophon*, of
seventy-four guns, and to maintain the unequal and desperate conflict until the *Saale*
could escape with the Emperor. But as this
would be sacrificing many lives to his personal safety, Napoleon declined the magnanimous
offer.

Leaving matters in this state of uncertainty,
Joseph retired from Rochefort to the country-
seat of a friend, at the distance of a few leagues.
He left his secretary behind, to keep him informed of all that transpired. Two days after
he received a letter announcing that the Emperor had taken the fatal resolution to surrender himself to the British Government. Joseph could no longer be of any assistance to his
brother, and he decided to leave France as soon
as possible. Under the assumed name of M.
Bouchard, he embarked at Royan on the 29th

of July, with four of his suite, on board the
bark *Commerce*, bound for the United States.
The vessel was visited several times by the
British cruisers without his being recognized.
On the 28th of August, 1815, Joseph landed at
New York. Captain Misservey, of the bark,
was not aware of the illustrious rank of his
passenger, but supposed him to be General
Carnot. The Mayor of New York, under the
same impression, called upon him as General
Carnot, to congratulate him upon his safe pas-
sage.

There were at the time two English frigates
cruising before the harbor of New York, to
search all vessels coming from Europe. One
of these frigates bore down upon the *Commerce*,
but the wind, and the skill of the American
pilot, saved the ship from a visit. If the English had succeeded in seizing the person of Joseph, they would have taken him back to Eng·
land, and thence to Russia, where the Allies
had decided to hold him in captivity.

It was not known in America until Jo·
seph's arrival that Napoleon had confided him·
self to the English. The illustrious exile,
much broken in health by care and sorrow,
assumed the title of the Count of Survilliers,

the name of an estate which he held in France,
and sought the retreat of a quiet, private life,
as a refuge from the storms by which he had
so long been tossed.

After having travelled through many of the
States of the Union, and having visited most of
the principal cities, he purchased in New Jersey, upon the banks of the Delaware, a very
beautiful property, called *Point Breeze*. Here
he lived the sad life of an exile, reflecting upon
the ruin and dispersion of his family, and exposed to every species of contumely from the
European press, then controlled by the triumphant dynasties of the old feudal oppression. It
was for the interest of all these regal courts to
convince the world that the Bonapartes were the
enemies, not the friends of humanity ; that they
were struggling, not for the rights of mankind,
but to impose upon the world hitherto un-
heard-of despotism ; and that in principles
and practice they were the most godless and
dissolute of men. In this they succeeded for a
time, and there are thousands who still adhere
to the senseless calumny. Terrible indeed is
the condition of a family when it is for the
vital interests of all the crowns of Europe
to consecrate their influence, and lavish their

money to blacken the character of all its members.

But the noble character of Joseph Bonaparte could not be concealed. His record had been written in ineffaceable lines. His illus-trious name, purity of morals, large fortune, simple and cordial manners, and his wide-reaching liberality, endeared him greatly to his neighbors and multiplied his friends. His wife was in such extremely delicate health that it was not deemed safe for her to under-take a voyage across the ocean. But his two daughters, the Princess Zénaïde and Charlotte, and subsequently his son-in-law, Charles Bona-parte, elder brother of the present Emperor, Napoleon III., shared with him his exile.

The entire overthrow of the popular gov-ernments which had been established by the aid of Napoleon, and the relentless spirit manifested by the conquerors, filled all lands with exiles. Many of the most distinguished men of Europe sought a refuge with Joseph, where they were received with the most gen-erous hospitality. When the tidings reached Point Breeze of the destitution in which Na-poleon was living in the dilapidated hut at St. Helena, Joseph immediately placed his whole fortune at the disposal of his brother. It was, however, too late, and the Emperor profited but little from this generous offer. A few years passed wearily away, when in May, 1821, Napoleon, through destitution, insults, and anguish, sank sadly into his grave. General Bertrand, who had so magnanimously accompanied the captive in his imprisonment at Saint Helena, and had shared in all his sufferings, communicated the tidings of the death of the Emperor to Joseph in the following touching letter. General Bertrand had returned from Saint Helena, and his letter was dated London, September 10, 1821:

" PRINCE,—I write to you for the first time since the awful misfortune which has been added to the sorrows of your family. Your Highness is acquainted with the events of the first years of this cruel exile. Many persons who have visited Saint Helena have informed you of what was still more interesting to you, the manner of living and the unkind treatment which aggravated the influence of a deadly climate.

"In the last year of his life, the Emperor, who for four years had taken no exercise, altered extremely in appearance. He became pale

and feeble. From that time his health deteri-
orated rapidly and visibly. He had always
been in the habit of taking baths. He now
took them more frequently, and staid longer
in them. They appeared to relieve him for
the time. Latterly Dr. Antommarchi forbade
him their use, as he thought that they only increased his weakness.

"In the month of August he took walking
exercise, but with difficulty; he was forced to
stop every minute. In the first years he used
to walk while dictating. He walked about
his room, and thus did without the exercise
which he feared to take out-of-doors, lest he
should expose himself to insult. But latterly
his strength would not admit even of this.
He remained sitting nearly all day, and discon-
tinued almost all occupation. His health declined sensibly every month.

"Once in September, and again in the beginning of October he rode out, as his physicians
desired him to take exercise; but he was so
weak that he was obliged to return in his carriage. He ceased to digest; shivering fits
came on, which extended even to the extremi-
ties. Hot towels applied to the feet gave him
some relief. He suffered from these cold fits

to the last hour of his life. As he could no longer either walk, or ride, he took several drives in an open carriage at a foot pace, but without gaining strength.

" He never took off his dressing-gown. His stomach rejected food, and at the end of the year he was forced to give up meat. He lived upon jellies and soups. For some time he ate scarcely any thing, and drank only a little pure wine, hoping thus to support nature without fatiguing the digestion; but the vomiting continued, and he returned to soups and jellies. The remedies and tonics which were tried produced little effect. His body grew weaker every day, but his mind retained its strength. He liked reading and conversation. He did not dictate much, although he did so from time to time up to the last days of his life. He felt that his end was approaching, and frequently recited the passage from 'Zaïre,' which closes with this line :

" ' A revoir Paris je ne dois plus prétendre.'

" Nevertheless the hope of leaving this dreadful country often presented itself to his imagination. Some newspaper articles and false reports excited our expectations. We

sometimes fancied that we were on the eve of
starting for America. We read travels, we
made plans, we arrived at our house, we wandered over that immense country, where alone
we might hope to enjoy liberty. Vain hopes!
vain projects! which only made us doubly feel
our misfortunes.

"They could not have been borne with more
serenity and courage—I might almost add
gayety. He often said to us in the evening,
'Where shall we go? to the Théâtre Français
or to the Opera?' And then he would read a
tragedy by Corneille, Voltaire, or Racine; an
opera of Quinault's, or one of Molière's come-
dies. His strong mind and powerful character
were perhaps even more remarkable than on
that larger theatre where he eclipsed all that is
brightest in ancient and in modern history.
He often seemed to forget what he had been.
I was never tired of admiring his philosophy
and courage, the good sense and fortitude
which raised him above misfortune.

"At times, however, sad regrets and recollections of what he had done, contrasted with
what he might have done, presented themselves. He talked of the past with perfect
frankness, persuaded that, on the whole, he

had done what he was required to do, and not sharing the strange and contradictory opinions which we hear expressed every day on events which are not understood by the speakers. If the conversation took a melancholy turn, he soon changed it. He loved to talk of Corsica, of his old uncle Lucien, of his youth, of you, and of all the rest of the family.

"Toward the middle of March fever came on. From that time he scarcely left his bed except for about half an hour in the day. He seldom had the strength to shave. He now for the first time became extremely thin. The fits of vomiting became more frequent. He then questioned the physicians upon the conformation of the stomach, and about a fortnight before his death he had pretty nearly guessed that he was dying of cancer. He was read to almost every day, and dictated a few days before his decease. He often talked naturally as to the probable mode of his death, but when he became aware that it was approaching he left off speaking on the subject. He thought much about you and your children.

"To his last moments he was kind and affectionate to us all. He did not appear to suffer so much as might have been expected from the cause of his death.   When we questioned him he said that he suffered a little, but that he could bear it.   His memory declined during the last five or six days.   His deep sighs, and his exclamations from time to time, made us think that he was in great pain.   He looked at us with the penetrating glance which you know so well.   We tried to dissimulate, but he was so used to reading our faces that no doubt he frequently discovered our anxiety. He felt too clearly the gradual decline of his faculties not to be aware of his state.

"For the last two hours he neither spoke nor moved.   The only sound was his difficult breathing, which gradually but regularly decreased.   His pulse ceased.   And so died, surrounded by only a few servants, the man who had dictated laws to the world, and whose life should have been preserved for the sake of the happiness and glory of our sorrowing country.

"Forgive, prince, a hurried letter, which tells you so little when you wish to know so much ; but I should never end if I attempted to tell all.   I must not omit to say that the Emperor was most anxious that his correspondence with the different sovereigns of Europe should be printed.   He repeated this to us sev-

eral times.[1]   In his will the Emperor expressed
his wish that his remains should be buried in
France; however, in the last days of his life,
he ordered me, if there was any difficulty about
it, to lay him by the side of the fountain whose
waters he had so long drunk."

Joseph loved his brother tenderly, and he
never could speak without emotion of the in-
dignities and cruelties Napoleon suffered from
that ungenerous Government to whose mercy
he had so fatally confided himself.   Anxious
to do every thing which he thought might gratify the departed spirit of his brother, he implored permission of Austria to visit Napoleon's son, the Duke of Reichstadt, that he might

[1] The Emperor was very desirous that his correspondence
with the allied sovereigns should be published.   He wrote to
Joseph from Saint Helena to secure their publication in the
United States if possible.   "It will be the best response," he
said, "to all the calumnies which have been uttered against
me."   During Joseph's sojourn in England, he learned from
Dr. O'Meara that the autograph originals of these letters addressed by Napoleon to the sovereigns had been offered for
sale in London in the year 1822; that they had been in the
hands of Mr. Murray, a well-known publisher; that the letters
relating to Russia had been purchased by a diplomatic agent
of that power for ten thousand pounds sterling.   There was
no longer any hope of obtaining them, since they were in the
hands of those interested in having them destroyed.—*Mémoires et Correspondence, Politique et Militaire du Roi Joseph,
tome dixième*, p. 231.

sympathize with him in these hours of afflic·
tion.   The Court of Austria refused his request.

In 1824, Joseph's youngest daughter, the
Princess Charlotte, left Point Breeze to join her
mother in Europe, where she was to be married
to Charles Napoleon Louis Bonaparte, the son
of Louis and Hortense, and the elder brother of
the present Emperor of the French.   The tastes
of Joseph inclined him to the country, and to
its peaceful pursuits.   He had, however, a city
residence in Philadelphia, where he usually
passed the winters.   While thus residing on
the banks of the Delaware, sadly retracing the
memorable events of the past and recording its
scenes, he received a proposition which surprised and gratified him.   A deputation of
Mexicans waited upon him at Point Breeze,
and urged him to accept the crown of Mexico.
The former King of Naples and of Spain in the
following terms responded to the invitation :

"I have worn two crowns.   I would not
take a single step to obtain a third.   Nothing
could be more flattering to me than to see the
men who, when I was at Madrid, were unwil-
ling to recognize my authority, come to-day to
seek me, in exile, to place the crown upon my
head.   But I do not think that the throne

1824.]   LIFE IN EXILE.   335

The Crown of Mexico.   Visit of La Fayette.

which you wish to erect anew can promote
your happiness. Every day I spend upon the
hospitable soil of the United States demon-
strates to me more fully the excellence of republican institutions for America. Guard
them, then, as a precious gift of Providence;
cease your intestine quarrels; imitate the
United States and seek from the midst of
your fellow - citizens a man more capable
than I am to act the grand part of Washington.[1]

When La Fayette in 1824 made his triumphal tour through the United States, he
visited Point Breeze to pay his respects to the
brother of the Emperor. Upon that occasion
the marquis expressed deep regret in view of
the course he had pursued at the time of the
abdication of Napoleon.

"The dynasty of the Bourbons," said he,
"can not maintain itself. It too manifestly
wounds the national sentiment. We are all
persuaded in France that the son of the Emperor alone can represent the interests of the
Revolution. Place two million francs at the
disposal of our committee, and I promise you

[1] Quelque Mot sur Joseph Napoleon Bonaparte, par Napoleon III.

that in two years Napoleon II.[1] will be upon the throne of France.'"[2]

Joseph, however, did not think it best to embark at that time in any new enterprise for the restoration of popular rights to France. The Bourbon throne seemed to be for a time firmly established. Joseph was getting to be advanced in years. The storms of his life had been so severe that he longed only for repose.

The following extracts from the correspondence of Joseph, while he was an exile in America, throw interesting light upon his political principles and upon his social character. General Lamarque was one of the veteran generals of the Empire. After the restoration of the Bourbons, he was highly distinguished for his eloquence in the Tribune as the antagonist of aristocratic privilege. Napoleon, when on his death-bed at Saint Helena, in view of his earnest support of popular rights, both on the battle-field and in the Chamber of Deputies, recommended him for a marshal of France. Those friends of the Empire who had been pros-

[1] The Duke of Reichstadt, son of the Emperor, then thirteen years of age, living at Vienna, in the Court of the Emperor of Austria, his grandfather. He died of consumption in July, 1832.

[2] Œuvres de Napoleon III., tome deuxième, p. 489.

ecuted for the part they took in the *Hundred Days*, had found in him a zealous friend. His devotion to the interests of Poland had secured for him the homage of that chivalrous people. The liberal party in France, with great unanimity, regarded him as their leader. Upon the occasion of his funeral, in June, 1832, the Liberals in Paris made a desperate endeavor to overthrow the government of Louis Philippe. The insurgents numbered over one hundred thousand. The attempt was bloodily repulsed by the royalist troops. On the 27th of March, 1824, General Lamarque wrote a letter from Paris to Joseph, from which we make the following extracts:

" MONSIEUR LE COMTE,—The memory of your kindnesses lives as vividly in my heart as on the day in which I received them, and I ever seek occasions to prove this to you. Already I have refuted, in many articles of the journals, the atrocious calumnies which have been published against you, and I ever avow myself to the world as your admirer and grateful friend. Be assured that your reputation is honorable and glorious. Truth has already dispelled many clouds; soon it will shine forth in all its brilliance.

22

"You do well to consecrate a portion of your time to writing your memoirs. It seems to me that the part most interesting will be your reign in Naples. You were there truly the philosopher upon the throne, which Plato desired for the interests of humanity. I recall your journeys in which you urged upon the nobles love for the people; upon the priests tolerance; upon the military, order and moderation. Not being able to establish political liberty, you wished to confer upon your subjects all the benefits of municipal régime, which you regarded as the foundation of all institutions.

"Under your reign—too short for a nation which has so deeply regretted you—feudalism was destroyed, brigandage disappeared, the system of imposts was changed, order was established in the finances, administration created, the nobles and the people reconciled, new routes opened in all directions, the capital embellished, the army and marine reorganized, the English driven out of the whole realm, and Gaëta, Scylla, Reggio, Manthea, and Amanthea taken.

"Your memoirs will be a lesson for kings. But that they may be received with the relig-

ious respect due to a great misfortune, it seems
to me that you ought to efface yourself from
the scene of the world, that your writings
should be like a voice coming from the depths
of the tomb, and that you should only ask of
your contemporaries not to calumniate and
hate the memory of a man who, having attained the height of all dignities, has descended
from it with serenity, with resignation, and almost with pleasure. As to Spain, were I in
your place, I should say but one word ; that
word would be regret in not having been able
to accomplish for Spain the good which was
accomplished for Naples.

"Like you, I have been proscribed. Like
you, I have wandered in foreign lands, breathing always wishes for my country. I know
how irritable and sensitive one thus is, and
how keenly one feels the attacks of his enemies. But upon my return I perceived that
in exile we exaggerate the importance of such
attacks. Let not the calumnies which reach
you, after having traversed the seas, disturb
for a moment your domestic happiness, and
the calm of your situation. They are the last
gusts of the tempest, the last noise of the ex-
piring waves."

In a letter to Francis Leiber, dated July 1, 1829, Joseph writes:

" Walter Scott wrote for the English Government, and from information furnished him by the Government which succeeded that of the Emperor Napoleon. Napoleon found France in delirium. He wished to rescue it from the anarchy of 1793, and from a counter-revolution. That he well understood the national will, his miraculous return from the isle of Elba will prove sufficiently to posterity. The English Cabinet always prevented the surrender of his dictatorship by perpetuating the war. Napoleon was thus under the necessity of assuming the forms of the other governments of Continental Europe, to reconcile them with France. All that which Napoleon did, his nobility (which was not feudal), his family relations, his Legion of Honor, his new realms, etc., he was under the necessity of doing. The English ever forced him to these acts, that he might put himself in apparent harmony with all those governments which he had conquered, and which he wished to withdraw from the seduction of England. Napoleon often said to me, ' Ten years more are necessary in order to give entire liberty. I can not do what I wish, but only what I can. These English compel me to live day by day.'"

As the tidings reached the ears of Joseph of the great Revolution of 1830 in France, in which the throne of Charles X. was demolished, he wrote to La Fayette under date of Sept. 7, 1830:

"MY DEAR GENERAL,—General Lallemand, who will hand you this letter, will recall me to your memory. He will tell you with what enthusiasm the population of this country, American and French, have received the news of the glorious events of which Paris has been the theatre. If I had not seen at the head of affairs a name[1] with which mine can never be in accord, I should be with you immediately with General Lallemand. You will recall our interview in this hospitable and free land. My sentiments are as invariable as yours and those of my family. *Every thing for the French people.*

" Doubtless I can not forget that my nephew, Napoleon II.,[2] was proclaimed by the Chamber which, in 1815, was dissolved by the bayonets of foreigners. Faithful to the motto of my family, *Every thing by France and for*

[1] Louis Philippe, Duke of Orleans.
[2] Napoleon's son, the Duke of Reichstadt.

France, I wish to discharge my duties to her. You know my opinions, long ago proclaimed. Individuals and families can have only *duties* to fulfill in their relation to nations. The nations have *rights* to exercise. If the French nation should call to the head of affairs the most obscure family, I think that we ought to submit to its will entirely. The nation alone has the right to destroy its work.

"I ask for the abolition of that tyrannic law which has shut out from France a family which had opened the kingdom to all those Frenchmen whom the Revolution had expelled. I protest against any election made by private corporations, or by bodies not having obtained from the nation the powers which the nation alone has the right to confer.

"Adieu, my dear general. My letter proves to you the justice I render to the sentiments you expressed to me during the triumphal journey you made among this people, where I have seen, for fifteen years, that liberty is not a chimera, that it is a blessing which a nation, moderate and wise, can enjoy when it wishes."

To Maria Louisa, daughter of the Emperor of Austria, and mother of the Duke of Reichstadt, Joseph wrote the next day, September 10, as follows:

" MADAME MY SISTER,—The events which transpired in Paris at the close of July, and of which we have received intelligence, through the English journals, to the 1st of August, remove the principal difficulties in the way of the return of Napoleon II. to the throne of his father. If the Emperor, his grandfather,' lends him the least support, if he will permit that, under my guidance, he may show himself to the French people, his presence alone will re-establish him upon the throne. The Duke of Orleans can rally around him partisans, only in consequence of the absence of the son of your Majesty. It is his re-establishment in France which alone can reunite all parties, stifle the germs of a new revolution, and thus secure the tranquillity of Europe.

" If I were in a position to unfold to your august father the reasons which render this step indispensable on his part at this moment, he could have no doubt of its imperious necessity. His ministry would perceive that the happiness of his grandson, that of France, the tranquillity of Italy, and perhaps of the rest of

---

¹ The Emperor of Austria.

Europe, depend upon the re-establishment of the throne of Napoleon II. He is the only one chosen by the voice of the nation. He alone can prevent a new revolution the results of which no mortal can foresee. I hope that the many misfortunes which we have encountered have not effaced from the heart of your Majesty the affection she has manifested for me under diverse circumstances. I can only offer to her myself for her son. For a long time I have been disabused of the illusions of human grandeur; but I am more than ever the slave of that which I deem to be my duty."

On the 18th of September, 1830, Joseph wrote a letter to the Emperor of Austria, which he inclosed in a letter of the same date to Prince Metternich. In his letter to Metternich, Joseph wrote:

"I do not doubt, sir, that you desire the welfare of the grandson of the Emperor whom you have so long served, the welfare of Austria, the tranquillity of Europe, and even of France, if these are all reconcilable. I am convinced that they are to-day perfectly reconcilable, and that Napoleon II. restored to the wishes of the French people can alone secure all these results. I offer myself to serve him as a guide,

The happiness of my country, the peace of the world, will be the noble ends of my ambition.

" Napoleon II. arriving in France under the national colors, conducted by a man whose sentiments and patriotic affections are well known, can alone prevent the usurpation of the Duke of Orleans, who, being neither called to the throne by the rights of succession nor by the national will, clearly and legitimately expressed, can maintain himself in power only by caressing all parties, and finally becoming subordinate to the one which offers him the best chances of success, whatever may be the means to be employed for that end."

Joseph's letter to the Emperor of Austria contained the following expressions: " The particular esteem with which the virtues of your Majesty inspire me, embolden me to recall myself to his recollection under circumstances in which the general welfare appears to me to be in accord with the sentiments of his heart, that he may restore to the wishes of the French people a prince who alone can confer upon them internal peace, and assure the tranquillity of Europe. This peace and tranquillity would be disturbed by the efforts which must be made to sustain in France a govern-

ment of usurpation like that of the Duke of Orleans, or even a republic, if the absence of the
son of Napoleon, the grandson of your Majesty,
should constrain the nation, thus abandoned by
the prince of its choice, to surrender itself to
another form of government.   Sire, if you
will entrust to me the son of my brother, that
son whom he enjoined, upon his death-bed, to
follow my advice in returning to France, I
guarantee the success of the enterprise.   Alone,
with a tri-color scarf, will Napoleon II. be proclaimed.

"Will it be necessary for me to speak of
myself to your Majesty to give him confidence
in my character?   Must I recall to his remem-
brance that, after the treaty of Luneville, he
communicated to me, through an autograph
letter to Count Cobentzl, that the opinion he
had formed of my moderation was such that
he would with pleasure see me placed upon
the throne of Lombardy?   I refused that throne.
I preferred to remain in France.   Since then,
at Naples, in Spain, has that character been
falsified?

"To-day, as then, I am guided by the single
sentiment of duty.   My ambition limits itself
to doing what I ought for France, for the mem-

ory of my brother, and to die upon my native soil a witness of the happiness of the grandson of your Majesty, which is inseparable from that of France and from the tranquillity of Europe. I can only contribute to that to-day by my wishes. May your Majesty second them by his powerful influence, and thus consolidate the peace of the world and the eternal glory of his name."

On the same day, September 18, Joseph wrote an earnest appeal to the French Chamber of Deputies.[1] The following extracts will show its character. " It is impossible that a house, reigning through the principle of divine right, should maintain itself upon a throne from which it has been expelled by the nation. The divorce between the House of Bourbon and the French people has been pronounced, and nothing can destroy the souvenirs of the past. In vain the Duke of Orleans abjures his house in the moment of its misfortunes. A Bourbon himself, returning to France, sword in hand, with the Bourbons, in the train of foreign armies, what matter is it that his father voted for the death of the King, his cousin, that he might take his place? What matter is it that the

[1] Œuvres de Napoleon III. tome deuxième, p. 441.

brother of Louis XVI. named him lieutenant-general of the realm, and regent of his grandson? Is he the less a Bourbon? Has he the less pretension of being entitled to the throne by the right of birth? Is it through the choice of the people, or the right of birth, that he claims to sit upon the throne of his ancestors?

"The family of Napoleon has been elected by three million five hundred thousand votes. If the nation deem it for its interest to make another choice, it has the power and the right to do so; but the nation alone. Napoleon II. was proclaimed king by the Chamber of Deputies in 1815, which recognized in him a right conferred by the nation. That he may be the legitimate sovereign, in the true acceptation of the word, that is to say, legally and voluntarily chosen by the people, there is no need of a new election so long as the nation has not adopted any other form of government. Still the nation is supreme to confirm or reject the titles it has given according to its pleasure. Till then, gentlemen, you are bound to recognize Napoleon II. And until Austria shall restore him to the wishes of France, I offer myself to share your perils, your efforts, your labors, and, upon his arrival, to transmit to him the will, the

examples, the last dispositions of his father, dying a victim of the enemies of France upon the
rock of Saint Helena. These words the Emper-
or addressed to me through General Bertrand :

" ' Say to my son that he should remember,
first of all, that he is a Frenchman. Let him
give the nation as much liberty as I have given
it equality. Foreign wars did not permit me
to do that which I should have done at the
general peace. I was perpetually in dictatorship. But I ever had, as the motive in all my
actions, the love and the grandeur of the great
nation. Let him take my device, *Every thing
for the French people*. It is to that people we
are indebted for all that we have been.

" ' The liberty of the press is the triumph of
truth. It is that which should diffuse general
intelligence. Let it speak, and let the will of
the great mass of the people be accomplished.' "

Again, on the 26th of September, Joseph
wrote to General Lamarque: "The Duke of
Orleans, by his birth, by his connection with the
reigning branches of the family of Bourbon,
which he in vain attempts to ignore, will soon
be suspected by the patriots of France, and by
the liberals of Italy and of Spain. The act
which places him upon the throne, not emanat-

ing from the nation, can not constitute him
king of the French. A few capitalists in Paris
are not France. He can not therefore have the
cordial assent of the liberals of any country.
He can not have the support of those who believe in the legitimacy of the elder branch of
his house. He can not have the assent of those
who have not lost the memory of the votes
which the nation gave to Napoleon, and to Napoleon II., whom the Chamber of Deputies
proclaimed in 1815.

"The Duke of Orleans, was he not a pupil
of Dumourier? Did he not, like Dumourier,
desert the cause of the nation? Did he not,
in London, in the presence of all the emigrant
French nobility, ask pardon and make the
amende honorable for having, for one instant,
borne the national colors? Did he not go to
Cadiz, sent by the English, to fight the French
troops who did not then wear the white cockade
of the Bourbons? Did he not enter France
in the train of the Allies, sword in hand, with
his cousins? Was he not rescued with them,
and did he not owe to the disaster at Waterloo
his return to France?

"The thirty-two individuals who called him
first to the lieutenant-generalship of the realm

would have called some one else if they had
not been greatly influenced by his rights of
birth. Was there no other man in France
more worthy to take temporarily the helm of
state? General La Fayette, who was at the head
of the provisory government, would he not
have given to the nation, and to the friends of
liberty and of order in the two worlds, stronger
guaranties than a prince of the House of Bourbon? The enthronement of the Duke of Orleans can be approved only by the enemies of
France. His illegitimacy, both in view of the
sovereignty of the people and of the partisans of
divine right, is so evident that he can only govern by being submissive to the will of the factions, whom he will be compelled to obey, now
one, and now another. The time for represent-
ative governments has arrived. Liberty, equality, public order can not exist where those governing are of a different species from those who
are governed."

In a letter to General Bernard, on the 29th
of September, Joseph uttered the following
prophetic sentiment: "You were deceived by
your informants when you said that the name
of Napoleon was not pronounced by the combatants. It was pronounced by them. It was

pronounced by the Army of Algiers. It is to-day pronounced by the people in the departments and will soon be by entire France. The artifices of intrigue and deception are temporary. The national will, sooner or later, must triumph."

La Fayette had been mainly instrumental in placing the Duke of Orleans upon the throne of France. He wrote to Joseph Bonaparte explaining his reasons for this. In allusion to the fact that he was compelled to yield to the pressure of circumstances, he said, "You know that in home affairs, as in foreign affairs, no one can do just what he wishes to have done. Your incomparable brother, with his power, his character, his genius, experienced this himself." He also expressed his strong disapproval of the dictatorship of Napoleon, and of the aristocracy which he introduced. Joseph replied from Point Breeze, under date of January 15, 1831 :

"MY DEAR GENERAL,—I have received your letter of the 26th of November. I am satisfied that under the circumstances you did that which you conscientiously thought it your duty to do. You have thought, as have I, and as did the Emperor Napoleon, that a republic could not, at present, be established in France.

You have recoiled before the confusion which it would introduce in the interior. You could undoubtedly have found a remedy for that in the family which the nation had called to such high destinies. But the hatred of foreigners against that family which France had chosen, inclined you to a prince between whom and legitimacy there was but a single child.[1]

"My reply is short. Let France preserve peace and liberty with that family. Let such become the *national will legitimately expressed*, and the conduct of the sixty-two Deputies, who have called the second branch of the House of Bourbon to power, will no longer be discussed by any one. Will this be done? Time alone can tell us.

"The portion of your letter in which you speak of the Napoleonic system as impressed with despotism and aristocracy merits, on my part, a more detailed response. While I render justice to your good intentions, I can not but deplore the situation in which you found yourself when released from the prisons of Aus-

---

[1] Charles X. abdicated in favor of his grandson, the Duke of Bordeaux, a child seven or eight years old. Should that child die, the Duke of Orleans would be the *legitimate* Bourbon candidate for the throne.

tria. That imprisonment did not permit you
to judge of the influence exerted upon the national opinion and character by the wretched
Reign of Terror. You had only seen the liberal system of America, and you have condemned the all-powerful man who did not transfer
that system to France. I remember that one
day my brother, in coming from an interview
with you, my dear general, said to me these
words :

"'I have just had a very interesting conversation with the Marquis de la Fayette upon
the subject of the disorderly persons whom the
police has sent from Paris. I have said to him
that this was done that they might not disturb
the tranquillity of good men like himself, whose
residence in France appeared to them one of
my crimes.[1] The Marquis de la Fayette does
not know the character of these people in whom
he interests himself. He was in the prisons of
despotism when these people made all France
to tremble. But France remembers this too
well. We are not here in America.'

"Napoleon never doubted your good intentions. But he thought that you judged too fa-

---

[1] The Jacobins wished all whom they termed aristocrats
guillotined or expelled from France.

vorably of your contemporaries. He was forced into war by the English, and into the dictatorship by the war. These few words are the history of the Empire. Napoleon incessantly said to me, ' When will peace arrive? Then only can I satisfy all, and show myself as I am.'

" The aristocracy of which you accuse him was only the mode of placing himself in harmony with Europe. But the old feudal aristocracy was never in his favor. The proof of this is that he was its victim, and that he expiated, at Saint Helena, the crime of having wished to employ all the institutions in favor of the people; and the European aristocracy contrived to turn against him even those very masses for whose benefit he was laboring. The French nation renders him justice; and the European masses will not be slow to say that Napoleon had ever in view the suffrage of posterity, whose verdict is always in favor of him who has only in view the happiness of his country."

On the 15th of February, 1832, Joseph wrote from Point Breeze to the Duke of Reichstadt as follows

" MY DEAR NEPHEW,—The bearer of this

letter will be the interpreter of my sentiments. He has passed several weeks in my retreat. They have been occupied with the souvenirs of your father, and of your future lot. I was born eighteen months before your father. We were brought up together. Nothing has ever diminished the warm affection which united us. At his death he entrusted to me the care of communicating to you his last wishes. But before my distance from you enabled me to fulfill that duty, his testament had been published in all the leading journals of Europe.

" When, in 1830, the house imposed upon France by foreigners was again expelled by the nation, I hastened to address to the Chamber of Deputies, and to his Imperial Majesty, your grandfather, the inclosed letters. But my distance from France still thwarted my wishes, and the younger branch of that same house was again imposed upon France by a factious minority. Innumerable calumnies, intended to alienate the nation from you, were scattered abroad with profusion. A chamber, controlled by the Government usurping the rights of the nation, proscribed us anew. But the voice of the people called you. Of that I have conclusive evidence.

"Let his Imperial Majesty consent to entrust you to my care; let him send me a passport that I may come to him and to you, I will quit my retreat to respond to his confidence, to yours, to the sentiment which commands me to spare no efforts to restore to the love of the French the son of the man whom I have loved the most of any one upon earth. My opinions are well known in France. They are in harmony with those of the nation. If you enter France with me and a tri-color scarf, you will be received there as the son of Napoleon.

"When you were born in Paris, the 20th of March, 1811, your father had become, through the love of the French people as well as through the obstinacy of the English oligarchy making war upon him, the most powerful prince in Europe. The English oligarchy foresaw the prosperity which France, governed in accordance with the liberal doctrines of the age, would attain if she had peace. That oligarchy feared the contagion of the example upon other states. Therefore it did not cease to employ the immense resources which the monopoly of the commerce of the world placed at its disposal to excite against Napoleon enemies at home and abroad, and to stifle, at its birth, the union of the peoples and the kings for the reform of the anti-social privileges of the oligarchy. It therefore provoked inces sant war, and thus rendered France every day more powerful, through the victories she obtained under the direction of your father, whom it accused of the calamities inseparable from a war kindled by itself, and with the sole object of maintaining its unjust privileges.

" It was at the close of a strife incessantly renewed, excited by the Government of a nation sufficiently rich to pay the soldiers of the others, and sheltered by its insular position against all attempts against itself, that, after the triumphs of twenty years, your father succumbed beneath the united efforts of the Allies of England, who perceived too late their fatal errors.

" Napoleon was the friend both of the peoples and of the kings. He wished to reconcile them to each other. He wished to save other states from the misfortunes which a bloody revolution had inflicted upon France. These were the reforms which he desired, voluntary ameliorations, commended by the increasing civilization of the world, and the widely-extended interests of all classes, and not violent commotions, which always pass beyond the end desired. His greatest vengeance against England did not exceed that which the advocates of the bill of reform seek for to-day.

"I think that now you are placed in a position to continue the work with which a divine genius inspired your father. France will accept you with enthusiasm. Factions will subside. The power with which your father was invested is no longer needful for the accomplishment of his designs. It was war which elevated upon the thrones of Europe the princes of his family. But it was not that he might give them thrones that he engaged in war. They were military positions occupied during the general struggle which the oligarchies had decided never to close but by the abasement of France. It was necessary to allow the conquered countries to be invaded by the republican system for which they were not prepared, or to cause them to be governed by men of whose devotion to France and to himself he was fully assured. And where could he find better guaranties than in his brothers, whom nature, as well as the favors which they had received from the nation, had destined to share his adverse as well as his good-fortune, both inseparable from that of France?

"To-day time has borne its fruits. Nations are more enlightened respecting their interests. They know well that the most happy nation is that in which the greatest number of men enjoy the most prosperity; which obeys a supreme magistrate whom it loves, and who himself has not the baleful power to abuse the life, the property, the liberty of the people, whom he represents only that he may protect the rights which they have entrusted to him. Such were the opinions, and especially the instinct, of your father. *Every thing for the people!* And at the general pacification which he desired with all his heart, *Every thing by the people, and for the people.* He did not live long enough.

"May I live long enough to see you return to our country, restored to herself, the worthy heir of his heart, all French, of his generous intentions. As for his immense genius, it is no longer necessary for France or for Europe. You are destined, by your birth, to unite peoples and kings, and to reconcile the old and the new civilization; to prevent new upheavings, to moderate all political passions, and thus to bring forward that prosperity of indi-

viduals and of nations which can only arise
from justice, from the free development of all
rights, from the equilibrium of all duties.

" Your father was accustomed to say to me,
'When will the time arise when justice alone
shall reign? When shall I finish my dictatorship?
We do not yet see that time. The English oligarchy will not have it so. My son perhaps will
see it. May that presage be soon accomplished.'

" This is also the fondest wish of my heart.
Receive it with the tenderness of the old friend
of your glorious father, at Point Breeze, State
of New Jersey, in the United States of America, where I live as happy as one can be far
from his country, in the most prosperous land
upon the earth, under the name which I have
adopted, of the Count of Survilliers."

The elder brother of the present Emperor,
Napoleon III., who had married the youngest
daughter of Joseph Bonaparte, died in Italy in
March, 1831. With his younger brother, Louis
Napoleon, he had joined the Italians in their
endeavor to throw off the yoke of Austria.
The young prince, who had developed a very
noble character, fell a victim to the fatigues of
the campaign. *By the vote of the French people,*
the Duke of Reichstadt was the first heir to

the throne of the Empire. In case of his death, the crown passed to Joseph Bonaparte. As Joseph had no children, his decease would transfer the sceptre to his brother, Louis Bonaparte, and from Louis it would pass to Louis Napoleon, his only surviving son.

When, in 1832, Joseph heard of the dangerous sickness of the Duke of Reichstadt, whose death, as we have mentioned, would constitute Joseph first heir to the throne, he with some hesitancy decided to leave his peaceful retreat at Point Breeze and repair to England. He hoped to obtain permission to visit his dying nephew in Vienna, and then to reunite himself in Italy with his wife, and with his revered mother, who was still living. Upon his landing in Liverpool he received the sad tidings that the Duke of Reichstadt had breathed his last on the 22d of July. He was twenty-one years of age, tall, graceful, affectionate, and of marvellous beauty. His mother and other friends wept at the side of his couch. Devoutly he partook of the sacrament of the Lord's Supper, and, with a smile lingering upon his cheek, fell asleep. We trust

"Asleep in Jesus, blessed sleep,
From which none ever wake to weep."

DEATH OF THE DUKE OF REICHSTADT.

CHAPTER XII.

LAST DAYS AND DEATH.

JOSEPH, finding himself in England in 1832, and his nephew, the Duke of Reichstadt, no longer living, took up his residence in London. He earnestly desired to join his wife and mother in Italy. But the jealousy of the Allies would not allow him, until he was absolutely sinking in death, to place his foot upon the Continent. His universally recognized virtues secured for him, from all classes of society, a cordial reception.

While Joseph resided in England, the celebrated Spanish chief, Mina, who had been one of the most formidable of the leaders of the guerrillas, made several visits to the ex-King, expressing the deepest regret that he had not sustained him. He stated to Joseph that his intercepted letters had so revealed his true character, that others of the leaders who had operated against him were now in his favor.

La Fayette wrote Joseph a letter of sympathy in view of his double affliction in the loss of his

son-in-law, Napoleon Louis, and his nephew,
the Duke of Reichstadt. The letter, from
which we make the following extract, was dated La Grange, October 13, 1832:

"MY DEAR COUNT,—I am deeply affected by
those testimonials of confidence and friendship
which you kindly give me. And I merit
them by all those affections which attach me
to you. It is with profound sympathy that I
share in your grief from the two cruel bereave-
ments. I should immediately have written to
you in London, had I not been informed that
you were on the route to Italy. I have, however, since learned that your entrance into
Rome has been interdicted to your filial piety
by a base and barbarous policy."

La Fayette also expresses his deep regret that
the Orleans Government persisted in the decree
which banished the Bonaparte family from
France. Joseph, in a reply dated London,
Nov. 10, 1832, writes:

"MY DEAR GENERAL,—I have received
your kind letter, and I thank you with all my
heart. It is true that I love, as much as you
do, the institutions of the United States. But
I am near to France, and I do not wish to see
it vanish from my eyes like a new Ithaca. I

prefer France to the United States as the residence for my declining years, and I rely upon your powerful co-operation to secure that for me. It only remains for me to hope to see my country as happy as that which I have just left—a country which I love above all others except my native soil. A day will come undoubtedly, in which France will have no occasion to envy even happy America. As soon as it shall be clearly understood that all ought to devote themselves to the happiness of all, the most difficult thing will be accomplished. May we live long enough to witness that, and may I have the happiness of renewing my long friendship in our common country, in sometimes speaking to you of the admiration and gratitude with which you are regarded in the New World."

The following letter from Victor Hugo reflects such light upon the reputation of Joseph Bonaparte, as to merit insertion here. It was dated Paris, Feb. 27, 1833:

"SIRE,—I avail myself of the first opportunity to reply to you. Monsieur Presle, who leaves for London, kindly offers to place this letter in the hands of your Majesty. Permit me, sire, to treat you ever royally, *vous traiter*

toujours royalement. The kings whom Napoleon made, in my opinion nothing can unmake.
There is no human power which can efface the
august sign which that grand man has placed
upon your brow. I have been profoundly
moved by the sympathy which your Majesty
has testified for me upon the occasion of my
prosecution for '*Le Roi S'amuse.*' You love
liberty, sire. Liberty also loves you. Permit
me to send you, with this letter, a copy of the
discourse which I pronounced before the Tribunal of Commerce. I am very desirous that
you should see it in a form different from the
reports in the journals, which are always in-
exact.

"I should be very happy, sire, to go to
London to clasp that royal hand which has so
often clasped the hand of my father. M. Presle
will inform your Majesty of the obstacles which
at the present moment prevent me from real-
izing a wish so dear. I have very many things
to say to you. It is impossible that the future
should be wanting to your family, great as has
been the loss of the past year. You bear the
grandest of historic names. In truth, we are
moving rather toward a republic than toward
a monarchy. But, to a sage like you, the ex-

terior form of government is of but little importance. You have proved, sire, that you know how to be worthily the citizen of a republic. Adieu, sire; the day in which I shall be permitted to press your hand in mine will be one of the most glorious of my life. While waiting for this your letters render me proud and happy."

The celebrated Duchess of Abrantes, wife of Marshal Junot, sent her *Memoirs* to King Joseph by the hands of M. Presle. The following extracts from the letter of the duchess to M. Presle shows the enthusiastic attachment which Joseph won from his friends. The letter is dated Paris, 1833:

"Will you be so good, sir, as to have the kindness to take charge of the book which I send with this, and also of the letter which I address to his Majesty, King Joseph? I earnestly desire that both should be transmitted to him as promptly as possible. I very much wish, sir, I could have the pleasure of seeing you. My attachment for King Joseph is so profound and so true, of such long-standing, so established upon bases which can never crumble, that I would give days of my life to talk a moment with persons loving him as I do, and speaking to me as I speak of him and think of him. As for me, to see him for one moment would be now the fulfillment of the most ardent of my wishes.

"With these feelings, you will perceive, sir, how happy I shall be to have him soon receive this letter, which I entrust to you. It contains my wishes for the new year. And I can truly say that there is not another heart in France more sincerely devoted to his happiness—his true happiness and his glory. Ah! sir, I assure him that in France there is one being who is warmly attached, sincerely devoted to him, as are all hers. My children have been cradled in the name of Napoleon, and that without concealment. The misfortune of their father has been an additional tie to attach them to the memory of the Emperor, and to all those who bear his revered name. The bust of the Emperor is in my alcove, by the side of the font in which I place my lustral water. There I every morning and evening repeat my prayers. Why should I not say this? I do it because my love for my country constrains me to fall upon my knees before that name which constituted its glory and its happiness for fifteen years."

On the 28th of July, 1833, the Louis Philippe Government, in reluctant concession to the almost universal voice of the French people, restored the statue of Napoleon to the Column of Austerlitz, in the Place Vendôme. It is scarcely too much to say that as that statue rose to its proud eminence, the whole French nation raised a shout of joy. A Parisian journal, *The Tribune*, intending perhaps to reflect upon the Government, expressed surprise in not seeing a single member of the Bonaparte family shaking the dust of exile from his feet, and coming, in the broad light of July, claiming a "just reparation." Joseph wrote to the editor from London a letter containing the following sentiments :

"I have read in your journal of July 29th the article in which you give an account of the solemnity which took place on the 28th at the foot of the Column of Austerlitz, upon the inauguration of the statue of the Emperor Napoleon. You attribute the absence of his brothers to very strange sentiments. Are you ignorant, then, that an iniquitous law, dictated by the enemies of France to the elder branch of the Bourbons, excluded these brothers, out of hatred to the name of Napoleon? Would

372   JOSEPH BONAPARTE.   [1833.

Restoration of Napoleon's Statue to the Column of Austerlitz.

you wish that, in defiance of a law which the National Majesty has not yet repealed, we should bear the brands of discord into our country at the moment when it re-erects the statue of our brother? *Every thing for the nation*, was the motto of our brother. It shall be ours also.

"Instead of speaking, as a hostile journal would have done, in casting the blame upon patriots proscribed, who wander over the world the victims of the enemies of their country, would it not have exhibited more of courage and of justice on your part, sir, to recall to the electors of France that Napoleon has a mother who languishes upon a foreign soil, without it being possible for her children to speak to her a last adieu? She shares with three generations of her kindred, including sixty French, the rigors of an exile of twenty years. They are guilty of no other crime than that of being the relatives of a man whose statue is re-erected by national decree.

" The name of Napoleon will never be the banner of civil discord. Twice he withdrew from France, that he might not be the pretext for the infliction of calamities upon his country. Such are the doctrines which Napoleon has bequeathed to his family. It is because the French people know well that his pretended despotism was but a dictatorship, rendered necessary by the wars which his enemies waged against him, that his memory remains popular Is it just, is it honorable that his family should still be condemned to endure the anguish of exile, and to hear even his ancient enemies reproach the French with the injustice of their proscription ?"

This law of proscription, dictated by the Allies on the 12th of January, 1816, and re-affirmed by the Government of Louis Philippe, was as follows :

" The ascendants and descendants of Napoleon Bonaparte, his uncles and his aunts, his nephews and his nieces, his brothers, their wives and their descendants, his sisters and their husbands, are excluded from the realm forever."

The penalty for violating this decree of banishment was *death*. Madame Letitia had been informed in Rome that the Louis Philippe Government contemplated abolishing the decree of exile, so far as *she alone* was concerned. In response she wrote, April, 1834, to a distinguished gentleman in Paris, M. Sapey, as follows :

"MONSIEUR,—Those who recognize the absurdity of maintaining the law of exile against my family, and who wish nevertheless to propose an exception, do not know either my principles or my character. I was left a widow at thirty-three years of age, and my eight children were my only consolation. Corsica was menaced with separation from France. The loss of my property and the abandonment of my fireside did not terrify me. I followed my children to the Continent. In 1814 I followed Napoleon to the island of Elba. In 1816, notwithstanding my age, I should have followed him to Saint Helena had it not been prohibited. I resigned myself to live a prisoner of state at Rome; yes, a prisoner of state. I know not whether that was through an amplification of the law which exiled me with my family from France, or by a protocol of the allied powers.

"I then saw persecution reach such a pitch as to compel the members of my family, who had devoted themselves to live with me at Rome, to abandon the city. I then decided to withdraw from the world, and to seek no other happiness than that of the future life; since I saw myself separated from those for whom I clung to life, and in whom reposed all my souvenirs and all my happiness, if there were any more happiness remaining for me in this world. How could I hope to find any equivalent in France, which was not already poisoned by the injustice of men in power who could not pardon my family the glory which it has acquired?

"Leave me, then, in my honorable sufferings, that I may bear to the tomb the integrity of my character. I will never separate my lot from that of my children. It is the only consolation which remains to me. Receive, nevertheless, monsieur, my thanks for the kind interest which you have taken in my affairs."

On the 15th of January, 1835, Joseph wrote to his brother Louis, the father of Napoleon III., as follows:

"MY DEAR BROTHER,— I have received your letter of the 27th of December. I am afflicted by the depression of spirits in which it was written. It is true that for many years fortune has been constantly severe with us. But it is something to be able to say to one's self that fortune is blind. And an irreproachable conscience and a good heart offer many consolations. They accompany us wherever

we go, and prevent us from being too severe
in our turn against fortune and her favorites
of the day.

"It is indeed true that there are but few
gleams of happiness to be met in this life.
The least unfortunate have still their storms.
There are but few privileged men. How many
there are whom we must admit to be more unhappy than we are. And we do not sufficiently take into account the sufferings of dishonor-
ed men, whose conscience will at times awake
and react upon those who have done it violence. Those who have borne arms against
their country, against their benefactor, who
have sold their services to foreigners, think
you they can be happy? The consciousness
of not having merited the abandonment of
which you speak, is not that a happy sentiment? It is necessary then for us to perceive
what we are in this life, and not what we could
wish to be. Being men, we are destined to
live, that is to say, to suffer. But we can preserve our own self-respect, and the esteem of
the friends who appreciate us. So long as that
continues, one is not absolutely unhappy. In
that point of view, no person ought to be more
satisfied than yourself, my dear Louis. All

other evils over which we have no control are hard to endure, undoubtedly. But their necessity, in spite of ourselves, should lead us to bear them. We ought to submit to that which we can not prevent.

"Still, I can say nothing upon this subject which you do not know as well as I do. But I am not writing a dissertation. I recount my sensations and my sentiments as they flow from my pen. The consciousness of not meriting the evil which one suffers greatly mitigates that evil. Adieu, my dear Louis. I love you as ever. We have not known any revolutions in our affections."

Soon after Joseph had established himself in London, he called his brothers Lucien and Jerome, and his nephew, Prince Louis Napoleon, to join him there. The acts of the Government of Louis Philippe and the intense opposition they encountered engrossed his meditations. Fully satisfied that the Government could not maintain itself in the course it was pursuing, Joseph deemed it important for the triumph of what he called the popular cause, to effect a cordial union between the Republican and Imperial parties. The Government thwarted this union by sending spies into the clubs, who,

joining those associations, assumed to be earnest democrats, and strove in every way to promote discord, while they extolled in most ex-
travagant terms the brutal deeds of Marat, St.
Just, and Robespierre. Joseph could not act
in harmony with such men, and the projected
alliance was abandoned.'

In a brief sketch which Louis Napoleon,
while a prisoner at Ham, wrote of his uncle
Joseph just after his death, he says: "In general, Prince Louis Napoleon was in accord with
his uncle upon all fundamental questions;
but he differed from him upon one essential
point, which offered a very strange contrast.
The old man, whose days were nearly finished,
did not wish to precipitate any thing. He was
resigned to await the developments of time.
But the young man, impatient, wished to act,
and to precipitate events.

"The insurrection at Strasbourg, in the
month of October, 1836, thus took place without the authorization and without the participa-
tion of Joseph. He was also much displeased
with it, since the journals deceived him respecting the aim and intentions of his nephew. In
1837 Joseph revisited America. Upon his re-

' Œuvres de Napoléon III., tome deuxième, p. 449.

turn to Europe in 1839 he found his nephew
in England. Then, enlightened respecting the
object, the means, and the plans of Prince Louis Napoleon, he restored to him all his tenderness. The publication of *Les Idées Napoleo-
niennes* merited his entire approbation. And
upon that occasion he declared openly that, in
his quality of friend and depositary of the most
intimate thoughts of the Emperor, he could say
positively that that book contained the exact
and faithful record of the political intentions
of his brother."

It will be remembered that Louis Napoleon,
after the attempt at Strasbourg, was sent in a
French frigate to Brazil, and thence to New
York, where he remained but a few weeks,
when he returned to Europe to his dying mother. At New York, under date of April 22,
1837, he wrote the following letter to his uncle
Joseph at London. The letter very clearly re-
veals the relation then existing between them.

"MY DEAR UNCLE,—Upon my arrival in the
United States, I hoped to havè found a letter
from you. I confess to you that I have been
deeply pained to learn that you were displeased
with me. I have even been astonished by it,
knowing your judgment and your heart. Yes,

my uncle, you must have been strangely led
into error in respect to me, to repel as enemies
men who have devoted themselves to the cause
of the Empire.

"If, successful at Strasbourg, and it was very
near a success, I had marched upon Paris, drawing after me the populations fascinated by
the souvenirs of the Empire, and, arriving in
the capital a pretender, I had seized upon the
legal power, then indeed there would have been
nobleness and grandeur of soul in disavowing
my conduct, and in breaking with me.

"But how is it? I attempt one of those
bold enterprises which could alone re-establish
that which twenty years of peace have caused
to be forgotten. I throw myself into the attempt, ready to sacrifice my life, persuaded that
my death even would be useful to our cause.
I escape, against my wishes, the bayonets and
the scaffold; and, having escaped, I find on
the part of my family only contumely and dis-
dain.

"If the sentiments of respect and esteem
with which I regard you were not so sincere, I
should not so deeply feel your conduct in respect to me; for I venture to say that public
opinion can never admit that there is any alien-

ation between us. No person can comprehend
that you disavow your nephew because he has
exposed himself in your cause. No one can
comprehend that men who have perilled their
lives and their fortune to replace the eagle upon
our banners can be regarded by you as enemies,
any more than they could comprehend that
Louis XVIII. would repel the Prince of Condé
or the Duc d'Enghien because they had been
unfortunate in their enterprises.

"I know you too well, my dear uncle, to
doubt the goodness of your heart, and not to
hope that you will return to sentiments more
just in respect to me, and in respect to those
who have compromised themselves for your
cause. As for myself, whatever may be your
procedure in reference to me, my line of conduct will be ever the same. The sympathy of
which so many persons have given me proofs;
my conscience, which does in nothing reproach
me; in fine, the conviction that if the Emperor
beholds me from his elevation in the skies, he
would approve my conduct, are so many com-
pensations for all the mortifications and injustice which I have experienced. My enterprise
has failed; that is true. But it has announced
to France that the family of the Emperor is not

yet dead; that it still numbers many devoted friends; in fine, that their pretensions are not limited to the demand of a few pence from the Government, but to the re-establishment, in favor of the people, of those rights of which foreigners and the Bourbons have deprived them. This is what I have done. Is it for you to condemn me?

"I send you with this a recital of my re-movement from the prison of Strasbourg, that you may be fully informed of all my proceedings, and that you may know that I have done nothing unworthy of the name which I bear. I beg you to present my respects to my uncle Lucien. I rely upon his judgment and affection to be my advocate with you. I entreat you, my dear uncle, not to be displeased with the laconic manner in which I represent these facts, such as they are. Never doubt my unalterable attachment to you.

"Your tender and respectful nephew,

"NAPOLEON LOUIS."[1]

In 1840 the health of Joseph began to be

---

[1] For a short time after the death of his elder brother, Louis Napoleon, in accordance with the understood wish of the Emperor, adopted the signature of Napoleon Louis. Soon, however, he again resumed his original name.

seriously impaired. In London he had an attack of paralysis, which induced him to go to the warm baths of Wildbad, in Wurtemberg. He was somewhat benefited by the waters, and cherished the hope that he might join members of his family in Italy. But the Continental sovereigns so feared the potency of the name of Bonaparte upon the masses of the people that his request was peremptorily refused. Thus repulsed, he returned to the cold climate of England.

In 1841, the King of Sardinia, who was strongly leaning toward popular principles, allowed Joseph to take up his residence in Genoa. He was conveyed to that city in an English ship. He had been there but a few weeks, when the Duke of Tuscany, commiserating his dying condition, kindly consented that he should join his wife, his children, and his brothers in Florence.

In 1842 Joseph bequeathed to the principal cities of Corsica several hundred valuable paintings, which he had received as a legacy from his uncle, Cardinal Fesch.

In 1843, the Government of Louis Philippe, with marvellous inconsistency, voted to demand the remains of the Emperor Napoleon from the British Government, and to rear to his honor, beneath the dome of the Invalides, the monument of a nation's gratitude, while at the same time that Government persisted in banishing from France all the members of the Napoleon family.

A very earnest petition was sent at this time to the Government, numerously signed by Frenchmen, praying that the decree of banishment against the Bonaparte family might be annulled. But the Louis Philippe Government declared in council that the resolution of the Government to prolong the exile of the family of Napoleon was positive and unchanging. Joseph wrote a letter of thanks in behalf of the Bonaparte family to the signers of the petition, in which he said:

"The elder branch of the Bourbons, brought back to France by foreign bayonets, we have ever frankly treated as enemies. They did not conceive the hope of degrading us in our own eyes. It has been reserved for the younger branch to call artifice to its aid—to glorify the dead Napoleon, and to traduce, to proscribe his mother, his sisters, his nephews, fifty or sixty French people, charged with the crime of bearing his name.

" Were Napoleon living to-day, he would think as we do. He would recognize in France no other sovereign than the French people, who alone have the right to establish such a form of Government as to them may seem best for their interests. The too long dictatorship of Napoleon was prolonged by the persistence of the enemies of the Revolution, who endeavored to destroy in him the principle of national sovereignty from which he emanated.

" At a general peace, universal suffrage, liberty of the press, and all the guaranties for the perpetual prosperity of a great nation, which were in the plans of Napoleon, would have been unveiled before entire France, and would have made him the greatest man in history. His whole thoughts were made known to me. It is my duty loudly to proclaim them. He sacrificed himself twice, that he might save France from civil war. The heirs of his name would renounce forever the happiness of breathing the air of their native country, did they think that their presence would inflict upon it the least injury. Such are the principles, the opinions, the sentiments of all the members of the family of Napoleon, of which I am here the interpreter. *Every thing for and by the people.*"

In the few remaining years of his life, nursed by the tender care of his wife Julie, who was to him an angel of consolation, Joseph remained in Florence, his mind entirely engrossed with the misfortunes of his family. He had become fully reconciled to his nephew, and keenly sympathized with him in his captivity at Ham. The glaring inconsistency of the Government of Louis Philippe in persisting to banish from France the relatives of a man whom all France almost adored, simply because they were that great man's relatives, often roused his indignation.

The thought that he was an exile from his native land—from France, which he had served so faithfully, and loved so well—embittered his last hours. Supported by the devotion of Julie, and by the presence of his brothers, Louis and Jerome, to both of whom he was tenderly attached, he awaited without regret the approach of death.

On the 23d of July, 1844, Joseph breathed his last at Florence, at the age of sixty-six years. He left his fortune, which was not very large, to his eight grandchildren. He also requested that his remains should be deposited in Florence until the hour should come when they could be removed to the soil of his beloved France. Queen Julie survived him but a few months. Her remains were deposited by the side of those of her husband, and of her second daughter, the Princess Charlotte, who died in 1839.

Joseph was eminently calculated to embellish society and to adorn the arts of peace. His literary attainments were very extensive, and in the Tribune he was eminent, both as an orator and a ready debater. Familiar with all the choicest passages of the classic writers of France and Italy, and thoroughly read in all the branches of political economy, with great affability of manners and spotless purity of character, he would have been a man of distinction in any country and in any age. To say that he was not equal to his brother Napoleon is no reproach, for Napoleon has never probably, in all respects, had his equal. But Joseph filled with distinguished honor all the varied positions of his eventful life. As a legislator, an ambassador, a general, a monarch, and a private citizen, he was alike eminent.

From the commencement of his career until his last breath, he was devoted to those principles of popular rights to which the French

Revolution gave birth, and which his more illustrious brother so long and so gloriously upheld against the combined dynasties of Europe.
This sublime struggle of the people throughout
Europe, under the banners of Napoleon, against
the old régime of aristocratic oppression, profoundly moved the soul of Joseph. The honors he received, the flattery at times lavished
upon him, did not corrupt his heart. "Under
the purple," says Napoleon III., "as under the
cloak of exile, Joseph ever remained the same;
the determined opponent of all oppression, of
all privilege, of every abuse, and the earnest
advocate of equal rights and of popular liberty."

In his last days, Joseph, whose conversa-
tional powers were remarkable, loved to recall
the scenes of his memorable career. With the
most touching simplicity, and with a charm of
quiet eloquence which moved all hearts, he
held in breathless interest those who were
grouped around him. With pleasure he alluded to the comparatively humble origin of
his family, which had counted among the members so many kings. He was fond of relating
anecdotes of the brother of whom he was so
proud, and whom he so tenderly loved. One

of these characteristic anecdotes was as follows:

"Joseph," said the Emperor to me one day,
"T——' has infinite ability, has he not?
Well, do you know why he has never accomplished any thing great? It is because grand
thoughts come only from the heart, and T——
has no heart."

Though Joseph was a man of extraordinary
gentleness of character and sweetness of disposition, the cruel treatment of his brother at
Saint Helena he could never allude to without
intense emotion. In speaking of the destitution of the Emperor in the hovel on that distant rock, his eyes would fill with tears, and his
voice would tremble under the vehemence of
his feelings.

The course pursued by the Government of
Louis Philippe, the whole internal and external policy of that unhappy monarch, arresting
the progress of popular rights at home and degrading France abroad, and especially its gross
inconsistency in lavishing honors upon the
memory of Napoleon, and yet persisting in banishing his descendants, roused his indignation.
We can not conclude this brief sketch more

[1] Talleyrand.

appropriately than in the words of Louis Napoleon, written when he was a captive at Ham,
and when his uncle Joseph had just died in exile at Florence.

"If there existed to-day among us a man
who, as a deputy, a diplomatist, a king, a citizen,
or a soldier, was invariably distinguished for
his patriotism and his brilliant qualities; if that
man had rendered himself illustrious by his
oratorical triumphs, and by the advantageous
treaties he had concluded for the interests of
France; if that man had refused a crown because the conditions which it imposed upon
him wounded his conscience; if that man had
conquered a realm, gained battles, and had exhibited upon two thrones the light of French
ideas; if, in fine, in good as in bad fortune, he
had always remained faithful to his oaths, to
his country, to his friends; that man, we may
say, would occupy the highest position in public esteem, statues would be raised to him, and
civic crowns would adorn his whitened locks.

"Well! this man lately existed, with all
these glories, with all these honorable antece-
dents. Nevertheless upon his brow we see
only the imprint of misfortune. His country
has requited his noble services by an exile of

twenty-nine years. We deplore this, without being astonished at it. There are but two parties in France; the vanquished and the vanquishers at Waterloo. The vanquishers are in power, and all that is national is crushed beneath the weight of defeat."

These words were written in the year 1844. The Empire is now restored. The decree of exile against the Bonaparte family is annulled. The heir of the Emperor sits upon the throne, recognized by all the nations in the Old World and the New. The time has come when the character of Joseph Bonaparte can be, and will be justly appreciated.

THE END.

www.ingramcontent.com/pod-product-compliance
Lightning Source LLC
Chambersburg PA
CBHW021530110726
47902CB00004B/822